TORLO HANNIS OF NOOMAS

by

CHARLES NUETZEL

The Borgo Press
An Imprint of Wildside Press

MMVII

FIRST COMPLETE EDITION

CONTENTS

To

Don Janess, lifelong friend,
who introduced me to computers,

and

CAG, Charles A. Gramlich,
who met me first on Noomas

Introduction

As a writer I come across many people with stories to tell, most of which are useless. In the case of two men I shall call Dr. Spencer and Dr. Donaldson, quite the opposite was true.

In the beginning they were reluctant to reveal what they knew, partly for fear of ridicule and partly because they wished to keep their experiments secret.

During a party, Dr. Paul Spencer, a full-bearded stocky man in his middle thirties, began talking to me about telepathy, a subject which I've found of interest, much as the rumors of flying saucers—neither of which I believe or disbelieve. Paul Spencer claimed that some years back he had come across an idea—theory if you will—which might make telepathy possible. (I won't go into the technical details because I'm not qualified to do so. The general idea is that since thoughts are electrical impulses, they can be picked up by an electronic tuner—like radio waves are gathered by AM or FM tuners—to be channeled through an amplifier, changed to another frequency which would tune them to another person's mental wave band. The theory was that telepathy is a reality but that each person's thoughts are on a different wave-band and thereby unable to be picked up by another brain. The tuner would work as a mechanical device to adjust one person's thoughts to the wave-band of another's—thereby making telepathy possible to anybody.)

I argued against the concept of telepathy merely for the sake of a good evening's discussion. Because he was feeling a little too high and it was a private party among friends, Paul Spencer claimed that he had done extensive experimenting on it with John Donaldson, who was a telepathically sensitive person.

"We have tapes which would curl your hair," Spencer explained, "but nobody would believe them. That's why we haven't told anybody. As it is, I've talked too much!"

Donaldson had just walked up to the bar to pour himself another drink. He was a tall, dark-haired man with large nervous eyes. "That's quite right, Paul. Nobody would believe you. So keep quiet!"

"You can't stop here!" I exclaimed; now determined to learn as much as possible. "If you have something—please go on! Look, I'm not about to laugh. The theory does sound fantastic. But...if you've evidence..."

Donaldson filled his glass with Scotch. "Maybe there isn't any harm in telling you, after all. Even if you did write about it, who would believe you?" He took a large swallow of the drink. "It would sound like science fiction!"

"And that's for sure!" Spencer nodded, his face wide with a serious grin.

But the conversation was interrupted at that point because our wives came into the den. Nothing more was said that evening. But the next day I continued to think about what hints they had offered; my writer's instinct was acutely sparked. Even if it was nothing but talk, there was possibly a kick-off point here upon which I could develop a story.

I called Spencer that night to ask if I could come over and talk to him about the telepathy tuner. He was reluctant at first but I explained my purpose and he finally consented.

That evening we met in his lab, behind the large house in which he lives in Woodland Hills, California. John Donaldson was there and they explained in more detail what they had been doing, most of which went completely over my head. The lab was a scattered assortment of wires, tubes, tools and bulky electronic equipment. Their explanations seemed as difficult to understand as this electronic collection of gadgets surrounding me. But in the end, they presented these facts:

"Once the tuner was developed," Spencer announced, sitting on a tall stool, playing idly with a straight-stemmed empty pipe, "I put John here into an hypnotic state, then placed the headphones, especially re-designed for high frequency, on his head. I ran the dial up and down the frequency bands and at one point noticed that he tensed, his lips started to move, then relaxed as I changed the position of the dial setting.

"Pin-pointing the frequency was a delicate job, taking a little more than half an hour. All the time, John was showing signs of deep frustration and nervousness, muttering to himself, as if having a nightmare. I almost brought him out of the trance, then decided against it.

"Once the adjustment was made, he said, very clearly, in a stilted voice, as if he were having difficulty forming words: 'My name is Torlo Hannis. Who are you?' He repeated this over and over again. I turned on the tape recorder and didn't disturb John for some twenty minutes.

"The question kept repeating itself. Nothing else. Finally I turned off the tuner and brought John out of it. After playing the tape back to him, he admitted to having strange dreams. In his mind had come this voice. Though he understood the words, it was hard to form them into English."

Donaldson explained: "It was as if the language sent were different, insofar as the organization of word patterns. I found it hard to reorganize them."

"My theory is," Spencer offered, "that this Torlo speaks another language and is projecting telepathically, we are picking up his thoughts, John is having difficulty retranslating them into English patterns—or at least he was in the beginning."

"How long have you been on this?"

"For three months. We have now learned much about Torlo Hannis but there is a lot more to learn. I've recorded everything. John can now talk quite rapidly, exchanging questions with Torlo Hannis. The voice pattern is different when he speaks for Torlo." After a moment to let me think this through, he asked: "Would you like to hear some of the tapes?"

I was most eager.

As Spencer threaded a tape into the machine, he said: "The major fact we have learned so far is that Torlo is from another planet, either existing now or far in the future or in some other dimension. Don't laugh! It's just that we have been trying to come up with some theory. Exchanging in-

9

formation with Torlo proves the following: he is human in shape and biology, there is ancient history which suggests that his race came from a planet much like Earth—or Earth itself. The culture which gave him birth spans the galaxy, though he is isolated on a planet called Noomas, where he was shipwrecked some years ago. Well, let him tell you through the voice of John Donaldson."

It is enough, here, to say I listened to the tapes, all of them, then insisted they attempt to contact Torlo. Their arranged meeting was not due until three nights later. In the following weeks and months, I was a fascinated spectator as the doctors continued their communication with Torlo Hannis. At my suggestion an organized method of work was established, so that we could get a clear picture of the world on which Torlo lives. My motive was to see if there was a story here that I might use.

In the end I had enough material to organize into a book which, though fantastic, contained a fascinating and exciting adventure. Only after weeks of pressure did John and Paul finally allow me to use the material, but only on the condition that if I referred to them at all it would be under fictitious names.

I present the following as nothing but a good tale, something with which to pass a pleasant evening. Most readers will say it is merely the imagination of a science fiction writer; and who am I to deny them this belief? As to the others who will believe—or want to believe—who am I to claim they are wrong? Dr. Spencer and Dr. Donaldson believe; I trust them. And therefore one must conclude that I believe there is a Torlo Hannis living in some other time or some other dimension, who through his own experiments in telepathy, has by some freak of fate made contact with Earth through the Spencer Tuner.

—Charles Nuetzel
Thousand Oaks, California

CHAPTER ONE

BORN INTO MYSTERY

I, Torlo Hannis, was born at the age of twenty-eight, without memory of my past life, without knowledge of the world in which I found myself.

Birth came from darkness, black as night-sleep, but without dreams, only numb awareness and then dull pain. Sound was next, but I could not understand it or trace from whence it came.

My thoughts were real enough, organized as a man's will be. I vaguely became aware that I lived, but with a feeling of amazement that life still breathed in my lungs. I tried to remember what had happened last, but all was clouded, covered by a misty black wall cutting off memory. I knew not my name, nor anything of what had happened to me. I was aware, alive. That was all.

Then the sounds, first of footsteps, movement, cloth, articles striking each other, then words. But understanding of the words would not come.

Light flashed across my vision, knifing the darkness for a moment, then disappeared.

I tried to move but felt as if every muscle were paralyzed. Panic set in, then fluttered away as a soft, delicate hand touched my forehead. The light burst across my eyes once more, then disappeared.

A woman's voice said something in a language I could not understand, and then was answered by a male voice. For a while conversation took place over me. Then I felt a pinprick on my right arm. Nausea gripped at the pit of my stomach, then convulsed away. The pain surrounding my head disappeared.

Abruptly my eyes were open and I was staring up at a high ceiling upon which had been painted strange designs and patterns in greens and blues. The images were fuzzy at first but finally came into sharp focus. Then a face, oval, framed in long black hair which fell in flowing locks around a delicate feminine figure. The eyes were large and dark, the nose small, upturned, the mouth wide, sensual, full.

She said something in a low, musical voice that sounded like, "Kat töri, la'ătio, maẏśati, ĵordas Ši."

I shook my head, said: "You're beautiful, but I don't understand a word you say."

She looked away, said something to another, then stepped back. The face of an aged man leaned over me from the other side. He had a small white pointed beard and thin mustache. His eyes were deep set, but kindly, the hair shock white around his temple, the top of his head totally naked. There were lines of age in his face around the eyes and thin, wine-colored lips.

"Who...are...you?" the man asked, his words hesitant, the lips forming them as if having difficulty.

"Where am I? Who are you? What's happened?" I fired back, sudden relief winding its way through my body.

The man studied me for a moment, his face contorting into deep wrinkles of thought. There was something familiar about his face, and I decided it was because he looked so much like the girl in facial structure.

"I am known here as Andon Janis, Proctor of Koris— that's Prince of Doctors." His words were flowing a little more smoothly as if he were now getting used to speaking my language. "This is Youi Janis, my daughter."

The woman leaned over again as he spoke her name. I thought to myself that I had never seen such a beautiful face in my life; then puzzled over that, for no memory of a past would reveal itself. I knew that in some way my memory was lost. Something had happened to lock the door of the past from my conscious thoughts. Yet I knew conclusively that I had never seen a woman of such beauty.

Andon Janis asked: "How do you feel, young man?"

12

Considering his question, I tried to sit up. He helped me. The room which we were in was small, with an arched closed door and an arched window which looked out upon what appeared to be a city of glittering jewels. I could recognize what I saw. Place names, objects and things; but that was all. Personal past history was a blank.

"Where am I?" My eyes turned to Andon Janis, who was dressed in a one-piece red robe which fell just to his ankles, revealing leather-sandaled bare feet.

"On the planet of Noomas, in the city of Bel-loniea. Federation charts label our sun as a second rate star—I've forgotten the serial number but—"

"What are you talking about?" I groaned, tried to understand, but found it impossible.

Andon Janis studied me for a moment, then nodded: "Well, don't let it bother you."

"What bother me?"

The edge of panic in my voice must have been pretty sharp.

"You've had an accident. Loss of memory is not unusual under such circumstances." He smiled in a fatherly fashion. "But I wouldn't worry about it. You're in friendly hands, luckily for you. If the Dianos had gotten you, you would probably be dead by now."

"The Dianos?"

"We're at war with them. But all in good time, my boy. All in good time." He turned to his daughter, spoke in her language for some moments, then said to me: "Youi will give you a shot and when you awaken you'll be able to speak the language of the Noomas."

"How?"

"We have a machine which is used for many purposes, one of them is teaching of language through mind symbols. There are several languages on Noomas...you will learn everything necessary at the right time. Now I'll leave you with my daughter. You'll rest for some time and awaken a new man, I would say."

He turned and went to the door, opened the wooden panel, then closed it behind him.

I turned to Youi, marveled at her flowing figure which suggested itself under the loose, shapely yellow gown draped from her bare slender shoulders. The neckline closed around her throat. A pattern of golden lacy design ran through the cloth like thousands of tiny jungle flowers.

She moved gracefully toward the stand next to the bed. A moment later she came toward me with a needle in her right hand. A small, shy, but warm smile played on her lips, which dimpled at the corners. She was so beautiful that I felt a choke of emotion at the very sight of her. As she reached out and touched my arm, a tingling sensation of pleasure surged through me. I knew instinctively about love between man and woman though could not remember having made love to any woman; and yet I would have given much to possess Youi Janis.

The needle slipped into my arm so skillfully that I hardly felt it. A moment later the room became misty before my eyes. The soft touch of fingers helped me lie back and soothed the momentary sense of panic. Then darkness settled down over my awareness.

I dreamed of a small boy who was myself, playing in a large yard, a tiny gun in hand, an ersatz playmate hiding in the bushes to the right, beeping softly so that I would know exactly where it was.

"Got you!" a high-pitched voice spoke from my throat. "Don't move or by the Law of the High Command I'll blow you to atoms!"

A tiny voice pleaded, "I surrender, oh great Agent of the Federation, don't blow me to atoms! I will tell you the secrets of the Lancers! You have saved the Galaxy from ruin!"

The garden of flowers and green-purple brush flickered away, and I felt the arms of a soft woman holding me, saying: "Have I been worth the cost, spaceman? Did you like me?"

A vagueness whispered away the dream and suddenly I was sitting up in the bed where Youi Janis had left me. The room was now dark but a soft glow of light came from the arched window at my right. For a moment I just sat there, not moving, taking in the smells of the world around me. The

14

delicate fragrance of blossoms, the scented aroma of spicy food subtly teased my senses, bringing to awareness a sharp pang of hunger.

Then carefully I lifted myself up off the bed, stood shakily. After a time, I moved to the window and looked out upon a sparkling expanse of glittering lights scattered along curving night streets glowing from doomed rooftops and through arched windows. A soft murmuring of voices played like some kind of strange music on the air.

The window was some two flights above the ground. On the street below I saw men and women walking in different directions, some coupled off, wandering like lovers on a moonlight stroll, others briskly dodging in and out around those people in less of a hurry, as if on important business.

Most were dressed in simple one-piece, form-fitting cloth, belted at the waist, long swords swinging from the left, small objects holstered at the right—the latter I automatically recognized as some kind of strange hand gun. The women wore robes, glittering in the dimness as if sprinkled with countless stars.

Laughter came from directly below and a gay feminine voice floated up to me: "Tal, you wouldn't say that if I was a Proctor's daughter."

"But you aren't!" her male companion laughed. "Come...let's go to a Tavern of Love."

"I'm shocked!" But the voice sounded delighted. Their laughter faded away.

I moved from the window, suddenly amazed that I had understood what had been said. The language was different, yet as familiar as my own.

Across the room I spotted a mirror. Moving to it, I felt an odd emotional excitement. What did I look like? The form of my face was as lost to memory as my past life.

I looked in the mirror, studying the features which stared back as if meeting a stranger.

The face was not bad looking. My hair was short, dark blond, the eyes deep blue like evening sky. The bone structure was angular, the darkly tanned flesh smooth and firm. There was a set determination to the form of my mouth,

15

as if it were used to giving direct orders and expecting immediate results. The nose was long, straight.

After a moment of staring at this stranger who was me, I decided that this was a face I could like, trust.

It was interesting studying my own face, objectively, as I might a stranger's. Not many people get the chance to meet themselves in such a manner. Normally a person grows up seeing a baby face mature slowly into an adult stranger whom they get to know very intimately. With me, I was getting to know a stranger who was as alien to me as the world in which I had awakened.

After some time I decided it would not be difficult to live with this face.

The door behind me opened and a light filtered into the room from the corridor beyond.

Andon Janis stood there, another man standing behind him. The two stepped into the room. Andon touched a wall stud and light brightened the darkness away.

"Well, I see you came out of it right on schedule." Andon Janis greeted, pleasantly enough. "This is the Proctor of Bel-loniea."

The person he indicated was a well-formed man who appeared to be in his middle fifties. It was not until much later that I was to learn that he was well over 500 years old. His face was square, the jaw angular, the eyes brooding with a look of constant worry. The set of his firm mouth had the appearance of grim kindness. There was that about the man which made one almost see the great weight of responsibility which fell upon him. Yet he seemed basically a gentle man. The alertness in his gray eyes suggested that nothing escaped their attention. He was dressed in a glittering purple robe which draped over his shoulders, the sleeves coming down to his forearms. A jeweled belt pulled the cloth tightly about his narrowed waist, supporting an intricately designed sheath for a gold handled narrow bladed sword. The weapon appeared more decorative than usable. Though this was not the case.

He looked at me for some time, then said:

"Andon Janis has said you come from his civilization. Is that true?"

I looked from Andon to the Proctor. My puzzled expression must have registered with the Proctor, for he glanced at Andon.

"He doesn't know what I'm talking about!" There was an edge of irritation to the Proctor's voice.

Andon explained: "As I told you, sire, he has no memory of his past. Only his language remained. When he first spoke I naturally recognized it. At first it was hard to form the words after all these years. But on my honor, you can believe me. Look at the evidence." He started ticking off each point on his fingers. "We saw the falling star, as you referred to it, and then our scouts found the wreckage of the ship. You had me brought to the scene and I identified it as a one-man interstellar space-flyer. A little more advanced than the ones I remember. But, as with the ship which brought my wife and me to your world, the polar static of this planet interfered with the ship's engines and it apparently went out of control. He's lucky to even be alive. Loss of memory could be shock reaction...in which case he will in time have a return of memory. If it is brain damage, which our machines show no real indication of, then it will be permanent. His clothing was much the same as those which I wore when you found me. You don't have to take my word for it, sire Romos. On the soul of my dear departed wife, your daughter, I swear there is no doubt about this. You need not fear that this is some trick of the Diano. They might be clever but not that clever. It could be possible to learn how I came upon the planet, and in some way managed to take a ship, and the rest—but one thing is for certain, the Diano spies would have no way of knowing the language."

Romos, Proctor of Bel-loniea, nodded thoughtfully, rubbed his clean-shaven chin, then turned to me. "You know nothing of your past, then?"

"Nothing."

"You are willing to commit yourself to our cause?" the Proctor inquired quite seriously, his eyes probing mine as if he were attempting to read my thoughts.

"I know nothing of your world. I know nothing of your cause. I know nothing of myself. But if you will explain, and I see no reason to consider your cause unworthy,

17

there is no reason I should not commit myself to it. After all, I do owe you my life." I stared honestly into the Proctor's eyes, attempting to show the man that I would neither be bullied, fooled or dishonest to the man.

The Proctor grinned as if pleased with my answer, then nodded: "Well taken. Andon Janis will take over the job of revealing to you all information as to our culture and world and our cause. But I must warn you that we are at war with a bloodthirsty nation which gives no quarter, and though it is against our basic principles to be so ruthless, it is necessary to fight on their terms or be overthrown." With that he turned and left the room.

CHAPTER TWO

BY ORDERS OF ROMOS, PROCTOR OF BEL-LONIEA

Andon Janis said: "There is much for you to learn, and we might as well start from the beginning. But first, I would imagine you are thirsty and hungry."

The suggestion of food brought awareness of great hunger and I nodded, thanking Andon Janis.

He went to the wall, where the light switch was, and touched another button under it. Shortly a man dressed in a simple g-string, without weapons, entered the room.

"You can bring food and drink for..." He turned, looked at me for a moment, then added, "We have given you a name, my friend. Youi has already been calling you the Lost One—though that would hardly be a suitable name...yet there is an ancient language, the root for most of the languages on Noomas. I think maybe Torlo Hannis would serve the purpose perfectly. You see it translates as the Lost One. How does that suit you?"

I shrugged, for it mattered little at that point.

"Bring Torlo Hannis food and drink," Andon Janis ordered the man.

Once the other man had left, he indicated a wooden table which was set against the wall opposite the bed. "There we'll sit."

There was a wooden chair on either side of the table and both of us seated ourselves.

Andon Janis took his time in starting the conversation. He stared at me for a while, then said: "It seems remarkable that another from our civilization should come

19

here. I was the first in the recorded modern history of Noomas. That another should come within the same century seems too remarkable...much too remarkable. But nonetheless you are here."

After a while he said: "Well, now. Let's begin from the point where I entered. My wife and myself were on a trip to visit her relatives on a distant world—Pioti V, some 50,000 light-years from our home planet. We were having a honeymoon of sorts—belated, of course. At the time there was a lot of pirating of space liners—though the percentages of liners attacked were one in a million. We were unlucky enough to fall in that low percentage. Most of the passengers were killed and the only thing which saved the two of us was the fact that I was a doctor and they had several wounded men—plus their leader had acquired a sickness which it was within my power to cure.

"We were with the pirates for some weeks, then they set us adrift in this areas of space—with a fifty-fifty chance of survival and being picked up. I believe they knew about Noomas and expected we would end up here. Something was wrong with the space-drive and I, not being educated in space mechanics, could only head for the nearest star which offered suitable planets.

"This solar system is charted but with only the notation that there is an Earth-type planet, second from the sun. The date of discovery was some 12,000 years ago. One mention of an expedition coming here is noted but no explanation as to its return or fate, My guess is that the expedition landed, much as I—and you—and built up this civilization we see here today. It's a logical theory.

"Nevertheless we headed here, and once within the gravity pull of the planet the ship acted crazily, as if going through a solar storm. Only with difficulty was I able to land. My wife was injured in the crash and died some days later. On the day I was burying her, a scouting party from Belloniea picked me up.

"For months I was held a prisoner, taught the language much the same way you were, and questioned thoroughly. Once they were satisfied that my story might actually be true, they gave me a certain amount of freedom of the palace here, though I was always under guard.

"In those first months I met a young woman called Ragee, and she took a liking to me. Guards disappeared and I was given a certain freedom of the city itself. In time Ragee and I arranged secret meetings. I never knew her identity until after we had secretly gone to a Muti—of which you will learn a lot of later—and were joined in marriage.

"The Muti knew who she was, naturally, but they have a code of ethics which is totally their own. The Mutis form a separate social division on Noomas—independent of all national loyalty, ruled by no Proctor, though they serve the people of Noomas as well as the Proctors. They are judges and teachers of philosophy, listened to by all—even the religious leaders, known as the Jis. Mutis can read your mind, tell some of the future, if you will pay a high enough price—or they find it necessary to stop an injustice. I have learned that Muti stands for Mutant in the old language."

At this point the man who had come at Andon's summons returned with a tray laden with a platter of food and two goblets of liquid. He placed this between us and then quietly disappeared.

"You have excellent servants," I commented, looking at the lush display of food before me.

"Slaves," Andon corrected. "Second generation Diano slaves."

I picked up what looked like breaded bird flesh from between generous helpings of gravy-covered yellow and blue vegetables.

"Here," Andon said, taking a small narrow piece of wood from the platter. He held the wood at one end and then pushed it under a vegetable, lifted it to his mouth and ate. "That's the way. They don't have the same kind of dinnerware we were used to in the Federation—but it works just as well. With meat, other than fowl, you use the small knife at your belt for cutting and eating. Of course, you won't be given such weapons until Romos is sure he can trust you. That will depend on our conversation."

I tasted the bird flesh and found it delicious, strongly spiced, heavily flavored.

Andon began talking as I ate: "Well, as I was saying, I married Ragee without knowing that she was the daughter of Romos. The Proctor was furious and threatened to have me killed on the spot when he discovered me in Ragee's bedroom the night of our secret marriage. When Ragee told him we were man and wife he went into such a rage that I thought he would kill both of us. He had me taken away under guard and I considered myself dead as of that moment.

"For two nights and days we were kept separated, I in the dungeons under the palace. Finally Romos and Ragee came down and freed me. Romos was reserved, but claimed that his daughter had sworn to kill herself if I was not returned to her with full honors. A sworn statement from the Muti to the fact that I had had no idea who she really was had saved me just as much as Ragee's threat.

"Since then, over the years, Romos and I have become close friends, and he has made me Proctor of Koris of Bel-loniea, a much honored title. Being of the Koris, I am not allowed the right to ascend to the throne, for it takes a warrior for such a post—or the son of the Proctor.

"Romos never had a son and his successor has not yet been picked; a duty which is pressing on him only lightly as yet. He will rule, if life is not cut away by the sword, for another two or five hundred of our standard Federation years.

"Life is extended here on Noomas for close to 1000 Federation years—though death will usually come at about 700 years. I was too old at the time to have the youth-giving drug work on me as it does with those under thirty. The drug has retarded aging to some extent over the years, and now I will remain as I am for several centuries. That is enough for a man who expected to die at 150 years or so. My body is aged outwardly but the passions of youth are much stronger than they would have been without the drug—so I have nothing to complain about.

"Nevertheless, the High Congress has pressed Romos about a successor. He is waiting for the right warrior to be picked by Youi for marriage. She is Proctoress II, and should under normal circumstances be next in line for royal rule with a suitable husband-warrior."

Andon looked saddened. "Such a weight on such small shoulders. I wish that she would find a young man of her own choice. There are many who wish her but none she is willing to bind her soul to through a Muti in marriage. At least we have in Bel-loniea a sense of honor and the elevation of women's rights. A common woman will never be forced to marry a man against her will. But a woman of royal birth, especially a Proctoress, will bend to the necessity of State. If after five years of mature womanhood she has not found a man she loves, her father or the Proctor will pick from his high-ranking officers those he considers suitable and give her an extended five years to decide which one. If, after that, she does not pick a man, he has the right to choose for her. Youi is now almost twenty, a few months short of the first five years. Shortly Romos will call a meeting with me and we will have to decide on a small number of possible suitors."

Andon sighed. "What can a father do? Romos is as saddened as I. It is the dearest wish of a father that his daughter marry a man she loves—but the affairs of state make it necessary for Romos to push this matter. He must choose those to succeed him—his first choice is, of course, through honor and love, Youi and her future husband."

I looked at the goblet in which was an amber liquid.

He caught the direction of my gaze. "This is Porshi. A liquor of mild strength but if one takes too much it will make you as sloppy drunk as a Stellar Cocktail."

I took a sip of the Porshi. It had a salty-sweet flavor, not at all unpleasant.

"Tell me, Andon," I inquired, putting the goblet down on the table between us. "What kind of world is this?"

"A primitive one in many ways. Some scientific gadgets still remain—the translator—grav-plates, which are used as a means of flying. Primitive. Just a large oval plate with sides and a top which can be pulled away. It's used in battle and hunting in a slightly different form. But for the most, this world is a series of city-states, walled colonies of people surrounded by rich farm lands. Bel-loniea extends for two hundred Federation miles in each direction, bound by mountains on one side, desert and forest on the other two

23

sides, and an ocean on the fourth. We have a perfect port here and the Dianos would give their Proctor's family for it. Though," he said with some humor on his face and in his voice, "they would much rather take it at the cost of Bel-loniea blood. War is the basic nature of the Diano."

"You believe in the honor of the Bel-loniea?" I inquired, now convinced that Andon was the kind of man anyone would trust with their life.

"It's a savage world of savage native beasts. In the far north there are natural alien inhabitants of the world which live a much more savage existence, half cave-creatures, who carry weapons and have a primitive sort of language. The humans of this world are much the same. They have a code of honor and a code of ethics. They live by the sword, distrust strangers, but at the same time will recognize bravery and honesty. We know little of the countries across the ocean, other than there are savage inhabitants of low culture living there. Survival on this world can be harsh!"

Then he added as an afterthought: "But Romos is an honorable man. And since you are trapped on this planet now, you might as well face the fact that you will be here for the rest of your life. It can be a very pleasant life. I have been happy. Under Romos' rule Bel-loniea has profited as a nation, explored new lands, made some colonial conquests. With what information I could give him on medical sciences, the people have been healthier, my fame as a Koris has spread across the known world. Other nations have paid highly for borrowing my services. A Koris school has been in existence for the last five years, and even the Dianos have paid dearly for sending their students here to learn the ways of my doctoring. The people of this nation are a good people, you will not find yourself in bad hands here. But you must prove yourself as a loyal servant to Romos. You're young, strong and, I would guess from your build, a fighting man. If you were to offer your services in Romos' armies as a common warrior, I'm sure that you would go far, fast. As memory returns to you—"

"If it does," I corrected.

24

He nodded like a wise old seer. "If it returns, and I see no reason to believe it wouldn't in time—how long, I don't know. But when it does, you will remember many things which will probably be of some use to Romos' army—or whatever else you might have specialized in with the Federation. In such events, Romos is quick to give honors. With luck you would be able to choose from some of the higher ranking young women of our nation. Life can be sweet for a man living in the Royal Society."

I didn't take more than a moment to make my decision. "You can tell Romos that I'll join as a common warrior."

"A hard but healthy life," Andon Janis warned. "You will have to learn the handling of weapons and hand-to-hand combat. It will be a six ten-day period of hard training, and sometimes you'll wish you were dead."

Before I could say anything the door opened and Youi Janis, Proctoress of Bel-loniea, stepped in. She smiled at her father, then looked at me, a veiled expression covering her eyes.

"Father," she said in a musical voice, gliding over to his side, "A Lord from the Outer Province has come here to have you attend to his illness."

Andon Janis stood. "I must go."

"Tell Romos I'll become a warrior," I announced, standing, my eyes on Youi.

"So it will be," Andon announced grimly. Then he turned and left the room.

Youi stood there for a moment, then asked politely, in a formal manner: "How are you feeling this evening?"

Her voice was musical and lovely to listen to.

"Better. Much better," I assured her, finding it difficult to control a sudden trembling.

How beautiful she looked, like some goddess from heaven. For such a woman, men would throw their lives away. The warrior who won her love would be very lucky, I decided, suddenly realizing that life could be really sweet on Noomas if the arms of Youi Janis were awaiting me at the end of each day.

I believe that it was then that I decided that if it were at all possible I would win the love of Youi.

"I hope we can be friends, Youi," I told her, looking into those beautiful innocent wide eyes, making no attempt to hide my true feelings.

For a moment it seemed as if she were pleased by my implied meaning. Then she abruptly became rigid. "We can be friends. But nothing more."

With that she turned and left the room.

* * * * * * *

The next day, without any ceremony, I was instructed by a grim-faced warrior that I must come with him. Shortly before, a slave had brought a generous breakfast of green mush and a drink of hot yellow liquid which helped to awaken the sleep from my body. I learned that the drink was called Ka. The warrior in simple leather harness and loin cloth, armed with sword and side-arm, came as I was finishing my meal.

"Come with me," he announced in a voice heavy with authority.

"Where to?" I inquired, standing.

"To the training barracks. We have been informed, Torlo Hannis, that you are to go into immediate training—by orders of Romos, Proctor of Bel-loniea."

Without a word I followed the man out of the small room in which I had been confined during my first night of consciousness. The corridor outside was large, with a high ceiling. The walls were covered with tapestries of brilliant colors, depicting strange and alien scenes. Some were battlefields massed with warriors cutting each other with swords, some of lovely women, draped in white, sitting in gardens or around sunken baths. Between the tapestries were weapons crossed over shields.

I tried to start a conversation with my escort but he commanded me to silence.

We were passed by dozens of men in robes of various colors, some armed with jeweled swords. A few women, escorted by slaves, came down the corridor, They were both

26

gay and beautiful, though not nearly so lovely as Youi. Thought of the daughter of Andon Janis, Proctoress of Bel-loniea, created a pang of regret because I was not going to see her before being taken into the Bel-loniea army. I had not believed they would move so fast. Now I had no way of knowing how long it would be before I would see her again.

Finally we came to stairs and the warrior led me down two flights. Then he turned left and entered a courtyard in which beautifully gardened flowers were spread around shortly clipped bluish grass. We crossed along the stone walk to the huge golden-gated entrance, before which stood two warriors, like statues, unmoving. They saluted the man escorting me by nodding their heads, then the one on the left opened the gate.

A moment later we were in the streets of Bel-loniea.

Everything seemed different in the daylight on the ground level. There was an air of business-like activity to the cobblestone streets, crowded with scores of people busy with their morning activities in front of smooth plaster walls, colored with bright designs. The buildings were built in simple lines, with arched windows and doorways. The voices of robe-covered, bearded men called out their chants of sale, pointing to the value and beauty of their products, as we passed open-fronted shops which brightly displayed foods and merchandise for sale. My escort ignored everything around, as if blind. He moved briskly in a quick military cadence as if used to years of marching.

Only when we passed the entrance of a large building, in front of which was a huge picture of a nude female, did he hesitate enough to call up a greeting to a dark-haired woman leaning out of a window on the second floor.

"Hail there, Geei...tell Opali I'll be there tonight."

The woman laughed down at him. "Who's the new recruit?"

"None of your business, woman!" he shouted back, good-naturedly.

"You're in an ugly mood today, Thora!"

"Tonight I'll take both of you on!" he yelled back. "With a little Porshi I won't seem so ugly!"

With that last remark he turned to me. "Women are the same the world over."

It was the only pleasant remark he made during the whole trip from the Palace of Romos to the Military Barracks of Bel-loniea.

We continued down the street until we came to the outer wall of the city which was five stories high, made of huge blocks of stone cemented with a bluish mortar. Here a large building was set against the wall. I was to learn that the wall was lined with such buildings—which kept the armies of Bel-loniea always alert and in position to protect their city.

Thora made his way to this building's entrance in front of which stood two armed guards, long spears clutched in their hands. They tipped the weapons as Thora passed. Inside I found myself in a small outer room, in which a desk was centered. A warrior sat behind it.

"I bring Torlo Hannis at the personal request of Romos, Proctor of Bel-loniea. He is to be given vigorous training." With that Thora turned and left the building.

The man behind the desk stood. "I am Prot of this training unit, known throughout Bel-loniea as the most demanding of officers in His Proctor's army. You will learn to hate me in the next days. You will at times want to kill me! But that is the way of the army. Afterwards you will understand and bless me." His voice was soft, gentle, amused. There was a light of respect in his eyes. "You are the one they found...the one all Bel-loniea is talking about...is that not true?"

"I am. They call me Torlo Hannis because I remember nothing of my past life."

"Then learn to remember. For as of this day you will have much to remember. But when I am finished with you, you will be one of the best warriors in Bel-loniea—or dead in the trying."

With that his attitude changed, hardened. He stepped around the table, then without warning his right fist swung out, hitting the point of my jaw like a sledge. "A warning!" he cried.

28

Even as I staggered backward, black stars blurring my vision, my body had taken on a defensive stance. Whatever training had been drummed into my brain in the lost past, now controlled every bodily muscle.

The Prot came forward, believing me too stunned to react. Instead he found himself walking into a chop to the neck, a second blow to the pit of his stomach. My hands moved without conscious directions. Each blow struck at him with every muscle of my body. He staggered back, amazement shocking his features.

Nonetheless, he came forward, now more careful. Before I could even recover from his first unexpected attack, I felt the point of a knife press into my stomach. Everything had taken place in but a few split moments.

"Remember, Torlo Hannis," the Prot announced savagely, "a man who is unarmed is helpless against an armed man."

With that he hit me with the butt of the knife, striking the side of my head.

I staggered under the blow, slumped down to the floor, stunned.

"You will learn, warrior. You will learn the true bite of Gora's training. Next time you strike me without orders to do so, I'll have you beaten with whips until your back is nothing but bloody scars."

He grabbed my arm, yanked me to my feet. "Now, when I bark, you jump. Stand at attention. Suck your stomach in. Chin out!"

He forced my dazed body into the position he demanded, then struck the point of my jaw with a large bony fist.

Stars sputtered in a flash of pain which was going to continue for almost six ten-day periods.

I was in the army of Romos, Proctor of Bel-loniea.

CHAPTER THREE

WARRIOR TRAINING

The next weeks proved far worse than I might have guessed, if there had been time to consider the matter. All the men in my training class were bunked in a large room of bare walls, sleeping on the floor on rough woven gray blankets. Weapons were always at our sides, sword and knife, hooked to the belted harness leather. Our garments were loincloth and harness and a cape which could be thrown around our bodies in cold weather. It was the uniform of all warriors of the low, common class. We ate quick meals in another room on a long wooden table. Usually mush was served, which had a heavy, slightly bitter flavor, and Ka for liquid. Water was never served during meals. There were twenty-six men in my unit, all of whom were far more familiar with the weapons being used. I had to learn from the beginning even how to hold a sword. Yet to my surprise, I picked up knowledge and skill with remarkable speed, as if partly remembering lost skills.

We were awakened before dawn every morning, quickly fed like a bunch of stupid animals, then taken outside the city wall for a morning exercise period. Our Prot, Gora, was assisted by two warriors who drilled us in marching, alternated by fast running, for most of the morning without rest. By midday we were taken back to the bunk and fed more mush and Ka. Then in the bunk room, now cleared of all blankets, which had to be rolled up and placed against the walls each morning, we were given instructions in the use of swords, knives and hand-to-hand combat.

30

Gora took an unnecessary delight in baiting me every chance he got.

The routine for this training ran thus: We would be lined up along the wall, then told to draw our swords. Then for several units of time we would be instructed through different maneuvers, lunging, attacking, defending ourselves against imaginary foes. If any of us made a mistake or tired or got careless, one of the assistants would pull them out in front of the class and demonstrate the use of the weapon. We were using naked blades, long and thin, needle-pointed, razor-sharp at the two edges. Our instructors made it a point to draw blood every chance they got. Under such pressure we learned fast.

Gora took a personal interest, and at times it seemed a delight, in hounding me at every chance he got.

"You must learn to keep your point up, see!" he would shout, lunging beyond my guard, touching my chest. "Watch out for this kind of trick." Then he would disarm me, touch my chest again with the point, drawing blood. "You must learn, coward! In battle you would have been killed several times."

After wearing us out to the point of exhaustion with the swords, they would start to instruct us in hand-to-hand combat, without weapons.

The first day I was exhausted to the point of hardly being able to move my muscles. Gora called me out of formation and announced: "Now, warrior, attack me! Try to kill me Here's your chance to get even!"

He stepped up, slapped my face hard with the flat of his hand.

"Come! Fight!"

I looked dazedly at him, trying to get the strength to take up his mocking offer, All the hatred burst to the surface and suddenly I leaped. But Gora wasn't where he'd been. Instead I felt the impact of his hand slap my face again—a blow which was insulting.

Then something happened to me that I could not explain at the time. My head cleared, all the anger washed away. I turned, faced Gora, calm, controlled.

Something in my eyes and manner must have warned Gora, for he tensed, took a defensive stance. All the cock-sureness had drained from his face.

"Come, coward. Kill me. Kill me!" he challenged, alert to every move I made.

I stepped forward, feinted to the right with my hand, then leaped in, left hand slicing at Gora's neck. My blow connected. Then my right slammed at his stomach, fingers stiff.

Gora doubled over, moaned as my knee connected with his jaw.

He crumbled to the floor, but before I could do anything else, his two assistants were on me like beasts. I slammed out with my hands like lightening, hitting the first one on the side of the head. He staggered back. Then his companion withdrew, pulled out the small hand weapon—a Kay-gun—from its holster.

"Don't move!" he warned.

I whipped around, then froze. I remembered what Gora had said that first day about attacking a man who is armed.

The other man helped Gora to his feet. The Prot stood there shaking his head for some moments, then turned and faced me. "You're a good fighter," he admitted, features still set in stone. There was no way of reading his true feelings. I half-expected him to have me beaten within a breath of death, but instead he merely ordered us back into formation and started lecturing on the basic methods of self-defense. Later he took on another man, whom he quickly defeated, throwing him around the room like a helpless baby.

His strength and ability as a fighting man was amazing. Not until having defeated half a dozen of us was he tired enough to call a rest period.

After that day he never engaged in hand-to-hand combat with me again.

One of my fellow trainees stepped up, said: "I'm Adt Dorta, I would be your friend, Torlo Hannis." He touched my shoulder in the common greeting on Noomas.

Adt Dorta was a tall, dark-haired young man with a slender, well-built body. He looked as if he would be a good

32

warrior and fighting man. There was that about his gray eyes which revealed an open honesty.

"I would be your friend," I assured him, touching his shoulder in the same manner.

"That was some attack you made against Gora. It's the first time I have heard of Gora being defeated in a training course. Where did you learn such tricks?"

I stared at the man for a long time, then shook my head. "I don't know. I remember nothing about my past."

Adt Dorta nodded as if remembering something. "Yes, of course. We heard about that. And your name...the Lost One in the old form. But you will make a fine warrior."

We sat on the floor, our backs against the wall. Adt Dorta told me, "It is said that you do not know from where you come, but that the Great Proctor of Koris, Andon Janis, spoke that you are from his world. If so, you will earn great honor in Bel-loniea. You have earned great honor by being trained by Gora—by His Royal Command."

I asked him what he meant by this.

"That is the Special Warrior School. When you leave here, you will be an officer in the common warrior class, with a ten-man unit under your command. Did you know this? Are you not aware that all of us here are either of the Royal Society or sons of honored rich men?"

"I knew nothing. I know nothing of this world. I know nothing of where I come from. I'm like a baby." I smiled grimly at this last.

"You fight like a trained warrior. Though," he admitted with a shrug of his broad shoulders, "you know little of the sword. But that will come. I'll help you any chance I get."

"Thanks," I said, believing his offer nothing but a groundless boast. After all, he was merely a recruit like myself, though of course he, like the others here, knew something about swords. Not until later would I learn that Adt Dorta was one of the finest swordsmen in Bel-loniea, and that his father was the Master Instructor for the Court. Though, nonetheless, he had to go through the formal training with the rest of us. In the days that followed, Adt paired off with me and I picked up many little tricks and pointers from him which even Gora didn't know.

He told me, "When we get out of this training period, I'll have to take you around the city and then to my family. I'm sure you will make many friends here. When you were brought to the city it became common social conversation to speculate about you. Great excitement. Two men from another world in the same hundred years. One was fantastic enough—but two—unbelievable!"

At that point Gora called us back to attention and we spent the rest of the day practicing with swords and knives. Just before darkness, we were given practice outside with hand-guns. These weapons are small, fitting into the palm of the hand, almost being concealed there. They shoot small explosive pellets. These Kay-guns are an ugly weapon but very effective.

After darkness fell, we were run around the city wall. The three moons of Noomas were high in the sky by the time this run was finished. Then we returned to the barracks, ate another meal of mush and hot Ka and went to bed. Sleep at night was short but total from exhaustion.

The routine continued day after day without break. Gora kept after me with the sword at each day's practice as if I were his personal enemy that he must destroy by endless cuts until I bled to death after days of such torture. When given the chance, I practiced with Adt Dorta. By the second ten-day period I had learned enough tricks to keep Gora's blade from touching me. Adt Dorta said at the end of the third ten-day period that I was showing amazing progress with the sword.

"My father, King Dorta, would consider you a prize student. I think he will like you."

There was little time for conversation during these long ten-day periods. But from the little exchange I was able to have with Adt Dorta and a few of our companions, during rest periods, I learned something of the customs and life of Bel-loniea and Noomas.

There were two basic social classes in Bel-loniea. The Commoners and the Royalty. But the division was not a hard dividing line over which nobody could pass. Royalty which became dishonored lost all its riches and honors and were as of then Commoners, living in the small apartments which made up the vast majority of the city. A Commoner who won honor in battle or through the earning of riches in business, could become of the Royal Class. Land owners, who were responsible for the farms, were from both the Royal and Commoner class. Slaves worked the farms under their supervision. All children, Commoner and Royalty alike, were raised together and given education in the Proctor's schools to the age of fourteen, at which time they were considered young adults, though without adult privileges. They were then prepared for full adulthood. First they worked as slaves, which was considered a social necessity. While slaves, they studied the religions of Bel-loniea and Noomas, of which there were many. It was a part of the belief of Bel-loniea religious law that each person should decide on their own what they believed insofar as a God or Maker of the Universe. The position of slave-servant during this time was considered a perfect position to study about the Gods of the Universe and Mind.

As a slave for one year they learned what it was to be both slave and master. At the age of fifteen the boys were trained in the use of weapons and in the jobs which their parents had chosen for them. By the age of sixteen, the men were considered adults and taken to the Government Houses of Love where they learned about love so they could be good husbands. This was considered an important part of their education, for slave women would be able to teach far more than classroom instruction from books.

The girls at the age of fifteen were taught how to care for household necessities, and considered from then on as mature enough to be married, though seldom did they do so before the age of sixteen, though they were many times in the company of young men whom their parents considered good companions and possible future husbands. But not until the age of twenty were Royal women ordered by law to pick a husband from a number of men felt to be a suitable union for them. They had five years to decide among these men— and if they fell in love with another whom their parents had not picked, they might marry if a Muti gave permission.

I tried to learn something about Mutis but was put off by Adt. "You will have to learn about them yourself. They are special."

The Mutis were a subject which Adt and my other companions would not talk about, as if some religious or superstitious fear surrounded these mysterious people. Adt did give me this much though: "When the time comes for us to join in the Special Corps as Full Officers of the Common Warriors, you will learn all there is to know about Mutis. It is against our custom to talk of them to the inexperienced—as you are."

He would not elaborate upon that. But I remembered what Andon Janis had said about the Mutis. They apparently had the ability to know what was in a person's mind. Telepathy? I wondered. Or were they merely faking some mystical ability? Andon Janis had said that Muti was short for Mutant. But where would a Mutant come from? What would cause a mutation? And what strange power did these Mutis have? Above all, if they were as powerful as Adt suggested, what kept them from ruling all of Noomas?

I could not help feeling there was more to the Muti subject that was suggesting itself on the surface. I determined to seek one out at the first chance I got. If they did have unnatural powers of the mind, then they might be able to unlock the past for me.

At the beginning of our fifth ten-day period Gora announced that it was time to test our skills in a proper manner, befitting a warrior of the Proctor's Special Corps.

We had been taken outside the walled city of Belloniea far earlier than usual. Normally the huge orange sun of Noomas streaked the south-western sky in deep reds by the time our morning meal was finished and we were lining up in formation. This morning the darkness of night was still upon the world, billions of stars pin-pointed the sky like diamonds sprinkled upon blank ink. At the southern tip of the horizon there was a huge bright star. Upon seeing it, I immediately recognized this as a super-giant, not far as intergalactic distances were concerned, and large enough to show as a distinct tiny disk. The information popped into my conscious mind like a pebble striking the surface of a peaceful pond. Immediately I probed deeper, trying to understand from whence that information had come. I could remember hearing nothing like that while on Noomas, and accepted the fact that this was some element from my past life surfacing. But the harder I attempted to seek out more information the fuzzier the thoughts became. It was like trying to chase a running man down a dark tunnel when you could only crawl after him.

Gora, standing in front of us, his two assistants at each side, said: "We will now hunt the Korda!"

A murmur sounded from those around me. There was no questioning the element of fear mixed with pride touching their voices. I tried to conjure up some mental picture of a Korda. The information which the translating machine had given me of the language of the Bel-lonieans offered only a vague image of some terrible, huge monster.

Gora waited for the men to recover from his announcement, then continued in a calm but grim voice: "There is nothing to fear with a Korda, if you do exactly as I instruct. You will be machines—without thought. You will strike at the Korda as I tell you, when I tell you. You will not question an order. Those who question an order will be killed, you can believe me. But if you listen, act without thought, you will kiss death into its lungs. This is the Holy Test before readying yourself for presentation before our Proctor's Muti. Only those with supreme courage and fighting ability will survive this test. And it is fitting that only the bravest best men will be members of the Special Corps." He hesitated only a moment, then said: "Remember that the eyes and a point behind the ears are sensitive to death. All else is like the hardest metal. The Korda is a creature of destruction. To hunt such a beast we will have to travel by grav-disk for many days march to the south. We will not hunt it in the day, for in the bright sun the Korda is less able to defend itself. The eyes see better at night. Our grav-disk will have a light-beam which one man will be in charge of, attempting to blind the Korda and illuminate the surrounding forest. We will have one unit of time to kill the beast!"

I had learned that the day of Noomas was broken into thirty units. The time given to make our kill would give little room for mistakes after the attack.

"As soon as the grav-plate flyer arrives we begin our hunt!"

The grim silence which settled upon the men created a depressive mood. I thought of Youi Janis, as I had so many times during the quiet moments while in training. I could not help but wonder if she had already picked some young man as her future husband. And all this time she was free to see any man of her choice; and here I was, unable to even let her know that I wanted her hand in marriage. Like so many times before, I tried to convince myself that she had been seeking such a man for almost five years and not found one and there was no reason to believe she would now suddenly fall in love simply because I had come onto Noomas. Nonetheless, a man in love does not reason with logic. I was falling in love with Youi. Why it did not seem strange to me that this should be, I do not know. Yet ever since that first moment I looked up into her eyes, I had loved her to some degree. Youi was that kind of woman. There was kindness in her eyes, beauty and grace in her face and body. I had no way of letting her know that I cared. Even if this were possible, I would probably have no way of winning her, for I was not born of the Royal Class. It would be hard, if not impossible, to break across the class line in time to be considered a proper suitor for her hand.

The soft purr on the wind sounded from above us and I looked up to see a huge black shape against the stars slowly passing over our heads. It circled and then gently lowered itself behind Gora. As it landed I saw a huge disk with sloping sides with a tent-like metal top.

Gora ordered us forward in marching cadence.

A ramp lowered to meet us and we were directly into the grav-plate flyer. The ship was bare inside except for a small cockpit in its front. This was where the ship's controls were located. Rings lined the side of the walls. To these a man could attach his harness so that when the top was rolled down there was no chance of being flung overboard if the flyer were turned over during flight.

38

Immediately after we were all boarded, the disk rose from the ground and shot off at amazing speed across the farmlands surrounding the walled city of Bel-loniea.

Chapter four

Battle to the death

This was my first adventure away from the immediate surroundings of the city and I looked forward to seeing something of the world in which I had found myself reborn without memory.

During the flight the military discipline was relaxed and we were allowed to settle down in little groups.

Adt Dorta and a man named Fita joined me. My first question was direct and to the point. "What is a Korda?"

Fita laughed nervously. "A beast, it is. A beast like you never imagined. I've never seen one close up but I've been told it takes a mighty man indeed to kill it single-handedly. That is why we hunt as a pack. Even then it will be a true test of our courage."

Adt offered in the serious manner he had gotten in the habit of when explaining something about the planet to me, "It is five times the size of a man at the shoulder. Huge fangs hang downwards from its mouth—the length of a man's arm, sharp as our swords. The head is large enough to gulp you down in one swallow. Six legs, four armed with hand-like claws, can crush a man's body to a bloody mass of bone and flesh. Their meat is delicious when roasted over a fire, and those of us who survive will dine on flesh for the first time since being brought into training. Its hide is black like night and covered with flat scales like the hardest steel of our swords. Like Gora said, there are but two places where it can be killed. The eyes, if a spear goes deep enough, and the points behind its ears. Either wound can reach the brain. But behind the ears the flesh is soft, and the bone paper-thin. A puncture will kill. But this is a hard place to get to. A man who can reach this place while the creature is still able to see, is honored greatly by his fellow warriors. A day of celebration is given him immediately upon returning home."

"But how could a man reach such a place?" I countered, immediately interested.

"Oh, but that's the catch. You must either leap from a grav-plate, or find a way up its scaly hide from the ground." Then Adt seemed to read my thoughts. We had talked some about Youi in the past days. He'd been shocked to hear how casually I assumed it would be possible to win the hand of the Proctoress of Bel-loniea, but had admitted it would be legal and ethical to offer myself as a husband if I had Social Position in the Royal Class. A great act of courage might give me this edge. I had sworn to take the first opportunity.

"I would not try that, my friend, for death would surely swallow you down. It takes great skill and experience to hunt Korda. And—above all, you would have to go against Gora's orders. Only success would be justification. If the Korda didn't kill you and you failed, Gora would make you wish you had been killed. No—such a feat would not be for a man with no experience with a Korda."

By now the gigantic sun had touched the southwestern horizon and the sky lighted up in deep reds. Clouds billowed in the fire of the heavens with such bloody, savage beauty, that for a moment everybody turned to watch the sunrise.

"It's a good sign," Adt announced. "Blood will flow from our blades before the hunt is up."

"Why do you say that?" I inquired.

"So is the Muti proverb. When the sun rises on a hunt with blood surrounding it, that is the promise of victory." His voice held no doubt.

We were flying low over a forest now and I looked out one of the half-dozen windows of the grav-plate flyer. A river made its way back and forth across the forest floor like some kind of meandering snake.

The rest of the day continued on quietly restful. Several times I slept, tiring of the view which continued without

41

relief. During the late afternoon, white-capped mountains turned into a tall, thick purple-green jungle beneath us.

Finally the grav-disk headed for a clearing along the river which we had been following throughout the day.

The sun was slowly lowering to the northeast. We had eaten twice of the hard Mio-stick, a tasteless brown dried food which was given warriors during times of war when they were away from their homes and unable to find food to hunt down. A ten-day supply could be kept in their harness pouches. Ka was served in small cups, cold but refreshing. Once we settled down on the river bank, Gora ordered us into formation and we were marched outside. Camp was set up with amazing speed. Several men were ordered into the flower-sprinkled jungle to gather dry wood while the rest of us arranged our sleeping blankets in a circle around a place where two others began digging a small pit.

"Here," Gora announced, "Korda comes to drink just at the break of night. Here we will make our kill and feast, if luck is with us. If not we will search the night and sleep the day."

That evening luck was not with us and so we were drilled on our roles for the hunt. Gora assigned me to the light-beam and one of his assistants instructed me on its use. It was a simple operation. The light was in the shape of a ball with a blunted front through which poured a beam of light, controlled by a trigger device underneath. The top of the grav-plate was lower and we drifted over the night forest, just topping the tallest trees. The hours dragged by without any sign of a Korda. As the sun rose the next morning all of us were exhausted from lack of sleep, but Gora ran us through exhaustive exercises, double-timing around the grav-plate flyer time and time again until we fairly staggered the last lap. Then he ordered us to sleep.

That day was a torment of restlessness. We were surrounded by a land of lush beauty, thickly laden with tangled undergrowth, flowering trees, brush of lacy purple leaves, twisting vines all blending together to create an intricate mosaic pattern of richly vivid colors. Birds sang and croaked gaily in a strangely eerie concert of incessant chattering. And then the insects came from ground and air at us like a loathsome army. They were malignant carnivorous creatures who industriously pecked and bit on every exposed portion of flesh. I finally rolled myself completely into the blanket, covering my head. Only then was it possible to find rest.

By the time the sun was setting, Gora was up straining his lungs. We immediately leaped from our blankets, rolled them up and went into a double-row formation.

"Tonight you will find a Korda or all of you will wish you had stayed back in Bel-loniea!" Gora growled. What he intended to do to make good his threat we never learned, because the bad luck of the night before was now reversed. We were just climbing into the flyer when a terrible roar sounded. The hairs at the back of my neck stiffened. Cold chilled my back as sweat burst from every pore.

The others murmured with excitement. Adt nudged me. "This is it, friend."

Automatically I touched the hilt of my sword, then released it at Gora's command that we take our posts. The top of the flyer was lowered as we lifted from the ground.

Gora commanded that we were not to strap ourselves in. "A test of courage!"

Another bloodcurdling roar grated from the jungle, followed by the crush of branches breaking against a rough hide. I turned toward the sound as I took my post at the light-beam at the front of the ship. I would be totally exposed to the Korda's attack and helpless to defend myself while handling the light-beam. Nonetheless I drew my sword and then held the trigger device in my left hand. At least I would attempt to put in a few counterattacks if the time came. At this post I had little chance to make any bold leap onto the Korda—a play which I had planned out, since success would surely win rewards of honor and possibly make it feasible to leap through the class line to the Royal level.

Then I saw the Korda and could not help feeling a sense of relief that the decision had been taken out of my hands.

The creature was even taller than Adt had suggested, and its front legs were quite long, double-jointed, giving them an almost snake-like agility. The huge eyes looked red-rimmed in the semi-darkness of twilight. The face was like

43

hard bone, the mouth splitting it almost to the ears. Two rows of sharp, pointed teeth revealed themselves as it snapped at the flyer. The long fangs just clipped the nose of the grav-ship, which leaped away with great speed. For a moment I had a sickening lungful of its nauseating breath.

"Spears one and two!" screamed Gora from my left.

Two spears were flung at the large eyes, one bounced off the nose, the other entered the softer flesh of the right lid. The creature tore the spear away with one of its huge claws, then struck at the flyer as it shot higher.

I looked own at that horrible black hide, shiny like a shell. Saliva drooled from those huge gaping jaws as they snapped repeatedly at us.

"Spears three, four, five and six!" commanded Gora as the flyer circled and dove toward the Korda.

"Light-beam!"

I squeezed the trigger device in my left hand, aimed at the Korda's huge black eyes.

The beast screamed, blinked, attempted to get away from the bright light as the spears were flung toward it.

Two spears bounced off its eyelids, another tipped the left ear.

"What a monster!" came a voice from behind me.

"Quiet, warrior!" Gora commanded.

Watching the Korda snapping and swinging around to follow our ship, I could see how difficult it would be to get upon its back and climb to the point where its pointed ears lay at the back of its head. Though at such a place a man would be safe from counterattack. Getting onto the back was another thing.

We dipped for attack after attack, doing nothing more than to enrage its anger as we kept just beyond its reach. Then finally a spear point managed to sink into the left eye, but not deep enough to make a kill.

A shout rang from the ship.

"Keep circling to the left," Gora announced. "We'll have our chance now!"

The ship made a deep dive to the left—on the Korda's blind side—and Gora ordered more spears thrown.

At the same time the Korda screamed, snapped, struck at the ship and before the pilot could cut away, one of the front legs connected with the side of the grav-plate with such force that we were almost overturned.

I felt myself thrown high into the air and away from the ship. At that moment it seemed that I was going to die. Luckily we weren't too high, having come low. Even then the impact of my body striking the ground was jarring. I rolled quickly forward, eyes alert, sword still clutched in my hand.

"Torlo Hannis!" came a voice not far from my right. I recognized it as Fita. Turning I saw him rushing into the bush.

A yell sounded from the ship and after a moment the light flashed in the creature's good eye, keeping its attention on the flying disk and away from me and Fita who had by now disappeared.

I came to my feet, discovered the Korda turned away. I was on its left side and saw my chance.

Rushing forward, I found the rough hide with my left hand. The scaly plates on the Korda's body were about the size of a man's head, making it easy to climb upwards, much as one might climb a ladder.

My body was between the Korda's head and the ship, so there was no chance of being accidentally struck by my fellow warriors.

I scampered up the side, then onto the back and toward the thick plated neck, one thought frozen into place: get up to the head behind the ear and plunge my blade deep in one swift movement.

Then I heard a terrible scream rumble from the Korda. It reared upwards, just as I was climbing up its long neck. It was all I could do to keep hold of the rough hide as the Korda thrashed around like a wounded, dying animal.

Then I was at its ear, holding my sword, poised to plunge into the soft pulsing spot which would immediately kill the creature.

With a convulsive shudder the Korda jerked away from the flyer, started toward the wide black river.

I then drove my blade at the ear, but in the rush missed the mark, then the next moment I was flung from its back as it suddenly collapsed with a last mighty jerk.

My body was thrown into the icy water and I frantically started swimming, sure that in a moment I would serve as an early night snack for this monstrous beast.

A moment later I stood on solid ground and saw the Korda was lying still, half in the water, head submerged.

The flyer settled quietly to the ground and a yell came from some twenty-seven throats as men poured from the grav-plate to surround me. Adt placed a hand on my shoulder, grinning from ear to ear.

"You are truly a brave man!" he exclaimed with pride.

Gora stood before me, his face was split with an admiring smile. "I thought you would be killed. And you have no knowledge of this world!"

I looked from one man to the other. "I didn't make the kill!"

Gora nodded. "But you might have if we had not been lucky enough to get a spear in its other eye a moment before you reached the ear. The bravery is in the attempt—success is simply a matter of luck."

Suddenly a couple of men lifted me onto their shoulders and paraded me around the flyer, shouting and laughing. But I felt little joy. If I had actually leaped from the flyer and then made the kill, it would have been different.

Nonetheless I was paraded around for a long time, then deposited in front of the campfire pit. They wouldn't allow me to help with the cutting-of-the-Korda ceremony or with the preparation of the meat.

I watched before the fire as my fellow warriors worked long into the night, laboriously hacking away a large portion of the hard hide and then slicing huge chunks of meat from the Korda's flank. The three moons were high in the sky by the time several warriors, under the leadership of Adt Dorta, who seemed an expert in trimming Korda flesh, came to the fire. They made a support with two large stones and then ran a sword through the huge flank of meat, suspended the blade across the fire over the stones.

46

The deep red meat was cooked until black charcoal on the outside, the flames eating hungrily away at the tender flesh. The sweet aroma which came from the cooking meat created a sharp pang of hunger. Then the meat was taken from the flames and set on some of the hard black hide which had been so painstakingly cut away from the Korda. After the meat had cooled a little, Gora approached with drawn sword, stood over it like some supernatural demon, the flames flickering highlights on the angular features.

"And, lo, the great hunters of Bel-loniea came and slew the dragon.

"And, lo, Torlo Hannis, the Lost One, bravely engaged the Korda.

"And, lo, his bravery is honored by these present.

"And, lo, he of our unit, has brought honor upon us all.

"And, lo, he who has brought honor, will eat of the first meat."

He had chanted the words in a sing-song fashion, his voice rising higher and higher toward the end. At the last word her lifted the sword high above his head and flung it downwards, slicing clear through the meat, cutting it in two equal portions.

"And, lo, Torlo Hannis will cut from the side he desires that portion he sees fit as proper reward for his bravery."

Adt explained: "By custom you deserve a full half, and may take any or all of that share."

I stood, moved to the meat, took out my knife and cut a slice which seemed quite enough to satisfy the hunger of any man.

Immediately the others formed a circle around the roasted Korda flesh and Gora sliced portions equal to mine. After everybody had been given a slice of meat we squatted around the campfire. The meat was delicious, tender, full-flavored like nothing I remembered tasting before. It was by far the best meal I had had on Noomas.

Afterwards, war chants were sung by my fellow warriors. Later we rolled up in blankets and fell into an exhausted sleep. By then I had decided that Gora was not such a bad fellow after all. He was the kind of man who would be good to have at your side in battle. The necessity of training us had forced him into the role of a sadist.

The next morning Gora was up early, shouting us awake. The relaxed good-natured companionship of the night before had come to an end. Our training began immediately with twenty laps around the flying disk. Exhausted, we stepped into the ship and it took off, heading for Belloniea.

Gora said, once we were high over the jungles: "Today you will take the Ceremony of the Muti and become true warriors. In the next ten-day period you will learn what it means to be a warrior. You can bet your bloodless swords on that!"

Under normal circumstances, I was told by Adt, we would be taken before the Muti of the Special Corps, touched upon the forehead and blessed. Then the next ten-day period would begin a serious instruction in killing. We would be pitted against captured slave-warriors to battle to the death; those who survived would become officers; the others would be buried with full honors.

But circumstances were far from normal in Belloniea, and our test-of-courage and skill would not be against slave-warriors; and there would be no Muti ceremony that day or for a long time in the future.

As we approached Bel-loniea it was to discover the city was under siege by a huge attacking army from Diano.

48

CHAPTER FIVE

THE INVADING DIANOS

The scene which we saw in the distance was beautiful in its primitive savagery. Colorful pennants flew from hundreds of spears around and in the city. Flying grav-disks were engaging in battle in the air along the perimeter of the wall. The Dianos were attempting to fly men into the city, but the Bel-loniea forces were holding them back. Brightly painted grav-plate flyers of various sizes dodged back and forth across the walls, driving in and out at each other, explosive gunfire exchanging from one craft to another. Several ships screamed up into the sky like wounded birds and then twisted over, men dangling by their harness straps as the flyer made a final plunge to the ground, crashing into a mangled pile of steel and flesh. Green and yellow tents were thickly scattered around the wall, surrounded by thousands of dots which were warriors preparing for mass attack.

Adt Dorta, at my side, said: "We're in for a great show!"

"I'd rather think we were cut off, in a very bad position!" I pointed out. "Wouldn't it be a simple matter for them to cut us down?"

Adt grinned, revealing strong even white teeth. "They won't be expecting an attack from this quarter. We'll probably circle around their forces, find the weakest point and shoot across before they realize what happened."

At that point Gora called us to attention, stood in the middle of the disk and announced: "What we've been expecting for some time has happened. By secret orders from our Proctor all ships which left the city were equipped with

Kay-bombs for just such an emergency. We were instructed, under these circumstances, to come in low, circling, dropping the Kay-bombs on the Diano forces on our return into the city. You're going to see a lot of action today. And remember that there's no better test of your worth than war. There will be no training games for you now. Each of you will be armed with Kay-guns and Kay-bombs. Drop bombs on orders and fire the guns at will. Try to kill as many Dianos as possible before we are shot down or manage to make our way into the city. We'll be flying low, just over their heads, so throw the bombs as far as possible. I'll be at the controls and call out numbers. You'll be given a number between one and four. When I call your number throw a bomb, the others will keep a continual fire at the Diano warriors below. Try to hit the tents and grounded flyers, because there will be the High Command and officers. We want to create as much havoc as possible. I'll keep flying until our bombs are exhausted, then I'll make a run for the wall. Now strap yourselves to the harness rings—and good luck to you all! You're all top fighting men, untried but well-trained. Before the day's up you're going to get a chance to understand the training we've given you. Live!"

Without another word he turned to the controls and took them from the assistant who had been flying the disk.

The rest of us clipped our harnesses to the rings as the top of the craft was lowered. Then the two assistants opened a compartment in the floor of the flyer and withdrew several boxes which contained small rounded egg-shaped metal balls. These they quickly handed out to each man. I ended up with a small pile in front of me. Then one of the assistants started counting off men.

"You're one, you're two, you're three, four, one, two, three, four..."

My number was two. Adt at my right, was three. I turned to him, asked: "How do these work?"

We had not received instructions on Kay-bombs but I had learned that most men born in Bel-loniea knew much about the weapons of war by the time they were ten years old.

50

"Just throw them," Adt explained. "They'll explode on impact."

"And we were carrying them in the ship while fighting the Korda?" I cried, realizing how dangerous it might have been while combating the beast.

"They were well-packed, and there's an electronic field in that compartment which keeps them from exploding by accident. There was no danger," Adt grinned. "In any case, it is the movement through the air which burns off the outer coating—another protective measure. We don't take chances like you suggest."

I nodded, checking the small hand-weapon which had been passed to me a moment before. I remembered from our training with Kay-guns that they held 50 explosive charges, the size of a coarse grain of sand. When the pellet was discharged from the powerful air-pressure gun it exploded only upon striking an object. A man struck by the pellet would have a good piece of flesh and bone torn away. It was a wicked weapon and not used in honorable combat between two men, unless so agreed in the beginning. Usually the Noomas warrior chose the sword because of the skill and bravery needed in it use; plus the fact that a man could come out of such an engagement with a mere scratch. But in war every weapon that would be brought into use was considered fair play.

Our flyer was now dropping lower and Gora ordered us all to silence. Every eye turned to the trampled farm fields around the city. I felt a sudden wave of deep excitement. It seemed as if I'd faced scenes of war all my life. War fell upon my consciousness as naturally as breathing. For a moment I had a flashing mental picture of some other battlefield, men in different kinds of uniforms, cigar-shaped flying objects which I recognized in a flash of understanding to be spaceships. Then the picture drifted away, running, fleeing from recognition. A moment later I was trembling, aware that cold sweat covered my body.

Adt shook me, "What's wrong?"

"Nothing."

"Don't be afraid to admit fear," Adt admonished. "We're all scared."

51

"It wasn't that!" I countered roughly, staring into his eyes, once again in control of myself. "I remembered something—from the past. It was only a reaction."

"Silence!" Gora shouted.

Adt went back to his post an arm's distance from mine. He leaned out over the edge of the craft. I followed his example to discover we were already almost over the outer fringes of the Diano forces.

Flyers were still battling back and forth across the wall, some crashing in the city itself. There was a primitive element of no-give on both sides, brutal and harsh. Battle cries mingled with screams of death.

"Fire at will!" Gora ordered as the ship lowered, skimming the edge of the enemy camp.

The soft crack of twenty-seven Kay-guns sounded in the air as I squeezed the trigger of my own weapon. Immediately small explosions pecked around the warriors of the Diano army as they prepared for battle in the back lines. Shouts of surprise and anger mixed with the screams of mortally wounded men. My shot went true to its mark, an officer giving orders to his men. The man's chest exploded red as he fell to the ground.

"Bombs-one!" Gora shouted above the noise of battle.

Seven arms flung out over the sides of the grav-disk and a moment later the staggered crack of heavy explosions came from all around. I saw a tent burst into flames and then rip to shreds. Men yelled in agony. Another bomb fell in the center of a group of warriors, blasting them in different directions, dead or badly wounded.

"Bombs-three!"

Adt threw at a small tent which burst with multiple explosions.

"An arms storehouse!" he laughed, pleased.

Gora continued toward the walls of Bel-loniea in a zigzag fashion. We hit the enemy and before they could adjust to this unexpected attack, our ship was far past them. By the time we had exhausted our bombs, the Diano were aware of the attack and most of the battlefield alert. Two flyers took off from the ground and started after us as one larger ship turned from the wall to attack.

Gora cursed, yelled: "I'm going under the big fellow—those at back cover our retreat. Up front aim at the grav-engines of the big one."

I turned and kept my attention on the huge flyer in front. It was a small battleship, Adt explained, armed with Kay-guns.

"We have little chance on this one!" His eyes frowned into squinted lines.

One of the guns on the large ship fired and the explosive shock of a near miss slammed the side of our grav-disk. Gora was knocked from the control, fell unconscious to the floor.

Adt tore himself from his harness ring and leaped to the controls as our ship started going out of control. Immediately he brought the ship back on course but headed directly toward the walls of Bel-loniea.

"Hold on!" he screamed.

One of the warriors at my side pulled at Gora and I helped as the ship twisted up, heading almost straight toward the high sun.

The sound of metal against stone brought warning how close death breathed down our throats.

All of us were dangling from our harness straps. I and the man on my right strained to keep hold of Gora. Time froze, stretched out as Adt kept our ship in the vertical position.

I heard an explosion and the craft slammed sideways, jerking us painfully on our harness straps. My companion's grip was torn from Gora and I felt our commanding officer slipping from my fingers. Not too many days before I would have welcomed such a chance to end the life of this man but now I strained with every muscle in my body to keep hold of him. Then the ship leveled off just as Gora was torn from my grip. He slammed across the floor to the other side of the ship.

One of the Dianos' small flyers side-swiped us, a rapid-fire Kay-gun riddled the deck to hit three warriors, killing one. Then we were over the wall, our own ships coming to our defense,

Adt headed for the first roof in sight upon which a busy hangar was located. Everybody shouted in deep-throated voices, unhooking themselves from the ship and surrounding Adt. Gora had now recovered and called us to order.

"We'll report to the first officer we see. You will probably be given men to command. War conditions force quick promotions. Use every bit of knowledge you have learned. Follow orders without question. You'll be given scarves which will inform every commander that you are new, inexperienced officers. They will give you as much instructions as possible. You're a good group. Live!"

He marched us off the ship and then toward the hangar, where warriors and officers were crowded, busy in the rush of war preparations.

We stood in formation while Gora approached a high-ranking officer. It was some time before he was given any attention. Shortly after that he returned with a handful of yellow scarves which were passed around.

"Tie them to your harness, at the shoulder, so they are in full view from front or back."

Once we had fitted the scarves as instructed, he marched us to a stairway and then into the building below. We were taken to a large room full of officers and warriors.

I asked Adt, " How long will the Diano continue their siege of the city?"

"Until they get what they are after or are defeated. That could be a along time."

"What do they want?"

"The Proctor's son of Diano has decided he wants Youi Janis as his woman. Not as a Proctoress but as a slave woman. He is already married—a marriage of state, I understand. But even if he were not married, he probably would attempt to steal Youi Janis and make her his slave woman. It's the kind of thing Aoji would attempt as an insult to our women and nation.

"The Dianos and Bel-lonieans have never been friendly as long as they have existed as separate nations. The

Dianos have the lands beyond the mountains. Originally they were part of our nation but a man by the name of Diano, second son of our Proctor some 500 years ago, attempted to overthrow custom, kill his brother and become Proctor of Bel-loniea. The attempt was stopped just in time and Diano was exiled with all his followers—which numbered in the hundreds. They went through the Beldon Pass and created a new nation on the other side of the mountains. Ever since then we have been at war with each other—though at times a truce is recognized for as long as a generation. During these periods open trade is encouraged and exchanges of students. Such a truce has just been broken off at the beginning of this year. Aoji came here to study under Andon Janis and learn the ways of our mighty Koris. He brought several young doctors to do the studying while he flitted around in our Royal social life. Most of the Royalty here snubbed him; especially Youi Janis. He went to the Pleasure House and escorted these women to social gatherings—something which is not done. It was an insult, suggesting that these women were as good as the Royal ladies of Bel-loniea. Taking them to Royal parties was as much to say your best women are not better than the lowest street girl. Finally, when he did this at a gathering at my father's house, Kigor Dorta challenged him to a duel, which was as much as to sentence him to death—for no Diano can stand up against the sword of Kigor Dorta, Master swordsman of Bel-loniea. The Proctor stepped in and politely suggested that Aoji leave and return home the next day. Bitter words were exchanged and Aoji announced that a state of war now existed between our two nations and that he would be back to take Youi Janis as his slave woman.

"Now he has kept his promise to invade our lands. It will be necessary to kill every man and woman in Bel-loniea to keep the other half. Even then, Aoji would only have a dead slave woman, for Youi has pledged before a Muti that she will take her own life in such an event. That pledge alone would have been enough to obligate every warrior to lay down his life in her defense—even if she wasn't so nationally popular."

As Adt had told me this, cold chills trembled down my back. Then hot anger burned violently.

A loud voice in the front of the room commanded silence. All eyes turned toward the man who was dressed in a flowing yellow robe. Small medals covered his right chest.

Adt said in a soft whisper: "That is Qui Shan, the Commander of our forces. We are honored."

"Men," Qui Shan said in a loud, deep voice. "You are here for one purpose, the defense of our Proctoress, and the organization of a counterattack outside the city."

He paused, then continued. "I have here a report about their forces from Gora—Officer of the Training Division of the Special Corps. A training ship under his command was on its way back from a Korda hunt this morning and made a victorious return, damaging the enemy. Any time you see a man with a yellow scarf on his shoulders, honor him, for he was a member of this newly trained group. They are unseasoned warriors. But battle will season them quickly. They are to be given a ten-unit to command. Pick your best men for this assignment.

"You are all commanded to counterattack and many of you will not return to the city. Sell your lives dearly. Cause as much damage to the enemy as possible, let them feel the sting of your swords and know that the men of Belloniea are deadly warriors. Let them realize how useless it is for them to attempt to take our Proctoress."

He stepped back and another officer, dressed in simple harness much like our own, but jeweled with sparkling stones, moved forward and started reading from a paper in front of him, calling off names, assigning them to a unit number.

I was named with five others and we were taken command of by another officer with jeweled harness. His name was Perl Cort. He took us to a small chamber down the hall, closed the door and then told us to seat ourselves in the chairs facing a desk.

"In one half unit time we will go up on the roof and take a flyer. There will be ten men under each of you and your fighting instructions are simple enough. Engage the enemy and kill as many as possible before retreat is called. You will not surrender under any circumstances. There is only one reason for capture, because you have been overwhelmed by numbers, disarmed and are helpless to resist. If you are captured, you must make as much trouble as possible for the Diano. That's your sworn duty to the Proctoress of Bel-loniea." He hesitated. "You wouldn't be the Torlo Hannis who came from off-world?"

Perl Cort looked pleased.

I heard a cry from the men. "For Torlo Hannis!"

"We are doubly honored. If you are as gifted in war as Andon Janis is in his profession, I believe that the Diano have a surprise waiting for them."

"I'm an untried warrior."

"Untried, but skilled, I would imagine. Gora is a great teacher. He said that his new group was outstanding. He speaks highly of all of you. I'll be expecting great things from you, Torlo Hannis."

"I thank you, sir, for your confidence in me—and hope it is not ungrounded."

"How could it be? You are from off-world!"

"That might be true, but memory has stayed off-world, too. I know nothing other than what has been taught me here in Bel-loniea."

"Nevertheless, you will see, Torlo Hannis," Perl Cort insisted stubbornly, "that I am right in expecting great things from you. It can be no other way!"

Such blind and apparently worshiping faith seemed groundless to me. Yet once he had made up his mind, there was no changing it.

Then he gave us last minute instructions, little of which made any impression on me, for I was thinking about Youi Janis.

CHAPTER SIX

THE PRICE OF DISHONOR IN BATTLE

I realized that the Bel-loniea nation lived naturally by the sword: but how must a young woman feel when she knows men are going to their death in her defense?

I did catch some of the last of Perl Cort's closing statement.

"If you are cut off from the ship, and the horn of retreat has been sounded from the city walls, try to reach the forest. There is no reason to throw your lives away uselessly or fall into the hands of the Diano, who would quickly bleed your back into slavery for life. Above all, look out for your men."

We were taken to the roof and assigned ten men each. The ones under me were strong battle-scarred veterans, with a senior warrior named Orra Jik who was in charge of the other men. It was Orra Jik who introduced the others.

I ordered Orra Jik to form them in a circle around me. We squatted on the roof top.

"First, I want you all to know that I respect your experience at battle and suspect you might have your doubts about me. Possibly you have heard rumors about Torlo Hannis, the Lost One. It is true that my past life is behind a closed mental door through which I cannot look. All I know is that what I have learned here in Bel-loniea and all I know about battle is from Gora and our little experience this morning upon returning to the city. You will feel assured that my first thought will be in the safety of you ten men. If there are any questions or doubts in your minds, speak up now. Later there won't be time for hesitation."

58

They all were grinning, as if please at some private joke.

"What is it?" I felt slightly irritated.

Orra Jik explained: "Rest assured, Officer Hannis, that we are proud to be your first command. We all volunteered and were lucky enough to be picked from several hundred top fighting men." He studied me for a moment. "There are many among the ranks of warriors who wonder how you will turn out, sir. There is much betting."

Immediately I saw the underlying reasons for their eagerness to be a part of this command. If I turned out a coward, they would be eye-witnesses to the fact; if I proved my steel in battle, they would be in a favored position in the eyes of a man climbing up in Bel-loniea society.

"And how do you vote?"

Orra Jik squinted, his dark brooding features unreadable. "I had my doubts before seeing you, sir." He fingered a long scar on his right cheek. "Now, I believe you will be a good officer. If you live."

There was a challenge in his voice; but it held the offer of friendship. I was beginning to get a picture of a society that was harsh on cowards, worshippers of success. At least these men, while curious, were pulling for me, though there was no doubt about the fact they were watching every move I made—one could not help understanding why they were wondering just how much they could depend on me.

Perl Cort called us to attention. Five other groups of ten men were now lined alongside us. Perl Cort said: "Our unit will be sent directly over the far wall with an escort of ten flyers—there will be twenty other such groups leaving at the same time. We're to create an island within their forces. Try to keep our group close together. Hold as much ground as possible. Live! May the mighty power of the Mutis of Bel-loniea go with you."

He marched up to a large grav-disk which had guns mounted on all sides. Once we had boarded the ship, I formed the men around me. "I want you to work in pairs, each guarding the other's back, so there is less chance of being cut down from behind."

Orra Jik nodded. "Good idea. Who will guard your back?"

"You." The glint in Orra Jik's black eyes revealed he was pleased by this choice.

The ship immediately lifted from the roof and was joined by the escort of small one-man scout flyers. They quickly formed around our nose like a spear point.

I pulled the Kay-gun from its holster and shifted it to my left hand, then drew the long-bladed sword. It would be the first time I had used the bladed weapon against an enemy I intended to kill. They say your first kill with the sword is the most difficult one.

To Orra Jik I said: "If you get any good ideas while in battle, don't hesitate to call out an order. I depend on your great experience."

The scar grinned into a jagged line. "You are an unusual officer."

"They say that the professional man-at-war knows more than the green officer."

He frowned. "It's true. But I've never heard an officer admit it."

"You've heard it now."

Our exchange was interrupted by the sound of Kay-guns. The air around us flashed with explosions, yells, curses. I looked over the bow of the ship and saw that we were already passing the city wall. Diano troops had begun mounting ladders along the wall in an effort to find a way to the top.

"Why don't they just drop troops over by flyer?" I asked Orra Jik. "Or land them on the wall itself?"

"They try—and succeed at times. But the old ways aren't forgotten, neither is a good means of attack ignored. They will use every method to get into the city. Those warriors know their chances are small but they get higher pay and the use of tavern girls, free, at the expense of their Proctor. Those who survive are honored. Many of these warriors are young boys trying to earn honor, or dishonored Royalty attempting to win back their social position—many are mercenaries."

60

"What good does the honor do for them if they are dead?" I wanted to know.

"They find paradise, so the Mutis tell us."

I was beginning to wonder who actually ruled on Noomas, the Proctors or the Mutis. It seemed that the Muti word was law—accepted blindly.

The flyer got past the escorts and dove at us. The ship's gunners shot it down before any real damage could be done. Three men were wounded; it might have been far worse.

On the ground the Diano foot warriors were paying close attention to our flight. By the time we were just above the ground, the Diano forces were already starting toward us to support those who would be first to feel the sharpness of Bel-loniea blades.

The gunners of our ship kept firing into the ranks of all Diano within range. By the time the flyer touched down, a fair amount of ground had been cleared away for our disembarkation. Dead Diano warriors were scattered all around us.

I leaped from the ship the instant it landed, expecting my men to immediately follow.

Almost at the same time a unit of Diano surged across the space upon which their dead companions lay. I fired with the Kay-gun, squeezing off five rapid shots before the others reached me. For all I knew, I was the only one off the flyer.

Then I heard the deep-throated yells of my men as the Dianos came within blade reach.

Suddenly we were surrounded by a score of warriors, their blades licking out greedily to touch our half-naked bodies.

The first man I engaged was awkward and off balance. I brushed aside his sword and then lunged the point of my own blade deep into the man's naked chest.

Another warrior was there to replace him. Now I found myself crossing blades with a more careful swordsman. Yet, to my amazement, he fell within the first couple of exchanges. A flash of light came from the right. My blade moved, instinctively, caught the edge of the other sword on the hilt twisted and then lunged. The man parried and slashed

61

brutally at my head. At that instant I was off balance, having expected the other's weapon to have flung away from his grasp.

Orra Jik's blade cut into the man's side and he fell dead at our feet.

I remembered the Kay-gun and fired several times into the enemy ranks. Then my blade was attacked by another warrior. During such an engagement I noticed that nobody ever reverted to the Kay-gun which all held in their left hands. Later I learned this was a code of honor. One could shoot at others, even if they fought with one of your fellows during combat, but never at the man you faced with naked blade. It was considered a cowardly act and brought disgrace to the man who did so.

Blood spattered my body from half a dozen tiny wounds. The Diano finally pressed back. The ease in which those warriors fell before the blade was mystifying. Yet, I could thank Gora and Adt for their training—for without that I surely would have died in those first moments of battle.

Orra Jik cried: "Drop to the ground!"

Automatic reflexes moved my body.

I turned, questioned Orra Jik silently.

"They're going to engage in Kay-gun battle. A standing man is a Korda before the glare of the sun."

There was no time for any more verbal exchanges before the small explosions of Kay-pellets kicked up the ground around us.

I returned fire. The enemy had formed a circle around our flyer. I felt cut off, helpless. How could we possibly expect to escape with our lives? Then the sound of rapid fire came from behind us. I glanced back to see the big guns of our flyer trained on the Diano.

The enemy fell back, half of their numbers dropped to the ground, dead. The flyers' guns chased after the Diano, killing half a dozen more warriors before they had taken cover behind a nearby flyer.

"What damage to us?" I inquired of Orra Jik.

"None seriously hurt, sir." He stated after making a quick sweep of the men in my command. :That was a brave thing you did back there!"

"What?"

"Leaping out first. The other officers were put to shame by your move. We were stunned."

"What's so strange about that? A leader leads, does not follow!" I announced in a matter-of-fact voice.

Orra's scar cracked into a crooked line. "But few take it seriously, sir. You've won the respect of every man on the ship. And the special pride of those in your own command."

I nodded; then turning my attention to the field in front of us, asked: "What now? Do we just lie here, waiting for them to attack?"

"What would you suggest?" Orra asked in a respectful but slightly mocking voice, as if there was nothing else to do.

"We could attack them."

"And be captured."

"That's what we're here for. Attack and make the enemy feel the point of our steel. Come, gather the men. We'll attack in two groups of five and six. You lead one and I'll take the other. You go to the right, I to the left—we'll meet on the other side of that flyer."

Without questioning the order, Orra Jik split the men into two groups, giving me five warriors. I started to object, then decided this was not the time to argue.

I gave the order to move fast in a zigzag fashion like a bolt of lightning. From the expression on their faces this type of move was new but they seemed to see the sense of it.

As we started forward, I heard a muffled call from one of the other officers. "What're they doing?"

The amazing thing was that battle information was filtering in from my subconscious mind—knowledge which I had probably known in the past. I felt at complete ease leading this charge.

The Diano seemed mystified at our move and at first did not fire, merely watching our advance on the flyer. A vague plan formed in my mind. Then suddenly we were dodging Kay-explosions. One of my men rolled to the ground, dead.

"Death to the Diano!" I shouted.

Then we were upon them. My Kay-gun was firing rapidly as we approached, then as we engaged the enemy I ignored the gun in favor of the sword. A wave of excitement charged through me. There was something savagely beautiful about fighting with a naked blade. Each man had an equal chance as skill, training and raw courage were brought to a test. My men were at both sides of me and there was one fact brought swiftly into focus: the Bel-loniea warriors were far better trained in the art of swordsmanship—at least these men. Probably, I reasoned, this had to do with Kigor Dorta's mastery of the blade. I determined to learn as much as possible from Adt's father, when I had the honor of meeting him.

I found in these moments on the battlefield while engaging in swordplay, the mind could work on two levels at once. With as little experience as I had with the sword, mind and muscles moved the weapon in and out like a licking whip, snapping with death. Abruptly there wasn't a Diano alive in the immediate area.

"Take the ship!" I waved my blood covered blade to the seven remaining men.

Orra Jik took up the call and we leaped for the Diano flyer, which was about the size of the training grav-disk that had been used to hunt the Korda: though this one was armed with four rapid fire Kay-guns.

"Can you fly one of these?" I asked Orra Jik.

He nodded and immediately went to the controls.

"To the guns!" I instructed four men. "The rest of you help me find their supply of Kay-bombs."

Four men went to the four guns as the other two, covered with the blood of battle, helped me lift a plate in the middle of the disk. In the compartment we found several boxes of ammunition, most of which was for the rapid fire Kay-guns. But there were two boxes of Kay-bombs.

"Lift off!" I ordered Orra Jik.

Immediately the ship lifted from the ground, just as Diano warriors came screaming in toward us.

I marveled at the quickness in which orders were followed, without any questioning. They were well-trained men. If I had known how strange my commands seemed to them, I might have marveled even more. These men-of-war, who believed in giving no quarter in battle, had apparently never considered the concept of using an enemy ship during such a battle. The idea seemed natural to me. If we had been able to do so much damage with the training flyer, it seemed obvious that in one of their own ships our chances were even greater for doing far more damage.

The sun was high and hot in the sky above as we leaped above the battlefield.

"Fire at will!" I shouted.

Orra Jik said: "What about our own flyers?"

"We'll have to chance it." Then I realized why another ship had never been taken from the enemy. Our own flyers might serve as a great danger to us. How could they know we weren't Diano?

Our guns were now already beginning to spread death among the enemy below.

I grabbed a hand full of Kay-bombs and the other two warriors followed my example. I pointed directions to where they should post themselves, then took a position near Orra Jik near the front of the ship.

"Keep low, so our guns can be most effective."

The scar on Orra Jik's cheek twisted in a tense grin. "You're a brave leader, Torlo Hannis. But we will surely be shot down before long."

"Not if you fly this craft at top speed and keep low enough, just over their heads. Then, even if we are hit and crash, our chances of surviving are pretty good."

I was throwing Kay-bombs as fast as I could at any object which looked like a good target, at groups of warriors, tents, flyers. The damage being done to the enemy below well-rewarded any chance we were taking.

Going back to the supply of Kay-bombs, I heard a cry from the throat of one of our gunners. "For Torlo Hannis!"

The cry was taken up by the other men. "For Torlo Hannis!"

"They won't die if I have anything to say about it," I shouted stubbornly, throwing a Kay-bomb at one of the larger tents which we were passing. "Head for the wall! We return!"

"You can't do that without the order to retreat! The horns have not sounded from the city wall!" Orra Jik admonished. "They'll arrest you!"

"The ship is more important. If we can get it to the city, it will serve a good purpose for our forces."

Orra Jik reluctantly nodded, turned the flyer toward the city wall.

"You will be arrested, sir!" Orra told me again.

"I don't think so!"

"Retreat under fire without orders is considered cowardly."

"I don't think we are being cowardly!" I countered. "Do you?"

"No," he admitted with a grin. "But they might think differently."

I turned to the men, surveying them as they fired upon the Diano below. "We return to the city with a captured Diano ship. Are you with me?"

There was hesitation as if the men were considering the strangeness of the order.

Then their voices cried out my name as realization set in.

"Orra Jik—take to the sky, high as possible. It is our best chance. We'll continue throwing bombs. That should warn our own ships."

Immediately the flyer screamed up at 45° angle into the sky, high over the battlefield, until the warriors below became mere dots.

"Get rid of those bombs, men!" I ordered.

The gunners left their post and started gathering the Kay-bombs.

As we continued toward the city in a swift flight, my men dropped the Kay-bombs on those below. How much real damage done was hard to tell. Thousands of Diano warriors had come to make war with Bel-loniea. We were only annoying a huge beast like an insect might bother a Korda. But damage was being done. By the time we reached our wall, our own ships reluctantly fell back. Obviously they were as puzzled by what was happening as the Diano.

"To the first roof hangar," I instructed Orra Jik.

The moment we touched the roof, the ship was surrounded by Bel-loniea warriors, swords and Kay-guns pointed in our direction.

An officer stepped forward, his face hard, the eyes cold.

"What's the meaning of this?" he demanded upon recognizing our uniforms.

I stepped forward with a friendly grin. "I bring a Diano flyer back. We can use it well, for they will think it is a part of their forces."

The officer ignored my remark. "You return before retreat is sounded."

"The flyer is more important!" I pointed out, surprised by his abrupt attitude.

"You are under arrest. Your men will be held for questioning. Come with me!" he announced in an authoritative cold voice. "The punishment for disobeying orders during war is death. You will learn quickly the price of dishonor in battle!"

I started to argue, then saw from the expression on the man's face that it was useless. With a shrug, I stepped from the ship and allowed warriors to disarm me. Then under guard I was taken down a stairway, away from my men, arrested for a deed which should have brought honors. We had fought bravely, damaged the enemy far more than might have been expected of us; and captured a Diano grav-disk. Yet they refused to understand the real meaning of our act.

I couldn't help but wonder sickly: What kind of people were the Bel-loniea?

CHAPTER SEVEN

THE PROPHECY OF THE MUTI

They placed me in a darkened room, below ground level, bolted the door and left.

The sudden change from hero to prisoner was numbing. I tried to understand, attempted to reason out a logical, acceptable answer. It didn't make sense that their code of ethics would be this unbending and unreasonable.

Then I remembered how strongly Gora had pointed out the importance of following orders. An army which is trained to blindly follow orders is an army which is like a machine. This is good for the nation but bad for the individual. In war there are too many variables; too many events take place too fast to make it logical to mindlessly follow an order which has been made behind the battle lines by officers who are not personally involved. My move had given the Bel-loniea army a flyer which would make it possible to survey the enemy activities during night and day, without any danger of being shot down.

Depression became bitterness.

I lay on the damp floor of the prison cell, surrounded by total darkness.

It was a tomb world of black, inhabited by silent ghosts who threatened the mind. This fitted my emotional mood to perfection. Thoughts escaped from the present, attempted to penetrate beyond the wall of hidden memory which was so much like this cell, without solid shape, without sound, other than the immediate breath which sighed in and out of my lungs. Finally exhaustion took over and sleep soothed all thoughts away.

Upon waking, I had, for the first time on Noomas, the distinct impression that something important had brought me to this primitive world. What that might be was impossible to surmise. For a long time I lay there trying to remember what might have been so important to take me from another world to this one. Nothing came. At last I accepted the fact that such small pieces of memory were pressing to the surface awareness that it was impossible to fit them together. A visual picture of a man and woman flashed momentarily before my mind but their features were blurred, the details indistinct. They were important, this much I knew. What ever mission had brought me to Noomas I was sure was involved with those vague faces.

How long I lay there trying to remember, I don't know. Suddenly there were footsteps outside the door and the bolt was slipped back. Two armed guards stepped into the cell, outlined by the dim lighting from the corridor beyond.

"Come with us." The voice was commanding.

I was convinced they had come to take me to my execution. The arresting officer had warned that justice would be swift.

But for what purpose should I be killed, without any chance of defending myself?

They led me down the ill-lighted corridor and then up a flight of steps. Finally we came into a chamber in which several high-ranking officers were gathered. Everybody turned at my entrance.

Perl Cort and Qui Shan were among the officers. It was an impressive audience. Another door on the opposite side of the room opened and Orra Jik was escorted in with two guards at his side. He was armed like the rest.

Orra Jik started to make his way toward me but was held back by his two companions.

Perl Cort stepped forward. His eyes revealed deep concern and a heavy tiredness. "You have created a problem, Torlo Hannis. Your acts on the battlefield are inexplicable— yet courageous. Andon Janis was brought into this and suggested we consider the situation as totally different than if one of our native-born officers had committed a breach-of-

69

orders. His words were honored by our Proctor, and because of this you are to have a Muti hearing. Only by the Proctor's orders would such a thing happen during war! Thus you are honored for acts of courage—but the death punishment will be swift if you are found guilty." He hesitated, then asked: "What have you to say in your defense?"

"I don't think there's any need for defense. My actions speak for themselves."

There was an astounded murmur from around the room. Qui Shan, Commander of the Armed Forces of Bel-loniea, raised his hand. "We must wait for the Muti!"

Silence fell like a weighted blanket.

I surveyed my surroundings, first studying the expressions on the faces around me. Only Perl Cort and Orra Jik revealed honest concern in my behalf; the others were reserved, their faces as if cut from hard stone. Qui Shan appeared annoyed by the whole event, as if his time were too valuable to be taken up with such unimportant details. I could not blame the man, since Torlo Hannis was only a name from among his lower-ranking officers.

The room itself had hangings of blue on the walls with the golden face of a Korda embossed on them. The Royal insignia of Bel-loniea.

I could not help but wonder at the strange attitude of these people. During the high point of a war they were taking the time to give a hearing to a man they believed to have committed one of their more terrible war crimes in battle— retreating without orders. The attention being given me seemed far out of line for the importance my life should rate during the war conflict. Apparently Andon Janis' word was very powerful in Bel-loniea. Still, why had Qui Shan taken the time to be here? From the expression on his face it could be by Royal order. What powerful forces were being put into play? Or was it simply that my act of returning before retreat was ordered so great an offense that it took a very high court to reverse the sentence of death? This latter, I decided, was the only logical reason for so high-ranking a hearing. My offense must have been truly great in their eyes! The fact that Orra Jik was still armed suggested that my men, at least, were not held responsible. And this fell logically upon my mind. If warriors were trained to follow orders, regardless—then their followers should not be held responsible for obeying those orders.

Finally the door through which Orra Jik had entered the room opened and a robed, hooded figure entered the room. The robe was of a deep green, striped on the edges by gold. Immediately every head bowed.

I followed the example of the rest.

The robed figure stepped up to me and then drew aside the hood.

This was a Muti, I realized with a gasp of horror.

The face was both eyeless and without a nose. Where the eyes should have been was a deep depressed layer of skin. Two holes served as nostrils over a flat expanse above the thin slit mouth. Tiny shriveled ears appeared just above the jaw-bones. The head was totally hairless. The flesh stretched over the angular bony structure of the face like parchment which has been dyed bright purple.

The lips moved as a rumbling low voice said: "Fear not Torlo Hannis. We mean you no harm—other than the harm you have done yourself and thus honorably earned. If you be innocent of any cowardly act, so it will be stated."

The Muti reached out a gnarled, bony purple hand, whose veins stood up like swollen rivers. I repressed an automatic shiver as the Muti flesh touched my forehead. The hand was ice cold, as if frozen in death.

Staring into that eyeless face, I could not wonder at the fear and superstitious awe the Bel-lonieans had for these Mutant creatures. They would need no more supernatural power than a normal fear of something strange and alien, plus an intelligent program which would condition the normal humans to worship rather than hate.

A low rumble purred from the Muti's throat. "You fear my outer shell. You fear what you see—without knowing the outer shell means nothing. Outer beauty can be the mark of inner cruelty. Physical ugliness can mark a gentle wisdom and all-embracing love. Never judge a man by his face alone. Judge only what is within the man."

The Muti was silent for a moment, then the hand lifted from my forehead.

71

"You are a man without a past. There is a great wall across your consciousness. My mind has touched that wall, reached in, looked through the blackness and seen shadowy figures, misty memories—but it would take time to read fully into your past. Time we do not have right now." He turned to the Bel-loniea officers.

"This is an honorable, brave man. He must be judged by what is inside him, not by the acts which might seem difficult for your minds to understand. I see honesty. I see bravery. There is no reason to kill him—or to punish him for acts which he knew to be brave and right. I need not know what he has done—as you all well know. I read what he has done from the meeting of our minds. He acted wise, well. The flyer in which he brought his men back to Bel-loniea will prove the greatest weapon any man could have offered in the protection of your Proctoress. Behold, I tell you of the past and present and let you look into the future."

The Muti raised his hands high into the air. "Let it be known that Torlo Hannis is yet to serve you in greater deeds. Even now men are spiriting your Proctoress away!"

Immediate pandemonium broke loose. Voices rose in protest.

I was alert at once, while at the same time horrified by this announcement. "Why did you not warn us sooner, if you knew this?"

The Muti whipped around, faced me. The features contorted. "How dare you question the action of a Muti?" he rasped loudly, his voice ringing around the room like a live thing.

Silence fell like black death around me.

"All those present here know," the Muti announced after taking several deep breaths, as if controlling a terrible rage which was all but overwhelming. "A Muti does not interfere with the happenings around him. He will only report facts as they happen—as a warning. I see with mental eyes— and I see you moving across the course of our Proctoress like a shadow following a shadow. I but report what the mental process of the universe reveals to me—but I will never interfere or enter into the political affairs of you states. I explain this only because you have no way of knowing these things.

For it was upon reaching into your immediate future that I read the present by implication. Your future moves you away from Bel-loniea. I saw what I saw. You are a shadow against the image of Youi Janis. Thus the future is locked. Thus I tell those present what has taken place now—that which cannot be undone. Thus I announce to those here that you are important to the future of Bel-loniea. I have spoken!"

With that the Muti turned and left the room in long fluid strides.

Immediately I was surrounded by officers, their faces awed with sudden respect. It was Qui Shan who brought order.

He faced me. "What is it the Muti spoke of?"

I shook my head, as puzzled as those around me. "But if the Proctoress is in danger..."

Qui Shan gave orders to an officer: "Send a unit to search for the Proctoress—bar all exits from the city. Allow no one to leave! Then organize a search." Then he faced me. "Is that what you mean?"

I nodded.

"You will come with me, Torlo Hannis. I would talk to you in private."

With a shock, I realized from all but an executed prisoner, I had become the center of Royal attention, a man to be highly respected. Just on the word of a Muti. It was impressive.

Qui Shan led me from the room, up the stairs and down several corridors and into a small office. There was a guard posted at the door, to whom he said: "Send word to the Proctor that an emergency has arisen and that I would be honored by his immediate presence here."

When the warrior had left, Qui Shan closed the door, instructed me to sit in one of the comfortable wood frame leather chairs.

His attitude was that of a man pressed under fantastic responsibilities, yet he faced me pleasantly enough.

"The Muti says you are a shadow across Youi Janis' path—that you are destined to leave Bel-loniea. I can read that only one way: You are the key to Youi Janis' safety. The order to form a search was merely for appearances. We will not find her. The Muti's word is law. Though how one man could mean so much to a whole nation and..."

"How can he know such things?" I countered, still dazed by what had happened.

"A Muti has limited vision of the future. He can look into a man's mind and read what the past actions will lead up to. It was explained to me in this way when I was a small boy," Qui Shan said in a gentle voice, as if instructing a child in a basic fact of life. "As we add two and two and get four, the Muti can reach into the future by adding all these events of the past and come to the end result of an equation. They read more than they reveal. It is the way of the Muti not to interfere with us, other than to keep anyone away from avoiding justice. Then they will reveal just enough to honor justice."

I puzzled over that for a moment, then asked: "They expect something important to take place in the future which will involve me?"

"Not that simple. The Muti read what the future held for you, and merely pointed this fact out to us."

"What would happen if he had not been there to tell you this?"

"Nothing that has not already happened. The Muti does not change the present or future. What happened took place because it could not have been otherwise. You cannot make two and two equal five or three. Time controls all things. Events become causes for new events. The future is nothing but the addition of all that has happened in the past. Even the moment of your death cannot be altered, regardless of the fact you might learn of that moment now. You cannot make two and two equal anything other than four—and if you are to die a certain way and were told how and when, this is part of the equation which will equal your death at that time and place—so the Mutis have told us. Your event on this world in a part on the pattern. It is not so much that it is written down—a belief which was at one time believed so—but that life and actions are like the elements of the mathematical equation. One act leads automatically to another act."

74

"That leaves no room for choice—no place for the split path!" I argued. "We are helpless in the tide of our past acts. That leaves no room for free actions."

"It is the way. It is life. We have free will, and that is part of the equation," Qui Shan pointed out with finality.

The door opened at that moment and Proctor Romos came charging in, a fury of emotion.

"My grand-daughter has disappeared!" he bellowed, as if announcing some vital new information.

"So it is told by the Muti!" Qui Shan said simply in a calm voice. "Your High Worship, listen, there is much here which concerns you—and this man from another world—Torlo Hannis—and Youi Janis."

CHAPTER EIGHT

THE WAR HAS JUST BEGUN

The Proctor frowned at me. He seemed to have recovered from his first emotional outburst. "What's the meaning of this?"

Qui Shan said, soothingly, "The Muti claimed that Torlo Hannis is like a shadow crossing over the shadow of Youi Janis. It was through reading Torlo Hannis that he saw the Proctoress was being spirited away. That's when he warned us."

Romos, Proctor of Bel-loniea, faced me once again, his features now serious, questioning. "What place do you, a stranger, have in my grand-daughter's life?"

"I don't know, sire, other than it is my dearest wish to protect her!" I spread my hands in the air. "I am a man without a past—yet your Muti claims that I have a future that involves Youi, the Proctoress. I know no more than you."

Qui Shan spoke solemnly: "This is a remarkable warrior. He captured a Diano grav-plate and returned to the city—even if it was before the retreat call. And—"

"Oh, yes, I remember something about that—one of my advisors said the ship might serve us well during the next days. I remember, Andon and Youi insisted on a Muti hearing to determine the disposal of the man. Yes, I remember it now. The pressure of war takes small details out of memory. So this young man is responsible—and he is of some importance to Youi's future? Well, give him anything he wishes. If he wants a legion of warriors, give it. If he wants a flyer, give it. I must believe the word of the Muti. Whatever place

76

he has in our lives, it is apparently important enough to honor his word.

"A remarkable act, taking the ship like you did," Romos announced, then dismissed me with a glance.

"I'll organize a massive counterattack on the Diano! I'll see you, Qui Shan, in my chambers within the unit. See to it this man gets what he needs. We must not stand in the way of any movement he might make in the future."

With that, the Proctor left. Both Qui Shan and myself were mystified, but for totally different reasons.

"What happens now?" I inquired, trying to adapt to the strange events taking place. "You can count on me to enter any campaign organized to rescue Youi Janis."

Qui Shan's eyes enlarged in surprise; his heavy features twisted into a contortion of wonderment.

"We but follow you. You are the light, the guard, the shadow which we must follow. Any counterattack will be more for face-saving—considered useless to the safety of our Proctoress. It will take time to organize a massive attack on Diano. The war has just begun! The Diano will leave the city, now that they have gotten what they are after." He paused, said savagely: "Those responsible for Youi's abduction will die terribly!" Then less emotionally, "If Youi still lives, it would seem that you are an instrument of the Mathematical Universal Plan. Thus you must be given free movement. But remember, the forces of Bel-loniea will be soon following.

"I will see that rooms are assigned to you, and any men you desire."

I requested Orra Jik and Adt Dorta.

"You shall have them within a unit of time. Come, I'll show you your quarters."

He led the way down a long corridor to a small suite of rooms. The other chamber was a waiting area, beyond which we came to a room whose walls were covered with tapestries, with lovely, graceful country scenes laced into the cloth. Tables and chairs were placed generously around this room. To the left of the entrance was a huge fireplace made of slate stone. A room beyond this was the bed-chambers.

"These are yours. The quarters of a high-ranking Royal Officer," Qui Shan announced at the entrance to the bed-chamber. "I'll have a slave bring food and drink. Orra Jik and Adt Dorta will report to you immediately. Will you need anything else?"

"Some authority to others to get what is necessary."

"I'll have one of my personal aids report to you within the Unit. He will see that you receive everything you need."

"The flyer which I captured—I might need it," I stated, a vague suggestion of a plan beginning to form in my mind.

He nodded, as if I had asked for drinking water.

With that, Qui Shan left and I sat down before the fireplace, trying to work out an intelligent plan which might serve to rescue the Proctoress. But what made it difficult was my lack of knowledge of Noomas.

Finally a respectful knock came from the outer door. I went into the waiting room and opened the door. A slave stood there with a tray of food. He set it on a table near the fireplace.

"Where are you from?" I asked.

"From the Palace of Romos," the slave announced, proudly.

"Originally."

"I have lived in the Palace of Romos most of my life. My mother was taken as a slave when she was a young woman. I was raised with the rest of her children," he explained.

"You were born here?"

"No—I was the child of a warrior she loved once, before she was captured by the Bel-loniea."

"From where does she come?"

"A nation north of Diano. She had been the woman of a mercenary who joined the forces of the Diano—and when he was killed she was taken as a slave woman. Later Romos bought her for a high price." His attitude of pride, rather than dejected hopelessness, surprised me.

"Do you not wish your freedom?" I inquired, studying the man's handsome features.

"Here in Bel-loniea the sons of a Proctor's slave woman—or of any Royal family—are well treated. We have all the freedom necessary to enjoy life—plus far better living quarters than would be ours as Commoners." He studied me for a moment then asked: "You are the man from off-world, aren't you?"

"Yes."

"Then you know little of the slave structure here, is that not right?"

"That's why I inquired about you," I pointed out, smiling.

"There are slaves and slaves. I serve the Proctor's family and his royal house and officers. I have no need to go to battle and be killed as a warrior might—and there are many young slave women who are beautiful. But I am lucky. The usual slave is not much better than a prisoner of war—for it is thus he is taken into slavery. To be thus is more terrible than being dead. To work for Royalty is to live a pleasant life. I am no worse off than many Commoners—and better than some. What more does a man want than food in his stomach, shelter over his head—especially if it is Royal shelter—and beautiful women to share his bed at night?"

With a bow he turned and left.

I wondered for a moment what kind of man could live under such conditions. He lived to exist. There was no hope of elevating his standing in life. He would never be his own master.

Then I wondered how many people truly were their own masters. We all marched to some pattern which held us in its cruel demanding grasp. For some men, though not I, possibly slavery in a royal palace, surrounded by beautiful woman, was not so bad a life.

I turned my thoughts back to the problems facing me. As I ate the delicious meat which was swimming in a deep brown gravy, I continued a mental struggle for some definite plan of action. There was no doubt that the flyer which we had captured would serve me quite well. At least I could get close enough to the enemy, possibly land among them. But beyond that point I was at a loss.

One fact plagued me: Youi Janis had sworn before a Muti to kill herself rather than let the Diano take her! What made everybody think that she even lived? Yet the Muti had suggested that I was important to the life of the Proctoress of Bel-loniea.

I was finishing the meal when as officer stepped into the room, unannounced.

"Qui Shan instructed me to report to you," the man stated in a reserved, tense voice.

I turned. "Your name?"

"Narr-Eld. I am also to report that the officer known as Adt Dorta cannot be found. He is either dead, prisoner or hiding in the forest—avoiding capture. The warrior named Orra Jik is on his way here, Have you any orders for me?"

There was something about the man's formal manner which bothered me. He seemed annoyed with the assignment.

"Would you have some Ka?" I offered, hoping to break through his reserve. "Or Porshi?"

"None, sir. Not on duty, sir." His voice was flat.

"There's no reason we cannot be friends. You seem uneasy here."

Narr-Eld shrugged. "I would rather be with sword in hand, fighting the Diano as they retreat from our lands."

"What? They're leaving?"

"They are beginning to break up camp. They are leaving. By the end of the afternoon they will be on their way back to Diano. And here I stand, playing service to a fellow officer." He sounded highly bitter, even angry.

"Narr-Eld, did Qui Shan tell you nothing of me?"

"Nothing, sire. Just to report and see that you got everything demanded."

"I am working on a plan to save the Proctoress from the Diano, though I have no sure method worked out as yet. Maybe you can help."

His handsome features brightened. I noticed for the first time that he was a strong built, clean-shaven man. "Then...this assignment might be far more important than— I'm sorry, sir."

"It is very important according to the Muti," I explained completely.

"You will let me go with you, of course!" Narr-Eld inquired eagerly. "This is in your service," he announced, his right hand touching the hilt of his sword. "And in the service of our Proctoress!"

"You know the ways of the Diano?"

"Well enough. I've had several Diano slaves."

"We'll need Diano uniforms, to begin with," I told him, the plan taking on a more firm dimension in my mind.

"What are you going to do?" Narr-Eld inquired. He ran a large hand through his black hair.

"Three of us will dress as Diano warriors and then join their forces. This is possible?"

"How do you plan on joining them?"

"The flyer we captured will serve as a means of joining up without their knowledge of who we really are. Can we fake it from there?"

"It's possible," he said thoughtfully. "There are many nations across the mountains. The Diano add to their forces from other nations. Many warrior mercenaries make it their life work to join warring armies. It would not be difficult to appear as a mercenary," Narr-Eld admitted. "But what then?"

"Find Youi Janis. Then escape. Return her to Bel-loniea," I announced with finality.

"That is impossible!"

"That is not impossible as long as I live to try it. We must try to find her and then we'll see what happens. Are you willing to go on such a mission?"

"In the service of our Proctoress I would die—and I can assure you that we will die before we manage to bring the Proctoress back to Bel-loniea." His total conviction on this point was unnerving.

A knock sounded on the outer door and I went and opened it.

Orra Jik stood there, his scar contorted into a crooked grin. "Torlo Hannis, I thought I would not be seeing you alive again until the Muti spoke."

I grabbed his shoulders in the more intimate fashion of two friends meeting.

"Come, Orra Jik, I'll tell you what I have in mind." Once the plan had been explained, he studied me seriously, eyes squinted.

"It seems impossible—but you are a doer of impossible deeds." He nodded toward Narr-Eld. "He is going with us?"

Narr-Eld answered: "Though I doubt the sanity of your plan, yet possibly it is better than following with a force of the Proctor's army. It is not dying that is important but rather the way one dies in the service of his country!"

"They won't expect us to come from within," I announced.

Narr-Eld shook his head: "No—that is where you are wrong. Their spies took Youi Janis and they will expect our spies to re-capture her. That is why it's impossible."

I looked at Orra Jik. The serious expression on his rugged features revealed that he agreed.

"But we must try."

"And," Orra Jik pointed out in a voice thick with awe, "I heard from the Muti that the shadow of Torlo Hannis crosses the path of Youi Janis. The Muti saw into the future."

"But did he promise success?" Narr-Eld countered as if he already knew the answer to the question.

"No," Orra Jik admitted. "But he implied that it was important that Torlo Hannis live and that he would serve Bel-loniea far greater than he had done so far."

"Come," I said, tired of the conversation. "We must act fast. We need three Diano warrior uniforms—of the lower ranks. We must get to the flyer and by cover of night join the Diano."

Narr-Eld nodded doubtfully. "I'll see to the arrangements."

CHAPTER NINE

IN PERIL'S PATH

The night sky of Noomas was clouded with bright stars, like millions of twinkling jewels lighting our way. Two of the three moons were already making their way across the heavens. The nearest, appearing twice the size of the sun, and said to be only a hundred thousand miles away, looked down at us from a naked and pockmarked orange face. Narr-Eld was at the flyer's controls and Orra Jik stood next to me watching the lights of Bel-loniea dwindle in the distance. I wondered if any of us would return; for none of us would without the Proctoress.

We were circling to the north, away from both Bel-loniea and the retreating forces of the Diano troops. The plan was to approach from the west, so there would be no hint to our true identity. The plain leather harness of the Diano common warrior was much the same as that of the Bel-loniea, except for the markings and red color of the loin cloth. The night air chilled our bodies and I had pulled the red cape around my shoulders to fight off the cold.

For a moment I tried to probe into my memory, attempted to understand what my past life had been, what important matter had brought me to this planet. A vague mental impression of a vast civilization spanning millions of civilized planets touched my mind, but that was all, other than the awareness that there was something very important which I had come here to do.

I pressed the thoughts away as Orra Jik said: "We should be changing course soon—then it will be but a short time before we join with the Diano."

I nodded. "The best thing is to circulate quickly. We will meet at the flyer in the morning."

"We went through all that several times, sir."

"Better get into the habit of calling me Torlo."

"Yes, Torlo. And you might get into the habit of thinking of yourself as a warrior from Kanns."

"Kanns, far to the north," I said, rehearsing what they had told me. "I have been away from it for 12 years. My father and mother were Commoners of Kanns. I left at 16 and joined the army of another nation, and since then I've been without a country. I don't want to talk about it, because the Kanns believe that a man's past is his own. Right?"

Orra Jik grinned. "You remember fast."

"I remember only details of the present—my mind is like a book without printing. I have a lot of pages to fill—and no memory to confuse learning. That is an advantage."

Narr-Eld called from the controls. "I see the forces of the Diano. Should I bank, drop lower?"

I moved to his side, looked off in the direction in which we were going. "Continue high, until you have come into their lines, then drop lower."

"That's a good plan. I'll begin circling once we enter their outer lines. Then they won't know from which direction we came."

"Remember, I want to get this done as swiftly as possible. The moment we land, we start circulating. From what you have told me about the Diano, it shouldn't be hard to get information—nor should it seem strange that we walk among the night."

Orra Jik nodded. "Many a restless warrior will walk the night after leaving the scene of battle. Especially the warrior-without-a-country, for he will be without desire for women—keyed up for spilling of blood. His real love is war—this is his mistress."

We continued in silence after that and I watched as Narr-Eld started circling above the forces of the Diano who had made camp at a proper distance from Bel-loniea. The plains upon which they were traveling toward the distant mountains were open, covered with short grass, spotted by tall, snake-like trees.

84

Slowly the ship lowered until we could hear the noisy mass voices of multiple conversations from the huge camp below. Fire-lights glowed by the hundreds with men and women gathered closely around them.

"They brought women along?" I asked surprised.

"Always on such a siege. They don't know how long they will be away from their wives," Narr-Eld explained. "Some even bring their wives. And the high-ranking officers buy the services of the tavern and house girls, who come along to keep the warriors of lower ranks happy. Remember to speak harshly of the Bel-loniea and praise the Diano victory. There will be some celebration, for many warriors can drink and love all night and still continue on the journey the next day without rest. Their heads will be splitting from too much Porshi, but their minds will glow with the memory of a war easily won. The professionals, who sell their sword to any High officer willing to pay, will be disgruntled, irritated that the war was so short and the pay cut off this quickly. Some of these will even pick fights. Be careful of such men, for they will, upon learning that you're supposed to be one of them, attempt to bait you into a duel, either with them or against some Diano warrior. Many times such duels end in death; it's a game played to let off the devils screaming inside them. Move carefully."

I was intrigued at the cost of moving such a vast army. "I should think they would have stayed until Bel-loniea had been reduced to ashes—or until they could sack the city of all its riches."

Narr-Eld laughed. "It would not pay in the long run. You can sack so many cities—and then there is nothing to bag. This way they come, fight, take what they want, and leave. We will be following their army soon with one of our own—all the way to Diano if necessary. The war will continue until one side decides they have had enough—or have been totally defeated on the battlefield. The Proctor of the defeated army will then pay a high price for any prisoners taken by the victorious nation. They will haggle for riches, the winner demanding enough tokens of value to pay for the expenses of the war and some extra for the vaults of the Proctor and Royal families."

The notion that I knew nothing about the money exchange on Noomas struck home at that moment. I asked Narr-Eld about it.

"We have Proctor tokens and half tokens made of light metals. Jewels of high value are used in international exchange—valuable metals such as copper and steel also serve as international exchange. Proctors Tokens are usually used within the nation itself. Though sometimes Proctors Tokens are honored by another nation for the purpose of buying products directly from the merchants who travel between cities. These nomadic tribes hail to no one Proctor but will at times align themselves to a noble or Proctor during times of war—and serve as spies."

"Then we are paid in Proctor Tokens?" I inquired

"You mean the warriors. Yes—and no. We are honored and respected. We can go into a tavern and order what we want and get it. Even the tavern girls will serve us in any manner we so desire. The Proctor pays the taverns and shopkeepers so much a year for these services. We are fed by the army and sheltered by the army. When we retire or decide to leave the services, the Proctor will allow us so many tokens for every year we served—the amount, naturally, depends on our rank upon leaving."

"Then we are allowed to take anything we want from the merchants?" I inquired, amazed.

"Not quite! We must sign for anything which cost more than five tokens—and this will be deducted from our Final Pay. Everything is all quite fair. A warrior is honored and given the freedom of not having to carry money around with him."

"What about when he is in another nation?"

"If it is friendly, he will sign for anything he takes, and his note will serve as a means of exchange and trade with his home country."

"And if you are in a city which is unfriendly?"

"You would be captured if you appeared to be from Bel-loniea. You play smart and appear as a warrior from a friendly nation, sign for what you want—and the only loser is the Proctor!"

"Isn't that rather expensive?"

"No—it is done both ways. Bel-loniea warriors gain riches from unfriendly nations and unfriendly nations gain riches from Bel-loniea. It cancels out—more or less. You see, Torlo Hannis, warriors shouldn't have to worry about anything other than fighting. When they get to the point where fighting is too much of a strain, they will quit the services, and find another means of support to live out the rest of his life."

"And this goes for the Nobles and officers, too?"

"That's something else. A Noble has honors and riches. Every honor bestowed upon a man is backed by a grant, gift from the Proctor. The grant can be as little as one thousand Proctor Tokens to a large apartment, or huge palace, depending on what his Honor was. But along with the grant or gift goes responsibilities. With an officer, he is responsible for his men, and will be given so many tokens a year to feed and clothe and arm them."

Narr-Eld now circled over a strip of land which was being used by the Diano for their flyers. As he started to drop lower our conversation broke off.

Once grounded, we closed up the flyer, set the door lock for early morning. After a last farewell warning, we separated, each heading in different directions.

The moment I was alone I felt an edge of panic, I knew so little about the customs of the Diano, other than what I had been quickly told in the few Units of time since we had devised the plan. My lack of knowledge of even the money exchange had brought home this fact.

Orra Jik had told me earlier that guards would normally be posted around the flyers, but on a night like this—right after a victory—a lot of celebrating would take place, leaving little room for the formal necessities of posting guards. Custom taught that there was no chance of an immediate counterattack, Nonetheless I did discover a campfire fairly near the area, with several warriors squatting around it. I slipped around several flyers, making a detour. Apparently the Diano weren't being completely lax.

Doubt plagued me as I left the flyer area. The campfires were bright and glowing, far larger than they appeared from the sky. Men and women warmed themselves against the chill of the night—some feasted on huge roasted animals which had been baked over the fires. A breeze was pushing hard across the plain and the laughing, singing voices of hundreds of men and women combined to create a loud pattern of noise. Flickering flames played on the laughing faces of those crowded around the roaring logs, creating sharp highlights which flashed on and off against the silhouette of their bodies.

I moved past several fires, listened to the loud gay voices. They seemed so normal that I felt a momentary moment of false comfort. It was hard to equate these merry people as enemies, for now they were fully taken up in the jubilant activities of victory celebrations. How wonderfully human and warm they seemed. There was nothing evil or cruel about their activities. Some of the men and women playfully teased each other. Some disappeared into tents together, staggering under the effects of too much Porshi.

Several men, like myself, were wandering from campfire to campfire, shouting hellos to those they knew, but continuing, as if either restless or going about some important errand.

Scattered between the fires were colorful tents which reflected the flames in bright orange and reds. Pennant flags flapped against the light breeze in front of the larger tents. Even in these hidden places the sounds of laughing voices mixed with those outside.

Two warriors came staggering out of a small tent and then brushed past me. One of them turned, a belligerent expression on his hard, battle-scarred face.

"What the Korda are you doing?" he grumbled. "Looking for a quick death?"

"Yeah," his companion cursed. "What you doing? Watch out!"

If they weren't being so serious about it, I might have laughed at their comic approach. They seemed more like two kids trying to act tough.

"You bumped me," I explained quickly. Then immediately realized the mistake I had made, as the two of them started to reach for their swords. Narr-Eld had warned about such an occurrence.

88

"Fellow warriors, I have no quarrel with you," I quickly assured them.

Then I added in hopes this would cool them down: "Foolish of me not to watch where I'm going."

The scar-faced one shuffled forward. "Are you a Korda, Bel-loniea coward—or a Diano warrior?"

I whipped out my sword, touched his chest with the point before he could move.

"If you believe that, you are a dead man!" I snarled, pressing the point against his flesh, drawing a trickle of blood.

"Come on, Eone—we have business with the prisoners!" The other man pulled on his shoulder.

Eone grunted. "Next time you feel the bite of my blade!" Then he turned to follow his companion. "Be watchful, warrior!"

I replaced my sword while watching the two men as they started off toward the right.

Having no other clue or destination, I decided to follow. What I expected to discover I don't know. But prisoners might mean that Youi could be close by.

CHAPTER TEN

HONOR IN WAR IS WINNING

I followed in the dark shadows, keeping as much out of sight of the two as possible. They led me across camp, through many wildly celebrating men and women. The abandon in which the Diano played out their celebration revealed a total lack of morality, I realized. Immediately I wondered where my standard of morality had come from. Little had been revealed to me about the Bel-loniea morality. This was, again, a piece of past memory floating up to the surface.

The two men led me to a huge tent next to several tall, bulky trees. Chained to the trees were men, locked by neck-irons in long lines, stretching out over a large area of ground. Here were the Bel-loniea prisoners. And from what Orra Jik had told me, they were headed for slavery, the best warriors to be used in testing the skill of Diano warriors-in-training in hand-to-hand combat, or placed into the Arena as entertainment for the Proctor and Royalty. Their future was bleak.

The cold reality of this life on Noomas, the warring instincts of its primitive people, set in deep as I looked across the darkness at the chained prisoners. The gaiety of the camp, which had seemed so normal, now took on a perverse form. War had created a hellish slavery for some, death and life-time crippling for others. What cruelty in the human mind could allow for such perversity? Man was created out of the love or passion of two human animals, born from the long agony of pregnancy, and raised with the soft love of a mother's arms, only to reach maturity and enter the harsh

90

struggle for survival which human society created for itself. Death came as an end to all struggles, either early or late—but always too soon. And for what purpose? Forgetting all purpose, Divine or man-made, what kind of madness could cause men to war upon themselves, making a hard life even more harsh and brutal? Survival, love of woman, love of nation, love of child—the necessities of life in food and therefore in land? Each hand grabbed out and claimed, "this is mine—you can't have it! I want it!" And then the killing, the violence, the injustice. Where was the honor in that? Where was the honor in the capture and slavery of human beings into a life without hope, without any purpose other than to keep the small spark of living matter within them still breathing, because an innate, built-in horror of death frightened the bravest man into a screaming child, calling out for the comfort of his mother's arms with his last breath of life?

Yet my own sword had ripped life away from faces which I had never seen before. I had killed without any personal hatred against those who immediately faced me. I had no real personal involvement with the people on Noomas, other than the fact I was isolated on this planet much the same as they were, and the Bel-lonieans had taken me in, fed and clothed me, given me comfort and protection—a home. And for that home I had killed—and for the love of a woman who might never return my love in the normal course of things. I stood as vile as those who tortured humans in a pointless life of slavery. I killed without emotional involvement. I murdered with but a thin thread of motive. My rationalization was self-survival. Yet was it vital that I engage in the mass murder of people I knew nothing about, simply to save my own face among those I adopted as my own people?

Such were my thoughts while looking at the prisoners. The night closed in oppressively, dampening all sense of duty, all rallying to a cause, all belief in a code of honor. It was the first time I questioned the world around me or wondered about the invisible pattern of life which seemed to have no purpose other than the destruction of lives. At that moment life seemed such a fragile thing, so much like walking an invisible line where one false move would be the step into eternity.

There were human beings, captive and captor. They all dreamed, breathed, hoped, loved, struggled for the same basic personal destinies and ideals. One was named friend and the other labeled enemy.

Yet was that not the purpose of Nature? The struggle, the violent war for survival where only the strongest lived to carry on the name of the species? Was it not through the struggle, seeking, war, that new knowledge was created out of the vacuum of the mind?

Again I realized that these thoughts and concepts were revealing knowledge and awareness of things which had not been learned on Noomas.

The image of Youi Janis, a young, innocent girl who had been taken against her will, because one selfish man decided he wanted her at all costs, formed like a sharp mental dagger. This man, named Aoji, son of the Diano Proctor, had created a war simply because of his greed for a woman who had done no personal harm to him other than state she was not interested in his attentions.. She had used her right of free choice, and he had decided to destroy that right. And men, like beasts-of-prey without sense of morality, had followed the call to blood simply for the pleasure of killing one another.

For such people, no considerations of morality could be justified. They deserved less rights than a mad animal.

I realized that here was the morality which set men against men. One picked sides because of the necessity of living with themselves and those they respected and honored and loved.

This moment of mental doubt slipped away and I once more saw the world through the eyes of a man of Noomas. Man either adapts to the world and society which he finds himself in or dies. He can neither truly change the worlds, nor can he reject it—but rather he must find that portion which suits him best, imperfect as it might be. The Bellonieans had an ethical code of honor, savage and unbending, but no more so than that of the world around them.

I focused on the prisoners and wondered if Adt Dorta was among them. The thought of this friend being a prisoner, chained there, was nagging. If there was anything that could be done to free him, I might have attempted it, but for the fact that such action would endanger our plans for rescuing Youi.

I was about to turn away when a voice from behind demanded: "What are you doing here?"

I turned to see a Diano officer standing there with two warriors at his side. Almost immediately I recognized the two warriors as those whom I'd followed.

"I wandered from the campfires," I quickly explained. "The end of the war makes us mercenaries restless. I wish to put my blade into the blood of more Bel-loniea Kordas."

"You'll get your chance, warrior, never fear. Romos will seek revenge—and war will continue." He stepped forward, stared at my face and then asked: "Where do you come from, warrior?"

"From the north. I sold my blade to the Diano."

"Which officer do you serve?" His voice was thick with suspicion.

I stared at him, uncertain. This was one question we had not been prepared to answer. Doubt touched my mind. I could not allow them to capture me.

"I asked you a question, warrior!", the man commanded, touching the hilt of his sword. "You will answer or die on the spot!"

"Aoji!" I blurted out, this being the only name which came to me.

The officer backed away, surprise mounting his gaunt features. "I did not know, sir. You will accept my apologies."

His face seemed to have drained of color.

"That's better, friend!" I snapped, pushing the unexpected advantage. "Now you will do the honor of directing me back to the Proctoress' quarters, where I am one of those female Kordas' guards."

"You are lost?" He sounded amazed, and I immediately realized I'd said the wrong thing.

"I wandered, restless. I must report to my post before the unit is up!" I retorted, authoritatively, hoping to bluff my way. "Or our Proctor will have my head."

The officer's attitude abruptly changed. There was now cunning in his voice. "How could you have missed it? Only a short distance back." He moved closer. "I begin to believe you are a Bel-loniea spy—a clever one—but a spy nonetheless. You will come with us and we'll see if you're what you claim to be."

"And," I announced stiffly, "you will see what will become of you for such insolence!"

"You speak well, warrior! But where is your metal of Aoji? I see only a plain warrior harness."

"I wished to dress as a Commoner—as I dress when unengaged by a Proctor!" I knew there was now little chance of bluffing.

There were three of them, and I had little experience with a sword and no knowledge of how skilled this officer might be, even if the other two weren't at his side.

His companions were beginning to circle away from him. I knew what this move meant. The officer had been playing for time, too.

Then, more in desperation than anything else, I whipped out my sword. Before the other guessed what I had in mind, the blade ran through his chest.

Immediately I turned to face the other two. But they were now in positions to approach from opposite sides.

Eone grinned sadistically. "I warned you, warrior. Next time!"

I faced him for two reasons. He seemed the most dangerous, and also stood between men and the Bel-loniea prisoners—which seemed the easiest route of escape.

I leaped at him, sword extended, feinted then lunged. I was more surprised than Eone when the sword slipped through his guard in one fluid movement and ran cleanly through his heart. What strange ability revealed itself in these skilled moments with the sword was a mystery I could not fathom—other than to assume that the Diano warriors had less skill with weapons than the Bel-loniea training had given me.

The second warrior pulled out his Kay-gun, fired. The explosive charge kicked up the dirt in front of me. I froze.

"You will drop your sword, warrior!" the man announced, triumphantly.

I turned to face him, weapon still clutched in my hand.

"Is there any honor in defeating a man with a Kay-gun?" I challenged.

"Honor in war is winning—the loser has no honor! We of the Diano learned that a hundred or more years ago. The Bel-loniea still play at games of honor and favor the sword—but it will be their downfall soon, for a sword is no equal to the Kay-gun!"

"I am not from Bel-loniea," I quickly countered in a heated voice. "I am from Kanns, far to the north."

"That might very well be, for the Kanns are of a brutal nature and certainly easy to anger. But we'll see. You've killed an officer in the army of Diano—a crime which can be forgiven only by a Muti or the Proctor Himself. If you truly be what you claim, there is nothing to fear—is there?" He grinned wolfishly. His deep set eyes seemed like dark pits of cold black fire. "You will come with me or die on the spot. Drop your sword!"

There was nothing I could do other than as instructed.

CHAPTER ELEVEN

THE DIANO MUTI

The immediate reaction to my capture was to create a total feeling of defeat. All hope slithered away. I marched in front of the Diano warrior with complete resignation. I knew that I was about to die.

The camp now took on the ominous feeling of personal threat. The celebrating Diano warriors and their women seemed like evil spirits dancing erratically in some mythical Hell, some supernatural pit of sin. My gloomy thoughts crushed all reason.

We went only a short distance from the place where the Bel-loniea prisoners had been chained, past only a half dozen fires, past three tents, one small area for flyers. There was a large blue tent in front of a roaring fire, before which squatted a score of warriors, alert, untouched by the poison of liquor. These were the Royal Guard of Aoji, I learned, as my captor announced: "You should have friends who will recognize you. If that is so, I will beg your pardon." Sarcasm was thick in his voice. "As you know, this is the place where the Royal Guard watch the Royal prisoner. They were hired by Aoji from the ranks of professional mercenaries who are honor bound to fight to the death in protection of any man who buys their sword. As you know such a guard is priceless, for they have never been known to dishonor their pledge for any counter offer. As you know—because, of course, you are one of them!"

He took me to the tent and then inside. It was divided into several sections by cloth partitions. I was taken into a

96

closed-in area where an officer was behind a small, collapsible desk.

All I could think of now was the fact that Youi Janis was within shouting distance and I was helpless to do anything about it.

My captor announced: "I am under-officer Nal, of the Verta Division. This man claims to be in your command, sir. Do you know him?"

The officer stared at me, then shook his head. "But I do not know every man in my command. I'll have the Chief Warrior-at-Arms come for an Identification. Wait here."

He left and then returned shortly with a stocky man with a puffy red face. "Do you know this man?"

The fellow glanced at me, then shook his head.

The officer demanded: "What's the meaning of all this?"

"He was caught looking at the prisoners and claimed to be one of your men. When we tried to take him to you, he killed Verta, my officer, and another warrior who was with us. I am alive here with him because my Kay-gun stopped his escape."

The officer glared at me. "Who are you, and no lying tongue!"

"Torlo Hannis," I announced without hesitation. "I come from Kanns, and don't like the attitude of this man. I have just arrived...hearing that you are—"

The man's right hand struck my face. "You lie! You're a Bel-loniea spy."

"Only a coward hits a defenseless man!" I spat out, holding back hot fury.

"For such as you, honor is not necessary!" the officer snapped back. "Take him away—chain him with the other prisoners!"

With that, the warrior shoved the Kay-gun into my back. Now I was considering the possibility of escape. Up until now the shock of capture had numbed my thoughts. This might be my last chance. The training in hand-to-hand combat had proved one thing: I had knowledge which was not known on Noomas. My attack against Gora during the first combat training period had demonstrated his inability to defend himself. Chances were the same would be true with this Diano warrior.

As we crossed through a more shaded area, I hesitated, as if stumbling.

As expected, he shoved at my back, and I whipped around, right hand catching his gun arm. With a quick jerk I snapped the arm back and then threw him off balance. The two of us slammed against the hard ground. My right hand hammered at the side of his neck. Then I stood and slipped into the shadows, leaving the unconscious Diano warrior on the ground where he had fallen, minus sword and Kay-gun.

I worked through the camp as fast as possible, without appearing conspicuous.

I was just passing a darkened tent when a hooded figure moved out of the shadows.

"Warrior," the rumbling voice of a Muti called. "Where are you going?"

The Kay-gun in my right hand rose, aimed.

The Muti moved so quickly that I was dazed. He grabbed my right hand and with amazing strength removed the weapon from my fingers as if taking a toy from a small child.

"How dare you threaten a Muti!" the voice rumbled. "Who are you?"

A hand reached out, touched my forehead, then withdrew as if burned by hot fires.

Total defeat choked me. It had been so close—now there was nothing to do but surrender helplessly. No trick would work against his brutal strength and lightning speed. I half expected to be shot down on the spot; but was completely unprepared for what actually happened.

"Go! Fast! Leave!" the Muti hissed, as if the words were distasteful. "Leave! Leave, Torlo Hannis!"

Mystified, I did exactly as instructed. Why hadn't the Muti captured or shot me? Again the mystery of the Mutis numbed my senses.

I slipped away, this time around the tent and into the dark shadows beyond the campfires, keeping in their cover until I saw the place where the flying forces of the Dianos were located. I thanked the Gods of Noomas that a lack of orders was in effect. Now the flyers were totally unguarded. Finally I made my way to the flyer which we had captured the days before.

I lay down next to the closed door of the grav-disk, wishing that the time-lock had not been set. At first it had seemed a good thing, but now I was exposed, and if anybody who knew my face discovered me here, there would be little hope of escaping again.

I imagined a mass search quickly taking place but as time slowly slipped by there was no indication of such a search. The camp noises slowly faded, as sleep took possession of the Diano forces.

It was early in the morning, the sun just creeping up over the horizon like some red-eyed monster, when I saw a shadowy figure slowly work its way toward the flyer. At first I believed it to be some Diano warrior approaching. Then I saw it was Orra Jik. He moved quickly to me side.

"They have captured Narr-Eld," Orra Jik announced.

"They almost captured me. Is he alright?"

"Yes, with the other prisoners. There was talk about another Bel-loniea spy who had been captured and then escaped. They made a quick but slight search and gave up. It is easy for one face to get lost in a sea of thousands of faces. Spies are common." He sat down beside me, asked: "Did you find out anything?"

"Only that the Proctoress is held by a special unit of mercenaries, and that their officer and Warrior-at-Arms Chief knows my face."

"That's bad."

"But...at least we've discovered where to look," I pointed out.

"What do you plan next?" He studied me through narrowed eyes.

"I don't know, yet. We have to make some attempt to get to Youi Janis—at least let her know that help is here."

"I heard some of the men talking...they have doubled their guard and swear they will die before allowing any stranger near the Proctoress."

I felt a deep wave of disgust. The only thing we had done was make it harder for ourselves. Maybe it was now impossible. But apparently she lived. But for how long? I felt the pressure of time closing in on me. What if I was too late even if I did reach her? The fact that we did know where to look for her was some gain against the losses.

"Do you have any ideas?" I asked.

"None." He shook his head.

Suddenly I remembered the Muti and explained what had happened.

"Why did he let me go?" I asked when finished.

"They will not interfere—unless it is of some use. Obviously a Muti can read something in your future which is immutable. I'd say his action speaks well for us. Apparently he realized there was nothing within his power to stop you."

"Or that I would be stopped in any case—in such a way which would be to the Diano advantage." I suggested.

"His horror—from what you said—would indicate otherwise."

"That could have been for my benefit. A ruse!"

Orra Jik shrugged. "The ways of the Muti are strange." Then he added on a lighter note: "But I believe he saw what the Muti in Bel-loniea saw—your shadow crossing that of Youi Janis. The future cannot be changed—not even by a Muti!"

I accepted that, mainly because I needed something to lift my spirits. "At least that's on our side."

"Maybe. The Mutis see the world in a different way than we normals. They see lines of movement, they observe, advise when called upon, and stay out of our political struggles. They merely observe and interfere when injustice calls for them to act." For some reason this last did little to soothe my depressed thoughts. "You will learn soon enough not to question the ways of the Muti."

In that last statement his voice had been thick with reverence and awe.

"You speak as if they are some Deity or—"

"They are no deity—they only look into the future and read what is there. They watch."

"But...they rule, too, don't they?" I was determined to push the matter—anything to get my mind off the frustration of our defeat.

100

"They do not rule. They only see with their minds. They watch, listen to the wind of our lives passing by. I have learned to accept and not question their ways or try to understand. It is safer that way."

"Then you fear the Muti?"

"One fears that which can see into your future. One fears the unknown—and certainly the future is unknown to normal man. The Muti sees what we cannot see. They walk among us without fear, with a sense of total power—as if they had the supernatural power of the Gods. And who knows, maybe they do. It is best not to dwell upon them. Accept and ignore—live your life as best you can—but don't question too deeply the ways of these creatures." Orra Jik was staring solemnly into my eyes, as a friend might who is concerned over the fate of another. Yet I could not help but think he had a great fear of the Mutis. I tried to question him on their origin but he shook his head, claiming they had always been here. It was difficult to keep from getting the impression that the Mutis were a stronger power in Noomas than expected. Possibly this was merely an off-worlder's reaction to their strangeness. Nevertheless they did seem to look out for the safety and lives of the normal humans.

I remained silent for a long time, then when the soft click of the lock behind me sounded, I stood, swung the door open. We stepped in, then slipped the bolt across the door.

"You know how to handle one of these flyers?" I inquired.

"Some, though I am not a trained professional pilot. A few of the larger ships are fairly complicated to handle. This—should be simple enough." He studied the controls. "I'll show you how they work."

The controls were quite simple. All one had to do was pull the speed lever, then grab a stick which was moved in the direction one wished to fly—back for up, forward for down, in the center to fly straight, right and left to turn in the desired directions.

"Here, let me try it!" I asked, going through a mock take-off, getting the feel of the movement. "Gentle!"

"Very gentle, until you hit a storm, then you're in for it." Orra Jik looked out the large glass windows which were placed so the flyer had a good view of his destination. "It's getting light, maybe we should take to the air."

"Why?"

"It might be safer that way, considering the fact that we are not really a part of any unit and don't know who to report to. In the air there will be no questioning our presence. If we take off now they will think we are scouts—or on some assignment. We can head in the direction of Diano, and then settle down, wait out the day and then join up at night."

"It's a good idea. Glad you're here. I wouldn't have thought about this."

"I'll take her up, now. Today I'll give you flying lessons," Orra Jik offered.

CHAPTER TWELVE

THREE BRIGHT MOONS
VIEW DARK DISASTER

Shortly we were flying high over the Diano camp—safe for a time. My mind rebelled from considering what we might do this evening. Every time I tried to figure out some scheme which might work, I was staggered by the difficulties facing us. Rather than exhaust my brain uselessly, since there was no real way of knowing what the situation might be this night, I turned my attention to other matters. Also I realized that the more my mind dwelled upon the problem the more exhausted it would become; while on the other hand the subconscious mind might serve up a solution, given time.

Once we were beyond sight of the Diano camp, I suggested that Orra Jik let me try handling the flyer.

"Just take it easy," he warned, as I took over the controls. "Easy."

The handling of the grav-disk was delicate but I took to it naturally, as if already experienced in flying such a machine. In fact, I had a feeling I had done something like this many times before.

The sun was high in the sky by the time I turned the controls back to Orra Jik. We settled down in a grassy clearing in the thick forest lands over which we had been flying for some time. Orra Jik managed to bring the ship under the shadow of a tall, gnarled tree, which served as a perfect cover from the air. We ate lunch of Mio-sticks and then I settled back against the end of the flyer to rest. Some time later I got up, paced the floor of the grav-disk.

Several possible plans formed in my mind but none seemed workable. Finally I decided it would be best to make a bold move. Slowly a daring plan took shape. I told Orra Jik what I had in mind and he admitted it had merit and at least as much if not more chance than any other method of freeing the Proctoress from the Diano.

"Though," he told me, "I doubt that even you can manage the impossible."

"Remember the Muti!"

"Even the Muti didn't promise success!" Orra Jik pointed out.

"It's the only plan that has any chance at all!"

"The only thing is, you are relying on the fact that she will be in the same tent, under the Proctor's personal guard of mercenaries," he told me seriously. "If you are wrong about that—what then?"

"I'll get out as fast as possible! If possible!" I laughed , more lightly than I felt.

"Can you handle the rest?" I asked.

"Getting a flyer will be easier than getting the prisoners free—that is if we manage to escape death and make final escape! But I'll need you along in the beginning—at least up to the point where we can see how difficult it might be to free the prisoners."

"Of course. But we'll have to move fast." I looked at the sky, seeing that the sun was already starting to dip out of sight. "We'd better start back. If we can cause enough confusion, quickly enough, there's a chance of success—and that's important. Everything will have to be timed perfectly."

Orra Jik took the flyer up and we were silent while the sun disappeared and night descended upon the world. Stars twinkled above us in a beautiful display, scattered thickly across the center of the heavens to bulk together in hazy brightness. I wished there were clouds to hide our approach and cover our activities but we were out of luck on that point. Though to the east I noticed that darkness was blotting out the heavens. I pointed this out to Orra Jik and he said: "As much as we need cover, be glad that darkness of that kind isn't here. That's a storm and storms on Noomas can be pretty frightening—especially if you're in a flyer."

It was late in the night by the time we spotted the campfires of the Diano. As we approached the camp, I could not help but once more wonder at the madness which had moved this vast army so far, at such obvious expense for but one purpose: the capture of Youi Janis. And now they were leaving because the main reason for their attack had been accomplished. I commented on this fact to Orra Jik.

"This is their full purpose, Torlo. They wish to insult the Bel-loniea nation by insulting their women through the act of degrading the most valued and worshipped woman—our Proctoress."

"But to do this to one human being, who has the right to happiness," I said feeling even greater hate burn in me. "She is innocent—Royalty through an accident of birth. Why should she be forced to suffer merely because she symbolically represents Bel-loniea!"

"It is the way of life!" Orra Jik said with a shrug.

I thought of how cruel life can be to the innocent.

After going over the plan with Orra Jik once more, I concluded: "The only real strong point is the fact that our plan is so bold, so daring, that it's possibly the last thing they might expect."

"Don't underestimate the Diano," Orra Jik warned. "They're clever Korda."

It was quite late now and most of the fires were dimmed, watched over by only a few sentries.

Orra Jik circled high over the camp until he spotted the place where the prisoners were kept. As he brought the ship down low, a safe distance from the prisoners, I wondered if we really had any chance. Freeing the prisoners might prove impossible—and capture would mean immediate defeat of our purpose.

I checked the charges in my Kay-gun and then slowly pulled the sword from its sheath. Orra Jik touched the ship down onto the ground like a silent shadow, just within sight of the prison area, but unnoticed in the darkness. The plan was for me to go with Orra Jik and make sure one man could handle this part of our moves alone. Then I would return to the flyer.

We lowered the ship's top and then leaped off the disk, moving quickly toward the prisoners' camp. Orra Jik had told me that one of the guards would have the keys to unlock the neck-irons. Everything depended on his being right about that.

When we were but a short distance of the prisoners, we dropped to our bellies and slithered along the ground like two Koillax.

Finally we were at the outer edge of the mass of chained Bel-loniea warriors. Orra Jik quickly awoke the first man we came to. "In the name of Youi Janis," he whispered, "where are the prisoners captured last night?"

The man looked up at Orra Jik, said: "At the outer end of this line."

"Prepare for escape!" I told him. "For the Proctoress! Pass it along."

The man looked confused but immediately started the message along the line of prisoners chained with him.

We slid along the ground to where Narr-Eld was supposed to be chained. We had almost reached our destination when a prisoner stopped me. I looked into his eyes and had to hold back a gasp of surprise.

"Adt Dorta."

"Torlo Hannis!" He moved closer, whispered in my ear. "What are you doing here?"

"Freeing you."

"But..." he looked doubtful.

"We have to free the Proctoress. Do you know if she is kept in the same place as last night?"

"I've heard little. But they have made no obvious changes I know of," Adt Dorta informed me.

"Adt—if we succeed, make as much confusion as possible. Attack—kill—and later try to escape. I'll need time—your men will buy that time—for Youi Janis!"

He nodded.

A guard's voice called out from the campfire a short distance away. "What's going on. Silence, slaves!"

He stood, surveyed the prisoners and then reseated himself closer to the fire. Obviously he had not seen wither Orra Jik or myself where we lay flat on the ground.

106

Now we made our way to the end of the chain. Narr-Eld was awake, watching us. We quickly explained our purpose and he nodded at each point. I gave him my Kay-gun and then slipped away, assured that Orra Jik could handle it from here on.

I regretted the necessity of leaving the scene at that moment but our plan depended on my being elsewhere when the prisoners made their break.

Returning to the ship, I went to the controls. A moment later the grav-disk was silently flying high over the camp. I had already located the tent in which we expected the Proctoress to be held prisoner. The whole plan depended on her being there.

Going off to the west, I started to bank the flyer, then circled, keeping alert for the first outbreak from the prisoners. The explosion of Kay-gun firing would signal me. Setting the controls in lock position, I quickly opened the plate in the middle of the disk and lifted out the box of Kay-bombs and Kay-gun ammunition.

Dragging the boxes to the controls, I opened them and took out a handful of small pellets which were used in the Kay-guns. Orra Jik had said that these would go off if dropped from a high enough altitude. Now I waited for the signal.

It had seemed to take forever and I was certain something had gone wrong. Then suddenly the dim sound of a Kay-gun firing broke into the still night air.

Immediately I threw the handful of Kay-pellets over the side of the flyer, grabbed more pellets while directing the grav-disk into a deep dive. The sound of multiple explosions came from below as the pellets landed. Three more handfuls of pellets flew over the side railing as the flyer dove lower. I pulled the ship up again and climbed high above the camp, leveled off, throwing pellets every chance I got. I was directing the flyer along the outer edges of the camp. Shouting voices, yells of pain sounded from below. Now I set the flyer controls in lock position and picked up the box of pellets, leaned over the side of the flyer and started pouring the explosives out. At this height the pellets had a chance to scatter on their way to the ground. Then I reached for Kay-bombs and started tossing them in every direction. I could imagine the confusion below. It would seem they were being attacked by a whole army—which they couldn't find. Sleep would cloud their reasoning long enough to give me the chance to rescue Youi Janis. Such were my prayers. Explosions sounded from below like the popping of giant firecrackers. Screams of agony followed the progress of my flight.

Once the Kay-bombs had been exhausted, I returned all attention to the controls and then dove low to the right, away from the original line of flight. Everything depended on timing. Once the controls were set so the ship would crash-land a short distance from the tent where Youi Janis had been held the night before, I went to the supply hole, took a line rope, tied one end to the tall harness ring, then the other over the side. Quickly I climbed down the rope and prayed it would be possible to hold on long enough.

The air whipped violently past, pulling the line far behind the flyer, which now skimmed close to the brush and tree-covered ground, toward one of the larger tents.

I just missed being smashed by a tree as the ship dove closer to the brush-speckled land below. Even at the lowest speed the flyer was incredibly fast. I began to doubt the possibility of surviving the leap. Then suddenly it was necessary to release the rope because the flyer was already too close to the outer fringes of the camp.

I held my breath, awaiting the impact. It seemed time froze as momentary terror gripped me. Then the ground struck with the force of a huge giant's hand attempting to crush life away.

I rolled forward, tumbling in an effort to absorb the shock. Skin was torn from my chest and arms. Then the forward surge of the fall stopped. For but a moment I took the time to mentally search for any sign of broken bones. Even though the impact had been jarring, stunning my mind, it was impossible to wait an instant too long. As I stood, it became apparent that no serious damage had been done by the fall.

I moved toward the large tent in which Youi Janis should be found. If luck was with me, a bold move would bring her to safety.

Then the sound of yelling voices, the clash of metal on metal came distinctly upon the air.

I was now in the shadows of the tent, approaching from behind. The three bright moons were glowing down on the landscape, and I cursed whatever perverse gods might be responsible for not giving the total darkness which was so badly needed.

Drawing the sword, I inserted it into the tent and made a small slit big enough to see inside. Darkness. I cut the hole larger and then slipped through it. Silence.

But the moment my feet moved, a muffled cry of alarm came from the right. I leaped, grappled with soft, feminine flesh. Hope swelled that this might be Youi.

"Speak or I'll kill you!: I warned. "Quietly!"

"Who are you?" a timid, unfamiliar voice inquired.

"Where is the Proctoress of Bel-loniea kept?" I hissed, holding the poor girl's arms in a brutal grasp.

"Aoji summoned her just before the attack," she sobbed in a voice trembling in terror. A choking sound came from her throat as fear threatened to take control of all reason.

"I don't want to hurt you," I assured the faceless shadow in my grasp.

"Please...don't," she stammered softly. "I'm merely one of the slaves in attendance to her. Don't kill me."

I cursed under my breath. "Where's the Proctor's tent?"

"The large pink one," she said, pointing to our right. "Just two campfires down."

Hating to do so, I firmly struck the girl at the point of the jaw, just hard enough to knock her out. Then I slipped from the tent.

What hope did we have now? Our plans had been useless. I was too late. There was every chance that Youi might already be dead by her own hand.

Sick with defeat, I moved into the shadows, away from the tent and camp.

The sound of battle came from beyond the tent and I realized that Orra Jik and the surviving prisoners had managed to reach their destination. They were to have served as diversion while I took Youi Janis out of captivity.

The bitter irony of it shattered me. All for nothing! Men were dying without any purpose or reason. Slavery and life would have been far better than this kind of useless death. A wave of personal guilt whelmed over me.

I stood there listening to the shouts of combat, knowing the men didn't have a chance to hold back the Diano for long, They would be killed or recaptured in moments and there was nothing I could do to save them.

Never had I experienced so great a moment of moral defeat as that instant. My own death would have been embraced. That thought spurred me to join my fellows. The least I could do was to share their defeat, while killing as many Diano as possible.

CHAPTER THIRTEEN

COUNTERATTACK

At that moment when I had decided to seal life for as many Diano warriors as possible, a new realization set in. The enemy would know that Youi Janis was safe in the Proctor's tent; they would guess what we were attempting, and smugly laugh at our useless efforts.

Suddenly there was hope.

The camp was in a state of confusion. There was a slight possibility of still gaining my goal by one final bold move. The fact that there was really nothing to lose offered moral strength.

I turned and started along the line of tents, almost immediately spotting the Proctor's, which was the largest and most beautifully decorated, with bold embossed pictures of warriors doing battle with strange and monstrous creatures; pennants flew freely from its top. Patches of light glowed through the tent's material, indicating sectioned off rooms. To the left of the guard nearest me was a long, narrow space of darkness where no light glowed against the blue cloth, suggesting the possibility of a corridor or hallway. This I decided was the best place to make my entrance. Guards were posted at all sides but just out of sigh of one another. I moved boldly toward the nearest one.

"Friend," I called a greeting, "I have orders to replace you. You're to reports to the officer-in-charge."

The man stared vacantly back, as if not quite sure whether to believe what I'd said. Before he could decide, my sword was deep in his chest. Withdrawing the bloody blade, I slipped it into the side of the tent, and then ripped downwards. There was no time to hesitate. Surprise would be on my side. Just before slipping into the tent, I swooped low, pulled the Kay-gun from the dead Diano warrior's holster. Then I moved into the tent.

To my relief I was in a darkened hallway of cloth walls. High-pitched murmurs of nervous excitement came from behind the thin partitions. Obviously the staff of the Diano Proctor was alerted to the unexpected night attack. Up until now apparently they had not discovered the extent of the enemy forces.

While standing there, I realized the rashness of my move. There was little way of knowing where Youi Janis might be. The tent was as large as a big grav-disk battleship with at least a dozen different subdivisions. I cursed myself for not having questioned the slave girl further. She might have known exactly where Youi could be found.

Since boldness had got me this far it seemed likely that it might continue to serve my purpose. Sheathing the sword and gun, I started forward.

Moving down the tent hall, I came to another passageway, lighted by glow-lanterns. Two guards stood before the flap of a doorway to the right. Otherwise the place was deserted. Outside of the voices in the tent, subdivisions, it seemed as if the place were completely empty but for the two men. The chattering female voices gave the illusion of not being a part of this grim silent hallway of cloth. There was an eerie sense of timelessness and my thoughts raced frantically to form the best approach to the guards. All senses were alive to everything, taking in each detail as if impressing it on a photographic plate.

As I stepped forward, the guards turned, grew quickly alert.

"Our Glorious Proctor wishes the Bel-loniea slave woman returned to her quarters—at once!" I announced authoritatively, gambling that Aoji would be occupied in directing the defense of his camp. I was ready to reach for either of the sheathed weapons. My guess was that this must be where Youi was being kept—or they would by implication reveal where she was held.

112

They stared dumbly at me like was statues. Their lack of immediate reaction was unnerving. I wasn't about to assume they could blindly accept my statement—yet if I could but stall them along enough to discover if they were actually guarding Youi Janis, it was worth any risk. Obviously I was a stranger to them and, if they weren't total fools, they would question my authority.

"I have orders! Do you wish to see them?" I offered in a reasonable sounding voice.

The closest said: "We are instructed to let no man in to see the Bel-loniea woman."

Mentally I sighed out my relief. My guess had been correct.

"The Proctor will be furious if you do not follow his orders!" I stepped closer.

"Who are you? I haven't seen you before!" the other warrior announced, his voice deep with threat.

"I haven't seen you before. Who are you?" I countered. My right hand was already tensing, ready to grab the Kay-gun. Speed would be more important than silence.

"What's your name, warrior?" The first guard started for his sword.

Now was the time to move. My hand grabbed the Kay-gun, aimed, fired two rapid shots. I was already past them as they fell to the ground and pushing my way into the room.

Another warrior stood there, Kay-gun pointed in my direction.

I fired, missed. He returned the shot while dropping to the floor. Once more I squeezed the trigger and half the man's head exploded away.

"Youi!" I cried, moving to a small figure huddled against a blanket-covered bed. The tiny female shape hesitantly looked up. She was dressed in a flowing colorful gown of expensive cloth, studded by rich sparkling jewels. There was a haunted, dazed look in her eyes as if the nightmare of captivity had drained emotional sanity.

She stared blankly at me, then looked at the fallen Diano warrior as if unable to quite believe what had happened. He large eyes returned to me, slow emotion beginning to flood into her face.

"Youi Janis—it's me. Torlo Hannis!" I grabbed her. "Come fast!"

At once she responded and without a word leaped from the bed. She clutched my arm like a small shadow hugging fearfully to another.

The softness of her small hand as I took it in mine sent a wave of tingling pleasure coursing through my body. How I wanted to pull her into my arms. The love which had begun that first moment I looked into her features upon awakening on Noomas now choked into harsh passion. The basic animal instinct to protect one's mate overwhelmed me—even though there was little hope of ever possessing this delicate, frail woman. I was filled with such all-consuming passion and love, I swore that for the rest of my life—be it for but moments or eternity—I would serve her in any possible way, becoming her slave if that was the only means open to me. It was startling to discover myself so fully infected—so completely helpless to these emotions.

We ran down the hall, then along the darkened passageway and finally to the slit in the tent where I had first entered. Screams had been sounding from around us ever since the first Kay-gun explosions but only now was I aware of this fact. Danger loomed too close—breathed down our throats. I heard footsteps running around the tent, then yells of warriors.

I pushed Youi through the small opening, then started to slip out after her as the footsteps came from almost directly behind us.

A moment later we were rushing for the safety of the dark impervious shadows. Not until we were some distance from the Proctor's tent, making our way toward where the flyers were being kept, did it seem so fantastic we had succeeded in getting even this far.

"Where did you come from?" Youi asked in a much stronger voice than I would have imagined possible. She seemed to have fully recovered.

"It's a long story!"

114

"Give me your Kay-gun!" she instructed in such an authoritative manner that it was impossible to even think of questioning the command.

Yet, I hesitated.

"I can use it well," she explained, soothingly. "You have the blade."

I gave her the gun and drew the sword. We continued to move under the cover of the shadowy trees, through the thick brush. The camp was actually located on the outer edges of the forest.

"Hurry!" I whispered a little later as we started across a more open area. In the distance I could see grounded flyers. It seemed incredible that we had not been captured. Still we were far from safety. As we approached closer to the flyers I saw they were under guard. The laxness of the night before had disappeared.

I pulled Youi into the shadows of a large tree, said: "You'll have to strip away some of that clothing. Can you make it look like a tavern girl's?"

Her features contorted in puzzled questioning.

The dress which she was wearing fell loose around her shoulders, almost to the ground, revealing little of her figure. Apparently the Diano Proctor had not had a chance to touch her before our attack.

Later I learned that he had just entered the room when Orra Jik signaled me with the Kay-gun. He had left immediately upon hearing the Kay-pellets, which I had dropped over the side of the flyer, exploding, believing the camp was being attacked by a whole unit of Bel-loniea warriors.

Youi studied me for a moment, as if attempting to fathom what I had in mind.

"We have to get past the guards—if you look like a tavern girl and I tell the guards we are drunken lovers returning to one of the flyers—wouldn't it make sense that they would believe us?"

She nodded and immediately started ripping away the outer clothing. "Look the other way, please."

I turned and listened as she tore at the cloth. A few moments later she said I could look.

She was now dressed in what appeared to be a plain common tavern girl's one piece gown, held about her waist by a sash, pulled up around her neck to only half hide her proud breasts. It was such a beautiful sight that I could not move. The moonlight was playing delicate lines onto her features and the curve of her figure.

For an instant I was hypnotized by the captivating sight of Youi. Delicate—yet youthfully strong. The speed in which she had recovered from the harrowing experience of captivity and what it might have meant for her, seemed amazing. Yet the firm set of her jaw, the almost eager light in her eyes, glowing brightly up into mine, created a thrill of pride. Just to be so near her, to have that gaze turned my way, seemed high enough reward for the dangers I had faced. Yet I found myself leaning forward, starting to reach out, irresistibly pulled by the enchantment of this moment as the two of us stood there on the outskirts of the Diano camp. What a time to be thinking the thoughts which raced through my mind! Such rashness could cause our recapture and death—or worse for Youi. Then as she seemed to draw closer, the desire began to throb at my nerves and muscles until it was almost impossible to ignore.

Then I remembered what I must seem in her eyes. I was a common officer without social standing. She was of the Royalty a Proctoress. This sobered the impulse to crush her to me.

"Come!" I said.

She hesitated then followed me. We made our way boldly toward the flyers.

"Act as if you've had too much Porshi," I instructed. "Keep the Kay-gun hidden as best you can."

"Do you take me for a fool" She sounded angry. "I'm of the Royalty of Bel-loniea, and know what is expected in such an emergency!"

Youi began singing a light, delicate ballad, but as if touched with too much liquor, slightly off-key:

> "The warrior and the maiden,
> Drank much of the Porshi,
> Slept on the moss lade,

With soft grasses of pishi."

The song was not vulgar in its words so much as its implied meaning, and my mind rebelled in surprise that Youi Janis would know it. Yet this was a common tavern ballad—and fit the purpose well.

Youi pulled close now, her arm circled my back and I felt momentarily weakened by such close physical contact with her. My voice sang out haltingly, struggling over the words in such a manner that my lack of knowledge of them sounded more like lack of ability to speak straight. But I was coldly alert, ready to fight my way through legions of warriors, if that was necessary for the safety of the Proctoress of Bel-loniea.

As we drew closer to the flyers, three seated warriors stood from a group of seven, moved from a small campfire in our direction.

"Where're you going?" one of them demanded. He was a brute giant with wide shoulders and thick rippling muscles. The idea of attempting to battle with just him alone in hand-to-hand combat was slightly unappealing, for I could easily see that he could break me in two pieces without even straining himself. Even in a sword duel it would take more than my limited experience with the blade to defeat him—for strength can sometimes play to the advantage of the one possessing it.

"Going...to...my flyer!" I announced in a loud voice, struggling over the words. I winked unnaturally dramatic.

"Kera," one of his fellows laughed, coarsely, "let them pass—you can see he's romancing the girl!"

The huge man glared at me closely, grunted and turned back to his fellows.

We continued singing and stumbling until we had passed beyond them, out of sight. Then I pushed Youi away and drew my sword. We had to move fast now, take the first unlocked flyer. Most of the grav-disks had their tops up, the doors locked. We made our way past a score of flyers before finding one with its metal top down. Quickly I half shoved Youi into the grav-disk and then leaped over the railing. Once at the controls, I set the lever for take-off and then

117

pulled the flight stick. Immediately the ship lifted up into the air.

Almost at the same time a cry sounded from below. There was no way of knowing if the voice came from the flyer guards or warriors from the Diano Proctor's tent who might have followed our trail this far. But I didn't plan on waiting to find out.

The crack of Kay-guns followed our course as I lifted the ship into an almost vertical position, heading for the skies. Youi clung to my harness for support until I leveled off, high above the camp.

The night had become chilly cold and a strong wind was beginning to whip across the heavens. The small craft buckled and then jerked under a sudden gust of wind.

Youi stepped back. "Where to, now?"

"Bel-loniea!" I announced, feeling a sense of elation. "Home!"

I turned, looked at her, saw she was studying me in a strange, thoughtful manner.

"I don't know how you managed all this, but..."

"There are a lot of warriors down there who helped in their way, probably dying." I told her, hating the necessity of leaving them behind. Then I explained what had happened to me since learning about her capture. It was necessary to relate the events in which I'd been involved with during the first day of battle around the city of Bel-loniea. She seemed openly impressed by my story.

When I was finished, she said: "You are a brave man. You will be much honored."

"And the others?"

"They will be honored. But you were the one who saved the Proctoress." She settled down on the grav-plate floor, smiled up warmly at me like a little girl. "You have learned much of our ways since we last met, Torlo Hannis."

"War teaches fast," I pointed out, mystified by her attitude. She seemed both regal and childlike—yet warm and friendly, as if speaking to a man she considered her equal.

The wind was increasing in force and the skies were beginning to cloud over. I looked behind us and discovered

118

that a couple of flyers had lifted from the Diano camp in fast pursuit.

"Our troubles aren't over," I told Youi Janis. "Not yet!"

She followed my gaze. "You didn't think they would give us up that quickly, did you?"

My attention was momentarily centered on the horizon ahead of us. I pointed, said: "Looks like a storm."

The other flyers were already gaining on us; obviously our craft was not built for great speed. I cursed the luck which had given us a slower ship.

"Our troubles aren't over," I told Youi Janis.

Youi Janis stood, moved to the back of the flyer where a small rapid fire Kay-gun was mounted.

"Can you fly one of these?" I called to her.

"Every man and woman in Bel-loniea can fly a grav-disk!" she announced with pride. "Do you take me, the Proctoress, for a child?" She turned, her expression haughty, hands on hips. Such pride and anger from so delicate a woman was strangely frightening.

"Get on the controls, I'll fire on the ships!" I commanded.

"Who dares give me orders?" she cried, angrily, not moving from where she stood.

I locked the controls and then grabbed and shoved her bodily to them. "Don't argue!"

Moving to the gun, I set the range control for maximum, sent out a couple of bursts at the pursuing flyers. The shots fell short.

Studying the sky, I realized that the storm would be upon us shortly. This might work to our advantage—if it was possible to survive long enough to escape the guns of the enemy flyers.

As the gap closed between us and the other grav-disk, I pressed the trigger. The shots fell short again.

"Shoot higher," Youi demanded in a very regal, contemptuous voice of authority, "so the shots will fall down upon them"

119

As she spoke, the cracking sound of Kay-guns came from the other ships. Little explosions broke way pieces of our craft's railing.

"Hold on," Youi cried.

I locked my harness to a ring just in time. The ship turned so sharply that my hands were ripped from the gun.

"What are you doing?" I cried, grabbing the Kay-gun.

"Counterattack! Keep to your guns, warrior!" Her voice was harsh, superior. "We'll see how good you are!"

CHAPTER FOURTEEN

THE CONFESSION OF TORLO HANNIS

The flyer dived, then pulled up at a sharp angle, directly at the two Diano flyers.

As the grav-disks drew closer, I fired, keeping the trigger depressed.

Youi Janis dipped the ship down under the first enemy craft and I aimed at its grav-plates. Almost immediately it exploded in bright red flame and then twisted toward the ground in a screaming dive.

Our ship jerked up, circled sharply and skimmed across the other Diano flyer. My gun kept a continued rhythm of fire as the enemy ship was riddled. Several men crumbled in death as Kay-pellets ran along its deck.

Youi circled again, turned for another attack, but the other ship was ready for us, and its guns burst a series of shots into our side. The angle of approach was such that I didn't get a chance to return the fire.

Again Youi banked, whipped us around so fast that I lost grip on the Kay-gun.

The Diano grav-disk came in low, this time apparently hoping to cripple our ship.

I sent a burst over their sides, then fired lower. A scream of pain sounded from below as the ship passed under us.

We turned, ducked low, right across the other's deck. I could see there were only a couple of warriors left, the pilot and another man, making his way to the bow gun.

I aimed as carefully as possible for the short time given as we whipped across the enemy deck.

121

This time the shots hit the pilot, his body exploding at several places as the Kay-pellets ripped soft human flesh and bone.

The ship dived out of control and the remaining warrior fell from its deck, screaming all the way down to the ground.

Youi turned course toward the south, away from Bel-loniea and the storm, as rain started flooding from the skies. Lightning flashed in the distance and a couple of seconds later thunder crashed loudly.

I went to the controls.

"Head away from the storm," she told me.

"That takes us away from Bel-loniea."

"Do as I say Torlo Hannis! The storm would dash us to our deaths!" She shouted above the gale of the wind. "If we ride with it we might get further from the Diano camp!"

She turned and rolled the top up. When this was finished, she came to my side as I continued struggling with the controls. Many times during this flight her body knocked against mine, yet she hung close, not moving away.

How long I fought the increasing power of the storm, the ship tossed like a feather on a tornado-plagued ocean, I don't know. But after the ship was almost overturned, Youi shouted: "Land, before it's too late! Fast!"

I started lowering the nose toward the ground. It was an agonizing struggle, demanding the use of every muscle. The wind and rain tore at us from black ugly clouds.

Lightning flashed against the horizon, outlining distant mountains. We were now being taken along the course of the storm, almost without any effort of the grav-plates. I now doubted it would be possible to land. The length of time between the lightning and the thunder shortened. Then a huge flash of electricity shattered the sky around us.

"Land!" Youi Janis screamed, clutching at my shoulders.

Cursing, I slipped the lever down, then to the left to avoid a grasping tree which loomed dangerously close. For a moment it seemed as if we would crash-land. Then the ship slipped in between two trees and slammed roughly into the ground.

122

We were knocked against one another, then thrown to the floor. Finally we stood, panting. Neither of us said anything at first, being too exhausted from the struggle against the storm. For the moment we were safe, and this fact alone was a lot to be thankful for. Once the storm had died, we could continue our flight to Bel-loniea. Home seemed very close at that moment—possibly because until now it had seemed more of a wishful dream than a possible fact. And for the first time that day I felt regret at the thought of returning, only because once Youi Janis had been reunited with her father and grandfather, there was little chance of being alone with her again like this.

Recovering, Youi moved to the center storage compartment. Then after opening it, she cursed: "Those Korda! No blankets or furs."

The chill of the night had become freezing cold since the storm had dampened our bodies.

I watched Youi as she curled up on the opposite side of the grav-disk, clutching herself with slender arms in an attempt to gather warmth. I moved close, and then sat down beside her.

"The storm can't last forever," I pointed out, trying to decide if it would be too bold to offer her the comfort of my arms and warmth of my body.

She looked up at me, very childlike. "It's cold," she announced, as if this were news.

I started to place an arm around her. Immediately she stiffened as if slapped.

"How dare you!" Her voice was sharp, eyes fiery.

"You said you were cold," I explained, a little miffed and hurt by her attitude. "I wished only to give what warmth was possible."

For a moment it seemed as if she were about to say something but instead looked down to the floor at her feet. Then she turned her gaze back to me, soft, almost innocent in its warmth. How much horror had she gone through in the last couple of days? Yet she was strong and brave enough not to have let it destroy her.

"You are beautiful," I suddenly blurted out, voice thick with emotion.

She didn't say anything to that, but her face revealed a mixture of surprise, shock and something else which I could not fathom.

"Youi," I said, the words coming out like flooding waters breaking through a destroyed dam. I could not control them any longer. This might be the last and only chance to let her know how I felt. "Youi, I've never known a woman like you."

Before I could continue she smiled, teasingly. "You could not remember, even if you had—unless your memory has returned!"

"Please, Youi!" I all but pleaded. "I must tell you something."

"Torlo, don't forget who I am!"

"I don't care if you were a Goddess—it would not make me love you more or less!"

A stunned silence followed my brash statement. I could hardly believe the words had been spoken. Youi, on her part, revealed no reaction—it was impossible to even guess what was going on in her mind.

"I had to let you know!" I announced explosively. "I've loved you since that very first day and—"

She shook her head, "No, Torlo Hannis. It is not right for you to speak this way to me!"

"Someday I will win a position high enough to make it right!" I cried stubbornly.

For some time we sat there in silence. I was struggling inwardly with wild emotions which would not settle down. The thought that she was totally within my power and it would be possible to take her, never tempted me, for I would have Youi only one way: totally and willingly, or not at all. After a long while she broke the painful silence which had fallen upon us.

"When we return to Bel-loniea there will be work for my grandfather to do. Those who took me to the Diano will be tried and killed!"

"Weren't they spies?"

"No! Curse them. If they had been spies, it would have been different. No! Cowardly Korda. They worked for the Kaska—a criminal organization under the rule of an un-

124

known mastermind. The Kaska has cells in most of the known countries of Noomas. Nobody knows who its leader is—but he was behind my capture." Her voice was contorted with rage, yet she looked even more beautiful. "But I know those who are directly responsible. and we will question them. My grandfather will kill them."

Savage as her words were, the voice which spoke them seemed to lack conviction. After a moment she looked up at me.

"How could you?"

The question came so unexpectedly that even if I'd known what she meant, it would have taken some time to recover enough to form an answer,

"I asked you a question!" she snapped, as if in anger.

"How could I what?"

She looked away, then blurted out: "Think...you... well, liked me from the beginning!"

Her cheeks were flushed a deep pink. Her eyes flashed as they returned to mine. Yet how totally feminine she was.

I gazed at her for a long time, hardly aware that she expected an answer to the question.

"Well?" she said hardly above a whisper.

"How could I help but love you?"

"Why should you?"

"Every man in Bel-loniea loves you—why should I be different?"

"Indeed, why?" she cried, furious.

Her reaction to this was totally different from what I had expected.

She whipped around and her right hand slapped me. The blow was far more stinging than one would expect from such a small hand.

The unexpected blow angered and surprised me so greatly that other emotions controlled my next actions so completely that I wasn't aware what was happening until I felt her soft lips under mine, her form crushed powerfully in my grasp.

How I'd managed to embrace her, I'll never quite know. A momentary insanity had blanked out all awareness.

Immediately I realized I'd gone too far, What the punishment might be for such an assault on the Proctoress I could only guess at. Yet it was impossible to stop now. The warm nearness of her soft yielding form made me dizzy with emotion.

I covered her lips and face with hot kisses, unable to contain this expression of my love.

Then I heard the sound of metal slipping against metal, then felt the needlepoint of a dagger press between my shoulder blades.

Immediately I froze. In that moment my thoughts raced over the distance of my life on Noomas, from the time I had awakened to see Youi's face suspended over mine, up to the present instant where my life hung in her hands. At first I believed that only a moment had passed since she took my knife—then realized that a long time had lapsed. This hesitation would have defeated her if I had desired to defend myself. But the realization of what I'd done made it impossible to find any mental defense which might be used to plead a case even to myself. This mad act of passion was no better because of its honest emotions than the fate which Aoji had planned for Youi. This made me worse than he, because she had trusted me.

In total acceptance of my death, I waited for Youi to plunge the blade deep.

Suddenly the point lifted away and I tensed for death. It was a long wait.

Then came the sound of the knife striking the floor. Youi slipped easily away, though not completely beyond my reach.

All I could think of was that she had not killed me. Why, was a puzzle I made no attempt to understand—it suggested much, though promised nothing.

My eyes focused on Youi's face, the high cheek bones, the wide eyes moist with tears, the full trembling lips.

"I'm sorry," was all I could manage.

She looked up at me, shook her head, drew her lower lips between even white teeth. Words finally stumbled out.

"I couldn't...couldn't!" Now her whole body trembled.

126

"You should have."

"I couldn't..." Emotion choked off any more words.

I stood, drew my sword and placed it at her feet. "This is yours for the rest of my life, Youi Janis. I hope it will serve you well. Take me as your slave or warrior and I will be there at your call!"

She stood, ignoring the sword. For a moment she seemed to lean close, then pulled herself stiffly erect. The expression on her features now glazed over, revealing no emotion.

Thunder shook the skies, lightning flashed close by, lighting Youi's face with sharp white strokes.

"Torlo Hannis. I am Proctoress—and someday I must be ruler of my beloved Bel-loniea, at the side of my future husband. This man must be of high Royal standing—a man who has won great honors and proven his worth. Such a man will have to be outstanding—able to rule a nation with justice and love." She hesitated, then continued more emotionally. "Such a man will be picked after I am quite sure he is able to stand at my side with equality."

There was something in her tone, the subtle turn of phrase, which implied she was attempting to tell me that which was impossible to state directly. My heart leaped with excitement. Could she really be saying I had a chance? Or was it merely my imagination reading what it wanted to hear?

"Do you understand why Torlo Hannis, a mere officer of the Proctor's Special Corps," she questioned in a firm, stiff voice, "is not in such a position?"

"I will not always be so lowly!" I announced harshly, for this last had hurt.

"Maybe not. But honors are won by deeds, not words! You have a long way to go, Torlo Hannis, before you have the right to speak to me of such things as you have this night." Then her face softened for but a moment. "Until then, Torlo, you will not speak of love. If such a time comes when you might have honors enough, you may take the right to speak again of such matters if it pleases you."

"Would it please you?" I inquired.

She merely turned and looked through the front window. "The storm is abating. It will not be long before we return home," she announced.

I wanted to move to her side but realized it would be a mistake. Her last words had offered much. Returning her safely to her people would surely offer many rewards. I wondered if it might be enough?

Youi Janis faced me again. "Torlo—if I was not the Proctoress..."

Then she whipped around, so I could not see her. After a moment she lay on the floor, back to me.

My thoughts were a mass of confusion as I lay opposite her. There was joy in the knowledge that she might someday be mine—if time and events played on my side. It was more than I could have expected.

The next day we would be safely back behind the walls of Bel-loniea, I thought, studying her back, taking in every beautiful line, curve and hollow, so that it would be forever impressed upon my mind. This would be the last night, I was sure, that she would be alone with me for a long time—if not forever. When sleep came, it was through total exhaustion, with the half-contented knowledge that Youi Janis was at last safe, and that there was some hope that in the future I might win the right to ask her hand in marriage.

If only I'd known the truth!

CHAPTER FIFTEEN

A SAVAGE STORM

A child who experiences his first storm will shiver in terror, cry in its mother's arms, shrink from every bolt of lightning, every groaning crack of thunder. A man, full grown, cannot do such things, even if he does not remember having witnessed such a frightening event. Still, the primitive instinct of raw naked terror of the unknown, basic in all living creatures, that causes virgin minds to shiver like cowardly babies in the wake of Nature's fury, was hard to control. I remembered little beyond my short existence on Noomas, and never before had the skies of this world contorted into the wild image of storm-fury since that day I was reborn here, a man without knowledge of any past life.

That lovely Goddess called Nature has a way of placing all living beings on the same helpless level of soft destructible flesh and bone, without the resources to combat the natural elements of the world in which they all selfishly fight the endless brutal struggles for existence. A man can take sword against beast and fellow human, having at least some chance of protecting himself. But what weapon would serve to combat the insane, tormented anguish of an atmosphere that can erode mountains, cut canyons, grind stone into powdery sand? The only defense against such power is cowering in the darkness with the blind faith that life will still breathe in your lungs when the gods have finished their little lesson in humility.

Such was my emotional reaction to the force of the storm which crushed around our little flyer. The wind screamed in agony, ripping through the trees, tearing at weak brush and grass.

I had trained as a warrior of Noomas, hunted the gigantic monstrous Korda beast, fought against the seasoned armies of the Diano and walked among the enemy camp to rescue Youi Janis, all with nothing but determination pushing me forward into action. But the power of Nature against the very world itself was able to rip aside my seemingly unlimited courage. Fighting man and beast was one thing; coming to terms with the possible supernatural elements of mythical or real gods was another! My life and strength were sworn to Youi as slave or servant. There was nothing I would not gladly face in order to save her from the slightest discomfort. Yet the violence of the storm was such that it sparked the very core of my animal terror.

I lay awake for most of the night, after a brief exhausted sleep, painfully conscious of how defenseless we were against this violent distortion of gentle Nature.

Lightning flashed overhead countless times, brightening the sky as if Noomas's huge sun had momentarily blinked awake. Rain sounded on the closed metal top of the stolen Diano grav-disk flyer that had taken us from the enemy camp.

Much to my shame, Youi Janis, frail, helpless appearing woman, did not move during the night. She rested peacefully throughout the great violence of the storm that tore at the world like a frenzied invisible demon, berserk with the desire to leave nothing untouched by its fury.

My first indication of real danger came when the flat bottom of the disk-shaped flyer started swaying. After a time it seemed to lurch away from its resting place. Immediately I went to one of the many oval windows that lined the interior of the disk. Outside all I could see was abysmal darkness beyond the thick downpour of the harsh rains flooding from the heavens.

The flyer rocked again and there was an unmistakable sensation of floating.

I stood there in silent astonishment, overwhelmed by this new evidence of the unbridled power that now held the world in its total power.

130

The sound of Youi sitting up drew my attention from the storm. She looked in my direction, large eyes wide with honest concern.

"The flyer—we're floating," her musical, soft voice murmured just above a whisper. She listened to the storm for a moment. "How long have I been asleep?"

"Most of the night—but it's still black outside," I informed her.

This time is was possible to take careful aim.

She shivered from the cold that pressed in around us like icy gnarled fingers attempting to freeze life away. The thin material of her clothing—so brazenly stripped down to give her the appearance of a common tavern-girl—was little protection against the freezing temperature. She reached for the warrior cape I'd placed over her sleeping form, and pulled it tightly about slender shoulders.

"The storm," I announced like a man who spoke from long experience, "will pass."

She looked quite unsatisfied by this statement. "Such storms can last for several days. In Bel-loniea, streets are constructed to drain off the overflow. Here, lost in the wilderness between countries, the land will drink water at a far slower rate than the storm will feed it—and all unattached things will make their way to the rivers and ocean."

The expression on her delicate, beautiful features appeared more concerned than frightened, but it was enough to create a great pang of protectiveness within me. How I wanted to move to her side, comfort that tiny form in gentle arms. But her words to me before going to sleep held off such action.

She was the Proctoress of Bel-loniea and I was a mere warrior. Already my actions had gone far beyond those even allowed a proper suitor. The passions that had caused me to embrace and kiss Youi Janis still burned like hot fires within every nerve; but the shame of having lost control, sent shivers of guilt to paralyze any further such dishonorable acts against her.

The flyer was now freely rocking from side to side, and there was the unquestionable surge of forward movement. The flooding storm waters already had us in their

131

grasp, speeding the small craft along an unknown course to a questionable destination. Any thought of taking flight was totally unworthy of any considerations. We had been forced down during the early moments of the storm, whose violence had multiplied many times since. Flight was impossible. All we could do was wait out the storm, hoping it would leave us undamaged.

I asked Youi, "Do you have any idea where we are?"

"Only in what direction we were going—away from the storm and home. In this direction is the ocean and to the north are the desert lands, bordered by dead mountains and the silent seas. As to where we are being taken by the storm waters..." She shrugged. "It could be to the ocean or to some of the rivers that feed the giant lakes beyond the territories of my grandfather's outer colonies."

I asked her to tell me something of the geography of Noomas, since up until now little or no knowledge had been offered and because it was better to talk about anything other than our immediate problems.

"As you know," she said much as an instructor teaching a small child, "Bel-loniea is bordered by desert, mountains, forest which finally blend into the Korda Jungles and the great ocean to the west, which stretches halfway across the world to a continent we know very little about. Beyond the mountains, if you go through the Beldon Pass, you come to the lands of the Diano, and beyond that are the territories of other great nations. To the far north are the Primitive Ones—whom we believe to be the first creatures of the world, though they did not develop as other species, becoming limited to an existence of cave dwelling. My father, Andon Janis, claims that they are probably the original inhabitants of Noomas, and that all human life came from his and your Great Civilization in the Stars. I know nothing of such matters, but must accept his explanation, since he is a great scientist who heals the sick, and all the learned Masters of Knowledge in the known nations of our world respect his word.

"The lands to the north are inhabited by the nomadic tribes. In the eastern slopes of the mountains are outlaws who have been exiled from their homes in disgrace—having dishonored themselves beyond the mere punishment of a lowering of social status, or criminals who escaped execution for their crimes, or slaves who have run away from their masters.

"Little is known of the rest of our vast world—except what small pieces of information learned from a few daring men who have taken it upon themselves to explore unknown regions. There has been rumor of a mysterious civilization, on the other side of the world, of great pyramids, golden cities of tall needle-shaped towers. But the man who reported this was half out of his mind, claiming the civilization was ruled by Mutis who enslaved all humans, ruling with a cruel, iron hand.

"Before our Proctor's Muti could come to prove or disprove the man's story, he died horribly, raving insanely. Of course, as you know, it is quite inconceivable that such a place could exist. Our Muti was told of the man's story, but said he knew of no such nation. That was several hundred years ago. Other explorers who have attempted to prove the story have disappeared, never returning. One cannot question the word of a Muti—and it is impossible to even consider the Mutis being other than the great, gentle voices that teach us normal humans the great wisdom of the future and the past, gently advising our greatest minds, humbly giving of themselves to all who but ask their help."

"Every one who has spoke of the Mutis seems to hold them in such awed respect—yet no one has really told me anything other than not to question the Mutis."

"The ways of the Muti are strange," she admitted with a shrug, as if reading from a book. "It is best not to dwell upon the subject. Learn to accept, they say, and never question the giver, for in receiving you give the blessing of pleasure to that person who has it in their hearts to be a giver. They thus claim it is as well to receive as to give."

A mental picture of her father's Muti assaulted my mind! The purpled face without real nose or eyes. How It had stared from hollowed sockets, shrunken, parchment-like depressions of flesh, seemingly unseeing, yet aware of far more than moral man could even guess at! My mind and inner soul had been ripped bare to its thoughts. Those deep-set eye-sockets blindly read what is inside you as if devouring a tiny book in a simple gulp. One felt stripped raw, revealed in such a denuded form that nothing was left unexposed, even down to the darkest depths of the inner mind. What details of my past could a Muti read? Did they know things about me that were locked way from my own consciousness? How far into my past had this monstrous creature probed?

Perhaps this was all fantasy illusion conjured up within my mind. The Mutis were supposed to have limited powers. And we all keep secrets locked safely away so even we are not able to remember them. Much like my lost past, life was tucked so totally beyond reach. Could the Mutis really probe that deeply into a person's psyche?

All I knew for certain was that the Muti had seen me as a shadow crossing Youi's life-path in the near future.

That was enough to rush shivers down my spine every time I thought of them.

Yet I was determined to learn as much as possible about these mysterious creatures of Noomas. Now, obviously, was not the time.

For some while we sat there on the floor of the grav-disk, each wrapped in our own thoughts. The storm continued to harass the world, flooding water pressed our flyer further from its original landing site toward a destination neither of us could be sure of. Still it seemed reasonable enough to assume that no matter how far the storm drove us, it would only take a short time to make our way back to Bel-loniea. Yet I could not fight away a nagging feeling that it might not be that simple.

I paced the floor of the grav-disk like a trapped animal. Several times I absently checked the charges in the small Kay-gun holstered on my right; twice I drew the long thin-bladed sword from its sheath. These were nervous reactions to the helpless feeling created by a long, stubborn storm. When hunger reminded me that we had not eaten since leaving the Diano camp, I offered Youi one of the Mio-sticks, that hard, dry food substance that is given all warriors when entering upon battle—hardly a delicious meal, but healthy. We ate twice that day, then slept.

The only outer difference between night and day was the deeper sense of dark that mothered the world outside. The storm never lessened—and at times seemed to burst into more open fury as it angrily ripped at the world. Sleep came through total exhaustion. By now I'd learned to accept the violence of Nature controlling the world, and anxiously embraced sleep.

During the night I suddenly sat up, startled awake. At first it was impossible to tell what had alarmed me out of the deep sleep. My body was shivering from cold, the dazed aftermath of total unconsciousness hugged my brain in a numbed embrace. Youi was curled up on the floor a short distance away, the warrior cape pulled tightly around her frail form. The flyer was gently rocking from side to side, moving along the course of the irresistible storm-flood waters that energetically pulled it.

Silence was so complete that it was some moments before this fact actually made any mental impression.

The storm had passed.

Moving to the front window, I gazed out upon the surrounding landscape.

The sky was crystal clear, sparkling bright stars twinkled down upon a watery landscape. I stared at the tiny point of the super-giant star that looked back unblinkingly. That star was almost an interstellar neighbor to our sun, but much too distant to give any special flow to the night sky. The bulk of stars were gathered tightly together into a distorted ball towards the center of the heavens to create a blurred cloudy haze of light. Two of the three moons were tipping up over the horizon, to bathe a streak of light across the world of water that immediately surrounded the ship.

To our right were the outlines of mountains, off to the left a jagged line indicated higher ground where thick forest reached up against the black of space, tall, gnarled trees lending a fantasy-like unreality to the scene.

I watched this silent world and attempted to probe my memory, trying to remember what life had been like before arriving on Noomas. Nothing new came. There were only the facts that had already revealed themselves in the short time since I'd awakened on this strange, primitive planet. I had

135

been born in a civilization that spanned the galaxy to form a vast federation of planets. I had apparently grown up to become a soldier, for a mental image had once formed of fighting in some fantastic battle where spaceships were as common as the swords and Kay-guns of the men of Noomas. Something involving a faceless man and woman had brought me to this world, only to crash-land and lose knowledge of past memory. Andon Janis had claimed that memory should return in time.

Living in such a mental shell is such personalized isolation. For one is restricted within the confines of their own consciousness. I was totally aware of the empty elements, like obvious voided places, blinded holes that revealed nothing except they were blank and empty of even shadow-memories. Yet shadow-dreams teased themselves across these blanks from time to time, to mock me with elements which never quite connected with my present reality. Would I ever discover the truth of my past; or would it remain a voided non-reality? I truly felt as if a Lost One!

Perhaps a Muti might, someday, help me remember—if it were able to read that deeply and, questionable at best, willing to share that information with me.

That thought was mysteriously disturbing.

Was it possible I didn't want to know the truth about my past life?

Turning to look at Youi, I wondered if it was really so important to remember the past. Andon Janis had said there was no way off this world, and that I would spend the rest of my life here—but that it could be a very pleasant life, if I learned the ways of this world and earned honors.

The rest of the night I sat looking at Youi. Life would be empty without this woman—it was a very possible future which lacked appeal. Honors and status came through great deeds. I had a long way to go before I would be in a position to ask for her hand in marriage before a Muti. And even then it might already be too late to have Youi Janis as mine. Affairs of state could easily force her into a marriage to a man picked by her grandfather. Yet I felt certain that if I now had the status needed, she would take my offer of marriage. This was a dream worth holding on to; something to believe in, no matter how unrealistic it might be. The next hours, days, might need such blind conviction. Hope, no matter how slim, is what our lives function on, what we use to motivate actions into reality—even when the immediate situation is hopeless. Maybe, someday, somehow the moment would come when I could win the right to fold her into my arms, into my life, into my very soul. For it seemed she held the same desires, unreachable though they might be. I told myself to believe that. I convinced myself that she could love a man without consideration of social status. She had almost admitted this by saying: "If I were not a Proctoress..."

As the sun was coming up, sleep took possession of my thoughts. When consciousness returned, a soft humming floated lightly on the air.

I turned to see Youi standing at the front of the ship, looking out, humming to herself.

She turned suddenly, as if aware that my eyes were upon her.

"You slept peacefully," her voice greeted lightly. A warm, friendly smile played on her generous mouth.

"How long have you been awake?"

"Not long. The storm has passed. We're floating along the banks of a river. The storm's water is passing off the land, making its way to the oceans and rivers. The sun should dry the ground by nightfall."

I stood, moved to her side, looked out at the world. We were just a short distance from a vividly colored jungle, thickly grown with huge, twisted, purple trees, creeping tangled vines, lacy blue ferns and brush, all gaily sprinkled by countless varieties of delicately pedaled flowers.

"Do you have any idea where we are?" I inquired, conversationally.

"I think this is the Toraniea River, which makes its way along the mountains, down through the outer fringes of the Quaine jungle—a narrow stretch of tropic land bordering the northern deserts. It's a place of terrible beasts, where no man has dared to go into on foot and return. If I'm right, we should be reaching the desert by tomorrow. The river normally dries up just beyond the jungle—though after such a storm as we've just survived, the river will cut its way through the desert, feeding the parched sands, until it reaches the dead sea to be absorbed into its thirsty dry floor, later to pass under the ground and make its way to the great ocean to the west," Youi explained with a tiny little smile, which seemed an attempt to show bravery.

"We'll not be around that long," I announced, moving to the controls.

Youi shook her head. "I tried them while you sleep."

My hands froze, just short of the control stick.

"They don't work!"

"What could be wrong?"

"Water-soaked," she explained with a shrug of her shoulders. "Possibly some damage was done to the grav-plates in the landing. We have to let the river carry us where it will."

Immediately I felt a surge of painful fear for her. What then? I wondered, alarmed. But determined not to reveal these inner worries to Youi, I shrugged.

"It will simply take just a little longer to return to Bel-loniea," I announced, lightly.

She was silent for a moment, then shook her head. "No, Torlo Hannis, it might take longer than that. The distance between the deserts and Bel-loniea is great—by foot it is at least five ten-day marches; and many dangers lay between those two points. If we survive the deserts, if we escape capture from the many nomadic tribes who would take us as slaves to be sold at the next city they come to, if we manage to avoid the beasts of prey along the way, find food enough to hunt, there is a chance that we might see Bel-loniea again—though a very slim one. I just want to let you know what dangers actually await us. On foot, with only a Kay-gun and sword to defend ourselves...there is little chance of ever reaching Bel-loniea."

"Maybe we can fix the flyer once we reach dry land," I offered, hoping this would give her some hope.

She shook her head. "It's probably been shorted out and only with a replacement part would it be possible to fly this craft again."

"Possibly the damage done is not that great."

138

"Perhaps. Anything is possible. It's even possible that by a miracle we might reach Bel-loniea someday." She shrugged, looked saddened, said: "But I don't believe in miracles, Torlo Hannis. I'm only sorry that because of me you must face the fate that now awaits both of us. For I will be a slave woman to some rich lord, and you will, if lucky, become an Arena-warrior, and die. It is surely not a fit reward for the brave deeds you have done in my behalf. You deserve honors, not death."

My throat choked at her words, for they held such desperate emotion that I was certain she would come into my arms right then, if she were other than the Proctoress of Bel-loniea.

And at that instant, I have to admit, I was tempted by the idea that if we were to die, what harm was there to claim this woman as mine for the few remaining units of time we might have of freedom and life. Her statements had carried a heavy burden of conviction which was impossible to reject. Youi was born of this world and knew its true hazards. It was beyond me to question this authority and knowledge.

Then I saw something in her eyes that told me similar thoughts must have passed through her mind. She appeared to take a step forward, then as I moved to pull her dear form next to mine, a low-voiced scream shattered the silence.

We both froze like statues cut from unyielding rocks. Then Youi's face drained of all color. She was looking over my shoulder, out through one of the back windows.

The flyer abruptly slammed to one side; both of us were knocked off balance, tangling against the floor. Under other circumstances her nearness would have been welcomed.

The ship was violently lifted from the water, swung high into the air. The actions created a sickening sensation at the pit of my stomach.

Youi screamed: "The gun!"

CHAPTER SIXTEEN

THE RAIDERS OF BAJI-NEY

I struggled to the Kay-gun at the end of the ship, which had been used to cut down a couple of Diano grav-disks two nights before. While grabbing the rapid-fire, long-barrel gun, I saw a monstrous slimy rounded head sway high above the craft. That first impression was enough to create a great shuddering conviction that we might not survive even this day. My hands closed on the Kay-gun, depressed the trigger, not even taking the time to aim. The long barrel swung toward that head, then the ship was overturned, flinging me bodily from the weapon, to slam against the top of the grav-disk. If the top had been down, our chances of survival would have ended then. As it was, out of the corner of my eyes I saw Youi knocked to the other side of the ship to bank unconscious against the deck as the flyer righted itself.

There wasn't time to do more than struggle back to the Kay-gun. I snapped the harness strap to one of the safety rings.

Now held in place, I gripped the Kay-gun. This time it was possible to take careful aim.

The flyer had been picked up and thrown back into the river by the long sleek tail of the deep green snake-like beast attacking us. In the moments of battle I had little chance to take in the full details of the creature, though later I mentally recorded its image. The head was split by a large, fang-lined red mouth out of which snapped a long whip-like forked tongue. This head was more than twice the size of an average man. The long coils of its thick body were wrapped around the flyer, crushing, attempting to squeeze the hard metal into a crumpled mass.

I depressed the trigger and saw huge pieces of the beast's head explode away in a burst of yellow blood as the Kay-pellets struck.

The head hit against the ship, tongue spurting with reddish foaming liquid—a deadly poison.

At this close range I squeezed off a long burst of Kay-pellets and was rewarded to see half the jaw pulverize away, and one of its three eyes explode into raw bony flesh. A moment later the creature slipped back from us, its long coiled body released its grip on the flyer. A convulsive shudder whipped through its snaky body, then the muscles stiffened in death as the river took command of the lifeless flesh, floating it alongside us.

Immediately I unstrapped the harness from the ring, went to Youi Janis' side.

She was lying on her back, a bruise on the right side of her forehead. Fear that she might be seriously hurt sent a wave of panic through me.

Then as I more carefully examined her, it became obvious she was only knocked unconscious. But as time passed, and she showed no sign of coming out of it, I felt the fears winding through my mind like hot fires. To have life taken from such a young, beautiful woman was too tragic to even consider. I knew that at that moment I would gladly die in her place.

I rolled down the top of the flyer. After tearing away a portion of the warrior cape, I dampened the cloth, then touched it to her forehead.

All during the rest of the day I watched over her. Even as the sun slowly set and darkness descended, there was no change in her condition.

Late in the night, she moaned softly. Shortly after that her eyelids fluttered. She looked up at me, a dazed expression on her face.

"Did...you kill the...Fiza?" she murmured, weakly attempting to sit up. I helped her while explaining what had happened.

141

"We were lucky the top was up," she observed as I pulled the cape around her shoulders.

Later she fell asleep, after a Mio-stick dinner, and I joined her, totally exhausted from the long day.

The next morning, when I awoke, it was to an immediate feeling of a change in our environment. The sun was baking hot from a clear blue sky. The air felt like the blazing breath of a furnace, pressing in around us with a fierce intensity. After the long days of coldness during the storm, this was almost a welcome condition.

Immediately I lowered the top of the flyer to survey our surroundings.

As far as I could see in three directions was a flat baked expanse of sand, broken only by a few rocks and strange yellowish bulbs of vegetation. The ship rested on dry land, where the waters of the storm had deposited us sometime during the night. Just on the horizon, I could make out a thin shadowy line which indicated the jungle through which we'd passed. From a world of water, we had entered a dry wasteland, a dominion of heat.

Youi came to my side.

"It's as I feared," she observed in a heavy voice. "The desert. We are a long way from home."

"And no water or food other than the Mio-sticks."

She shook her head. "Those plants are cups of water. The desert tribes subsist on their juice and flesh. Here, give me your sword."

We stepped out of the flyer and made our way to the nearest yellow plant. It was bulb-shaped, surrounded by a wall of thorns. Youi swung the sword skillfully over her head, moved it in a wide arc that lopped off the top of the bulb.

"The water-plant, the desert tribes call it," she explained with a grim, brave smile. Her courage was as great as the beauty of face and figure that Nature had given her.

Now, before us was a bowl of water about the size of a man's head, clear and sparkling. I waited while Youi satisfied her thirst, then cupped my hands into the small bowl. The liquid was sweet-tasting and most refreshing. I had not realized how great my thirst was until that moment.

142

"In which direct should we go now?" I inquired, fighting back the total desperation of helplessness that assailed me.

"To the south is Bel-loniea—but first we must go west, toward the ocean. Once there, we can turn south and continue in that direction until we reach the Bel-loniea seaport." At that moment she seemed so hopeful that the wave of depressive defeat left me.

She made it sound so simple that I managed to forget her warning of the day before. All we had to do was walk home, avoiding whatever dangers might stand in our way. Luckily I had no concept of what lay before us. This momentary sense of light-hearted attitude toward our situation would be the last we experienced for a long time.

With a good-natured smile, I sheathed my sword and then bowed low, in mocked gallantry. "After you, my lady."

Happily she played out the role, bowed and then started off to the right, west toward the ocean, leaving what we now both silently accepted to be a useless flyer to rust away on the desert floor.

Every time we passed one of the water-plants, a swing of the sword opened the door to quench our constant thirst. Outside of the unrelenting blare of the hot sun, it was not an unpleasant morning stroll. Fortunately the deserts of Noomas, while quite hot, are not impossibly heated—and can be endured with only a small amount of discomfort. By mid-afternoon we stopped to enjoy a well-earned rest and eat of one of the water-plant's inner rind, which tasted slightly bitter, having fed all its sweetness to the water. But it was a change from the more or less tasteless Mio-stick that had served as our steady diet since escaping the Diano war camp.

We were just finishing when high-pitched squawking sounded from overhead.

I looked up to see a swarm of huge birds swooping down upon us.

The unexpectedness of it was even more horrifying than the fact that we were so totally exposed. Each bird was gaunt and bony, a little larger than a human head. Their long, pointed beaks were bright orange, the small eyes fiery red, the feathers a gray, dusty color.

I hardly had time to draw my sword before they were upon us, beaks snapping hungrily, tiny claws attempting to attach themselves to our exposed flesh.

I swung the sword frantically around the two of us in an attempt to ward them off. It seemed a hopeless struggle, even though half a dozen fell before the razor sharp blade in the first moments of their attack.

Somehow I managed to throw Youi to the ground, face down. Standing over her, I attempted to take on the flock of greedy winged horrors. Possibly because she did not move after that, they paid full attention to my efforts to battle them off. But it was like trying to fight a whole army. My flesh was covered with blood from dozens of wounds inflicted by their sharp beaks and claws.

How long I continued to cut at the air, chopping at these winged scavengers, I don't know. It would not have been possible to last much longer. How they had approached, seemingly out of nowhere, was almost a puzzling as the endless quantity of their numbers. All I could think of was to somehow reduce them totally before they had weakened me beyond the point of further struggle. The mental image of Youi Janis' bones pecked clean, bleaching in the desert sun for eternity, gave strength to my sword arm even while it seemed only a few moments before I would dizzily pass out.

Then suddenly there was a loud cracking sound from behind us, which immediately repeated itself, multiplying into a continuous rhythm. Blood, flesh, feathers, bones, scattered around me in a heavy hail, and suddenly the few remaining birds flapped off, climbing high into the sky until their shapes disappeared in the distance.

Dazed, I stood there, breathing heavily, covered with blood, sword still raised in the air as if to strike at some invisible foe.

Youi came to her feet. "Torlo, Torlo!" she cried, sobbing. "I...thought..."

Her voice choked to silence as she suddenly stiffened, stepped away. She was looking over my shoulder, face contorted in an expression of resignation, defeat.

I turned to see a strangely savage sight.

144

Coming towards us were robed men riding large, slender, four-legged mounts. These desert riding animals had a long thin neck and small pointed heads; their hides were splotched with black patches on a white hairless surface. The men carried long Kay-rifles, the first I'd seen on Noomas. Their robes were bright yellow, pulled over their heads, strapped into place around their waists by a leather harness that supported sheathes for long sword, knife and Kay-gun.

The caravan moved swiftly across the desert floor, causing a heavy cloud of dusty sand to gather up behind them. As they came closer, I saw that the men wore long, pointed black beards, their faces were lean, narrow, the bone structures creating a gaunt, sunken appearance in their features. Straight noses cut like knives between close-set large black eyes.

When they reached our position, they moved in a wide circle, until they had enclosed us completely by a ring of mounted warriors—women and children remained in the back.

One rider moved forward, slung his rifle into a sheath on the right side of the saddle. He stopped immediately in front of us.

"You fight well, warrior!" he greeted, eyes studying mine with amusement. Then he glanced at Youi; a quick gleam of intense interest flashed across his grimly austere features. "She is a beautiful women to be dying in the desert. She'll bring a good price in the slave-market!"

"You'll have to kill me first!" I announced, raising my sword and touching his chest with its point.

He didn't move. A slow scornful grin spread across his face, then the thin-lipped mouth opened wide, exposing heavy, yellowed teeth as a low-voiced roar of laughter welled from the bearded face. The laughter was taken up by the ring of mounted warriors, becoming a thunderous roar of mockery.

Finally the man raised his right hand and a deathly silence fell upon the desert.

"You will die, surely, warrior, if I but lower my hand in one quick motion." His cavernous eyes glared callously down at me. "You fight well, you will bring a good price

145

from some Arena Master. I see no reason to kill you, warrior. But the choice is up to you. As we say in the desert, there is always hope as long as life breathes in our lungs. You cannot possibly stand up against the sixty guns of Baji-Ney's men." Then he shrugged indifferently. "Though I'd rather see you alive, for the price of Kay-pellets is high; and many were used to save your life. Decide fast!"

I looked at Youi, unsure what to say. I was about to announce Youi as the Proctoress of Bel-loniea, when she stated:

"Master, it is useless." The expression on her face was shaded in warning, her eyes guarded, voice sharp. "As he said, you cannot fight them all—and life holds more hope than death."

I studied her for a quick moment, then made my decision.

I announced: "This woman is my slave. I'm a mercenary from Kanns. My sword is yours for as reasonably long as you decide will cover your expenses."

"You are either a fool or take us a fools!" Baji-Ney announced nastily. "We of the desert have no use for men like you, since we have great fighting men in our own ranks. Are you mad or know you nothing of the world that gives you life?"

"I know enough to claim there is not a man among you who could defeat me in a bare-handed combat!" I challenged, sure that his pride would bait him.

He studied me for a moment, then nodded. "Let it be, then. We could use some entertainment. Tonight you will learn that life as a slave would have been far better than slow, painful death at the hands of a desert warrior. You will die in anguish, warrior."

"I think not," I countered. "And if I win?"

"If you win..." His smile was treacherous. "Why you can keep your slave woman until we reach the slave markets—otherwise, I will sample the goods, as will all my chiefs, before throwing her worthless body to the Korda city-dwellers."

I slowly lowered my sword from the man's chest, and then reluctantly waited while two of his men dismounted and came to disarm me. There was nothing else that could be done; as he had pointed out, life was better than immediate death. At least I'd bought some time—and if I could continue to buy time, there was at least hope. Two men roughly tied my hands behind my back, then took Youi off to where they kept other slave women.

I was thrown over the side of one of the mounts and a rider pulled himself up behind me.

Baji-Ney cried: "We must hurry to reach camp before darkness."

With that he screamed loudly, and the caravan bolted forward as one unit, taking an automatic formation behind their bearded leader, tracing a swift way through the late afternoon desert.

For me, this ride was a mental as well as physical torture, for the battle against the desert birds had drained all strength and I had nothing to look forward to except a fight to the death—one that might very well end my life and leave Youi Janis a helpless plaything for the bestial passions of these harsh men of the desert. The prospects for the future seemed cruelly lacking in hope.

CHAPTER SEVENTEEN

AND INTO SLAVERY...

The night sky was much as it had always been, though it seemed even more glorious on the desert—a perverse, mocking beauty to add a final artistic stroke of splendor to the setting for a battle to the death. The caravan of desert nomads had reached a small water-hole, surrounded by low bush trees just before darkness folded night down upon the world. Brightly colored tents were quickly placed in a circle about the pond's calm waters which dutifully reflected the night stars like a glassy mirror. All three moons rose to light the world in a soft glow, soothing away any harsh shadows cast by the flickering blaze of the huge bonfire that had been lighted in the middle of a ring of chiefs' tents.

I had not seen Youi Janis since our capture. They had placed me on the desert floor upon arriving, bound hand and foot by the tough leather thongs which cut cruelly into the flesh. Neither food nor water was offered by my captors. Upon requesting some, I was told there was no use in giving valuable food and drink to a dead man.

Once camp was set up, small fires had been built in front of each tent and the people of Baji-Ney's tribe settled down for their evening meal. Children played between the tents, and finally after the feasting was over, they were taken to bed. The men now slowly gathered in the large area in front of the main fire and their leader's tent. Small skin bags were passed around, in which I learned was the distilled liquor of the water-plant, a powerful drink which before the night was up would make many of the men of Baji-Ney half mad.

By the time the moons were high in the sky, most of the men were getting fairly drunk, some even fighting among themselves. Finally, Baji-Ney brought about order, taking a stance in front of the large fire which was kept supplied by slaves with slowly burning branches of the trees around the pond. He held a bag of the Gouto-liquor high in the air, cried for silence, swaying some from the effects of his drinks.

"Warriors of Baji-Ney, we have a slave who boasts that he can kill any one of you with his bare hands." His voice was thick, but formed the worlds clearly and loud. "We have all seen him in combat with the Shillos, and know he is a fine warrior with the sword, brave—a man who it would be an honor to kill. I have picked one of the greatest fighters among you—my own son, who will someday lead you to even greater glories and riches when he takes my place. Tonight he will show you his bravery, strength and skill by dispatching this braggart! Come, Rha-Ney—prove to the warriors and chiefs of our people that you are truly a mighty fighter."

A tall, lean young man with firm, wiry muscles, with only a loin-cloth about his middle, stepped from Baji-Ney's tent. He moved with a cat-like fluid step, sure of himself, confident as the young will be when facing the world at the peak of their youthful glory. But I realized he could easily be well past two hundred Federation years, for on Noomas the young are given the youth drug which allows them up to 1000 years, if administered before they reach their thirtieth year. One look at him revealed that he was a fighting man in his prime. Unlike his fellow clansmen, his eyes were brightly alert, untouched by the madness of the liquor. He took the engagement seriously. At least the man I would fight did not have contempt for his battle-partners.

"My son, when you have killed this man, you will be rewarded with any stallion among my private stock."

The tall young man shook his head. "I would have the new slave woman."

"Of course, she will be given you the night after I have enjoyed her ripe young body," his father generously offered with a grand wave of his hands.

"I would be first!" Rha-Ney persisted. "She is young, and should know a young man—the victor of her former master."

"You would rob your father of the delights of such a lovely maiden?"

"Only for this first night!" Rha-Ney announced in a firm, loud voice so that it carried to every man present.

A shout sounded from one of Baji-Ney's followers. "Let the young one have his way. He'll earn it."

Several other yells supported the suggestion, and father looked at son with a fiery anger burning in his sunken eyes. "How can a father keep from thus honoring his first-born's wishes?" The voice which spoke those words was deadly, soft, filled with such anger that I could almost feel the trembling rage mounting the bearded leader's body under the light weight yellow robe. "It shall be—then she will be brought to my tent before the night's up."

I was yanked to my feet by two tall warriors who swiftly cut the leather thongs which had bound wrists and ankles.

"You expect too much," I yelled, stepping forward. "Neither your son nor you nor anyone here will touch my slave!"

All eyes turned toward me for the first time.

"That is," I continued, moving toward Baji-Ney and his son, "if your honor and word is as great as your bestial passion for a helpless woman! Though how one can trust the honor or words of such a man, I don't know."

Rha-Ney tensed into a fighting stance, feet slightly apart, arms up, forward, every rippling lean muscle knotting. "You dare question the word and honor of the men of Baji-Ney?"

"I question the honor of any man who would take a woman against her will—or desire a woman who was not his to desire—or look with desire upon a woman who would not return that desire. Only stupid animals take their primitive pleasures with a female of their species by force of muscle. Only a mindless beast is so much without honor as to assume this kind of role. Have not you men of the desert enough charm to win your women—or are you like the brainless beasts of prey? Is that the way your women are treated—taken simply because they are considered possessions like the rags on you back, to be used and discarded when their usefulness is over?"

As I'd spoken, the emotion whipped across Rha-Ney's face, deeper and more violent as each statement struck him like a physical blow across the face.

My insults were calculated to anger him, for a man who fights with his emotions has lost part of the battle before even entering it. I was not fool enough to believe that the same standards they had for slave-women would stand for their own women. Life is cruel, and for the victor all spoils of war are automatic just rewards; the vanquished has no rights—such has always been the law of Nature. The strong crush the weak. I had accepted that during my first days of battle on Noomas. But I had learned that the men of Noomas had their code of honor, and pride in that code. The women of Bel-loniea were never forced to marry against their will to a man they did not love. Even Royalty was given a choice, restricted only to the necessities of state. I doubted very much that these men of the desert would be very much different—though their social structure might take on a variable form.

Rha-Ney's reaction to my words proved I'd guessed right about his code of honor towards women of his own kind.

It was Baji-Ney who spoke first.

"Do not be baited," he warned his son, wisely, "for you but play the fool!"

The knowing expression on the older man's face revealed a more kindly and respectful attitude as he turned to face me.

"You would make a great desert warrior," he said regretfully. "But such is not to be—for my son is a fine fighter who killed his first man at the age of fifteen with his bare hands. He has killed many since then and knows all the tricks a man must know about such matters. You will die painfully, warrior. But know that my respect follows you to your grave."

151

"I don't think I'll die," I retorted, mouth dry, parched from lack of drink. Weakened though I was from the encounter with the desert birds, and lack of solid food and drink during the afternoon, I did have one edge of which these men of the desert were not aware. While memory of all past life was behind a misty wall through which it was impossible to gaze, instinctive battle-conditioning and fighting knowledge was drummed into the very fiber of my nerves and muscles to such a degree that they took command of all actions under the stress of combat.

"We will see," Baji-Ney announced, parting the outer folds of the robe to reveal a long, curved knife. "We will see who dies this night. The rules are simple. I will throw this dagger high into the air, between the two of you, and then the man who obtains the knife first will have an edge over the other! And, warrior, I can assure you that my son is an expert with such a blade and can cut a man to pieces in a way that death is painful and long in coming. He moves swift like the winds of the desert. His every thought, every instant of young life has been teethed on such combat. You will learn quickly enough that your mouth has torn too large a chunk of flesh to swallow down without choking to death."

He raised the dagger high over his head. "Enough of such talk. We begin."

His right arm swung around and around, then suddenly the curved blade was flung high into the air, spinning upwards in a flashing arc, whistling against the light night breeze.

Rha-Ney moved with a trained sense of direction, eyes watching the darkness above, head cocked in such a way that it was obvious he was listening to the sound which revealed in which direction the knife would fly.

Apparently the idea was to get the knife first, but I wasn't about to allow him this pleasure—nor could I expect to be able to obtain it faster than his trained senses would carry him to where it landed. The only other solution was to keep him away from the knife—finish the fight in its first few seconds.

With a leap, I moved after the young warrior, intent on stopping him before it was possible to get any further.

152

There was no doubt that once he was armed my hopes of an equal chance of survival would be trimmed naked. My only desire was to be finished with this whole affair as quickly as possible—honor be damned. This was for Youi!

I'd taken but three steps when my feet stumbled over the extended foot of a spectator.

After the knife—not the man!" the bearded face laughed mockingly.

My body coiled, and at the same time I pulled the leg out of the way in such a manner that the man slammed backwards. I twisted, snapping the bone.

A yell of pain sounded as several of his fellows pulled him back out of sight.

Then I turned all attention to the running figure of Rha-Ney, who was already half across the clearing to where the curved knife had fallen to the ground. There was no chance of stopping him now.

A roar of approval sounded from the tribe of Baji-Ney as the son of their leader swooped gracefully down, grabbing the knife, then swinging around, without once reducing his speed. He now moved to the middle of the large ring of robed warriors, stopping there to bow contemptuously in my direction.

"You will die painfully, warrior," Rha-Ney said with a twisted grin. "And your woman will know what it is to have a man within the next unit of time."

He didn't move now, only awaited my approach. "Come, man with a big mouth. Meet your death bravely—for that is all you have left in life, an honorable death!"

CHAPTER EIGHTEEN

BAJI-NEY'S OATH

I started carefully forward, eyes alert for any sign of movement in the other's muscles. There was no way of knowing how long he would stand and wait. With the knife in his hand, he had the advantage and could approach me at will, confident that I would be helpless to defend myself. Or, it was highly possible, that he might decide to throw the knife, which would end the combat swiftly; though I doubted this last possibility. He would probably want to put on a good show, work up a neat sweat to make his session with Youi that much more rewarding.

I circled his tall form until the flames of the large fire would be behind my body, lighting his face, making me a dark silhouette whose face could not be seen or read.

Sweat already covered my body, and the multiple wounds inflicted by the desert birds were beginning to hurt with throbbing pains from what could be nothing but infection.

Slowly my feet stepped forward, ready to move into action the instant Rha-Ney made his play. It would take every trick I knew to even get an equal chance.

Voices chanted rhythmically from the surrounding robed warriors, some mocking and challenging to me, others encouraging to Rha-Ney. I ignored everything other than the man in front.

"Come, coward," Rha-Ney encouraged, a thin grin spreading across his narrow face. "I will make it less painful if you put on a good fight."

154

"A baby, even with sharp teeth is still a baby," I taunted. "Not a man!"

"Enough!" He leaped like a cat, springing with such speed that I was taken off balance. Not by so much as a flicker of an eyelash had he given a hint. The knife point flicked out, lightly touched my right shoulder, drawing only a trickle of blood. His control of the blade was masterful.

"Now what do you think, warrior?" he mocked, retreating almost immediately beyond reach.

"You don't kill a Korda with a pick!" I growled back.

He danced gracefully to the left, bounded in once more, knife arm extended, wrist whipping, directing the curved blade across my exposed chest. But this time I didn't stay long enough to feel the needle-sharp point. My body slid right, left foot swung up, catching the extended arm at the wrist.

The knife flew from Rha-Ney's fingers, but instead of falling to the sand it shifted to his left hand. Immediately the blade licked across my stomach, just breaking the skin.

"A pick cuts!" he said, hardly above a whisper.

I said nothing to that but merely kept my attention on what he was doing. His agility and skill were remarkably displayed by that swift recovery and I wasn't about to side-track my mind with foolish conversation. I couldn't help but admire him, even while being the victim of his artistry with the blade.

"I didn't cut your tongue," he taunted, dancing in for another jab at my body.

As I dodged away, he laughed. "Next time. Can you not speak?"

Again his knife arm flashed out. Blood trickled from a shallow would inflicted on my left shoulder.

As he started to leap back, I moved in, as if charging madly without rational thought. Rha-Ney did exactly what would be expected of a skilled knife-fighter, prepared to let my body's own movement drive me onto the knife's point. It was also what I'd hoped he would do.

Coming short, I feinted at his head with a right fist. This threw him off timing just enough to give the opening needed. My right hand chipped sideways across his exposed neck.

Staggered by the unexpected blow, Rha-Ney stumbled sideways. I grabbed his left wrist, twisted, pulled the arm around his back, brutally twisting.

The next thing that happened, I was being flung off balance by a sharp blow to the groin. I rolled, agonized by convulsions, doubled over as vision blurred, mouth screaming in terrible pain.

I'd made the mistake of underestimating Rha-Ney and overestimating the surprise of my attack.

In those next split moments I was sure death would cut me down. Time seemed to splinter, freeze solid, as I fought desperately to clear my head of the ringing pain that coursed through every nerve and muscle.

As had happened a couple of times before on Noomas, when under great emotional and physical stress, my mind opened, the wall holding back past memories disappeared just long enough for a mental impression to surface before slamming back into place.

I was a small boy. An elderly woman, tears streaming down her cheeks, stood over me, hands on my shoulders. "You're so young...why? You are such a young one to have twice suffered so great a loss." Then her explanation about my father and mother disappearing in space became a hazy, disjointed memory. Superimposed upon her face flashed the image of a hardened, scarred man, old with age, tired and defeated from long years in prison.

That was all. I attempted to probe deeper, tried to lift the impregnable wall across my lost past, but nothing came. It wasn't enough to explain anything—yet apparently was important to me, otherwise why should it have surfaced?

Then the sound of the deep-throated voices brought all thoughts away from the mental and physical pain.

Looking through a blaze of blurred shapes, I spotted Rha-Ney getting to his feet, moving forward. There wasn't time to consider what had slowed him down, other than accept the implication that apparently his counter-attack had been mere reflex action as he crumpled under my blow to his neck. It was the only thing which had saved him.

156

But now he had recovered and came like some savage beast, movements whip fast.

It felt as if my own muscles were sluggish, without direction. Yet my fingers found and clasped around a bone-hard wrist.

Rha-Ney's body was weighted upon mine. I felt the coldness of sand at my back and guessed what position we had taken, more than actually being aware of it because of any visual impressions.

How long we struggled on the floor of the desert, my nerves aware of only that wrist holding the long curved knife just a breath from my throat, I don't know. Finally the pain cleared away to make it possible to think more logically.

With my left hand I slashed across his right side, hitting him above the kidney. He groaned, the pressure of the knife-hand lifted slightly, then I chopped at his neck, shoved upwards, twisted his right arm around so that he couldn't use the knife. Ignoring it, I stood, dragging Rha-Ney up to his feet, then jerked his arm, throwing him bodily over my head. Immediately I grabbed at the man again and once more he fell in a crumpled heap on the sand. The third time I reached for his dazed form, it was to be stopped short by a bare foot kicking up at my chin.

Stars sputtered and I was flung backwards. Once more I had made the mistake of underestimating him.

The roar of approval from the warriors of Baji-Ney warned that Rha-Ney was once again armed.

Staggering to my feet, I turned to face Rha-Ney, who was still a little dazed by the punishment he'd taken. At least he was slowed down; though he still possessed the weapon. Now he approached carefully.

I stood waiting, taking this chance to clear my head. Then as he came closer, I leaped, feet flying outwards, high in front of me, connecting on his chest with all the force of my full weight.

He staggered violently back, landing on the ground, by all appearances stunned. Yet, still holding the knife.

I kicked the weapon from the man's fingers, then fell upon him, hands making a ring around his throat. Almost immediately his knees slapped up against my back, then he twisted, hit me in the stomach. I held his neck with a vise-like grip, squeezing brutally at the windpipe.

Then his knee attempted to slam into my still agonized groin. Pain erupted as the flow made partial contact with its intended target.

A moment later I felt an arm circle my throat. With one mighty yank I threw him over my head, then leaped on him. My arms went under Rha-Ney's, and back up to grip his neck from behind. In such a position he was helpless. I bent his head downwards.

What caused me not to instantly kill him I don't know. Had the advantage been reversed he wouldn't have hesitated to break my neck.

Yet, I held off.

Silence fell upon the desert; all eyes froze on the two of us. Baji-Ney took half a step forward, as if to come to the defense of his son. I could see the total inner defeat on the man's harsh features. He was too proud to beg for his son's life; too much of a leader of men to allow emotions to rule reason. Still his eyes unconsciously pleaded with me, but no words would move those harsh thin lips to speak, even though he was mentally screaming to do so.

There was something about these desert people which, though unyielding, was likable—savage, brutal, but men with a touch of greatness. Baji-Ney lived by a very harsh code, yet I could not help but believe he was good to his people, a great leader—a warrior. He had shown respect for a fellow warrior in his last remarks to me before beginning the fight. Somehow I could not help but believe this was the type of man I could learn to like—if there was ever a chance to make friends with him.

Yet it was not this which continued to hold me off, nor was it the desperation revealed in Baji-Ney's face as he stood there helpless to do anything to save the life of his first born. Honor could be the only thing which restrained him from ordering me killed by a Kay-gun. A man of honor I could understand, respect, like.

In a loud voice, I called to Baji-Ney. "If I let him live, what will you give in return?"

158

For a moment the only answer was a soft sighing of the warm desert wind.

"What do you offer for your son's life?" I demanded once again.

Baji-Ney straightened to his full height; his face swept around to take in the gathering of his warriors, surveying their attitude. Not one man had reached for a Kay-gun—no hand or voice was raised in Rha-Ney's defense—and there was no question about the fact that this was as it should be. The duel had been fair; I had honestly won. Baji-Ney was not looking for a defense of his son, but rather testing the faces of his men to see how far his natural father's instinct could allow him to go in dealing with me in an honorable way. He was weighing the necessities of leadership against a father's love for his son.

Then in a clear, level voice. Baji-Ney spoke, eyes now grimly meeting mine. 'Your life and freedom while in route to the nearest slave-market, and the protection of your slave-woman from the demands of my warriors. Nothing more or less than promised this day. The word of Baji-Ney will not be broken, changed nor tampered with. You are victor and by the rules of combat may have the life of this man I call son. Either way the results will be the same. Freedom under constant guard, safety for your woman, and then sale to the slave market. There will be no bargaining."

"And you, Rha-Ney, what is your offer?" I hissed in his ear?

A choking voice sputtered; "My father's word...will be honored."

There was no pleading, no begging for life.

I released my hold on Rha-Ney's neck, stood. Slowly he came to his feet, faced me. A dazed look of amazement was printed on his narrow, sun-tanned features.

He reached out and touched my shoulder as a friend will do on Noomas.

"You are a mighty warrior. I am honored to have done battle with you, and not shamed at being defeated. If you were of the desert people I would be honored to call you friend."

"Why must it be any other way?" I offered, mystified by his attitude.

"It must be as it always has been. There is no other choice, warrior. What do you call yourself?"

"Torlo Hannis."

"I will honor you in my prayers, Torlo Hannis, and beg the Gods to give you and you slave-woman a good master." He turned to face his father. "I would be honored with the responsibility of this man's guard while we travel."

"Let it be as you wish," Baji-Ney said in an emotionally thick voice. "I bless you, Torlo Hannis, for the life of my son. The Gods will be bribed to watch over you."

I was tempted to reveal Youi Janis' true identity then, and offer a great reward for her return to Bel-loniea, but decided against. it. Youi would have done so in the very beginning if there had been any hope of this information making any difference. My claim that she was a slave had been automatic, without detailed consideration, but I realized now that it had been motivated by an inner conviction this would be the best possible way to protect her from some worse fate—though what that might be, I could not imagine. I determined to talk to her about this at the first possible moment—when we were alone long enough to have a private conversation.

CHAPTER NINETEEN

HONOR AMONG THE RAIDERS

Baji-Ney raised his right hand, said in a clear voice heard by all, "Bring the slave-girl for Torlo Hannis. She is his until we reach the markets." He turned to his son. "You will see to it that they are both fed of the best foods, their thirst satisfied by either water or liquor and that they have decent sleeping quarters with at least a partial amount of privacy—just not enough so they can manage an escape. Remember that even if you are my son, your life would be forfeit if you allow them to escape while they are your responsibility. They belong to the tribe, and the tokens and goods we will receive for their bondage into slavery will be shared by all. To lose such profits makes all suffer. But this Torlo Hannis has earned the privacy of a tent with his slave-woman for at least these few nights allowed him before being sold to an Arena Master."

Baji-Ney faced me, stepped very close. "If it were up to me," he said in a low voice, "I would give you freedom in reward for not taking my son's life when it was within your power to do so. But it is the law of our people that the profits on the sale of all slaves is to be shared equally. To free a prisoner taken by the tribe is to rob all members of the tribe. Even I, their leader, cannot break that law. If you were my personal property it would be different. Though I could do nothing about the woman, in any case. It is the custom my people that a female slave is either kept for all the men to enjoy or sold at a high price at the slave-market. But I will do my best to see she gets a kindly master."

161

I studied him for a moment, mystified by this obvious offer of friendship.

"I would not take freedom without her, even if you could offer it, Baji-Ney," I told him. Strangely enough it seemed more as if I were conversing with a friend than an enemy. And in a perverse way, probably this was true. He had offered friendship in the only manner open to him under the circumstances.

I placed a hand on his shoulder, the universal action of two friends in meeting on Noomas.

He returned the gesture, a pleased expression on his gaunt features. "What kind of man are you that holds so loyally to a slave-woman, who so willingly accepts your enemy as friend?" His voice was thick with sudden emotion.

"A man who honors those who wish to be friends. She is more than a slave-woman—she is a companion and friend. I am more than her master—I am her friend." Those lies fell easily from my mouth. "As for you...you are a man of honor, who keeps his word and follows the code of his people, even when doing so would cause the death of his son. Such a man deserves the respect of friendship."

He nodded as if that made sense.

"Come, we will visit my tent." He turned to Rha-Ney. "You will set up quarters for him and his woman. He will be sent to her shortly. But first—I must talk to this man who has befriended his enemy. This man of honor. You intrigue me, Torlo Hannis."

I smiled, feeling a sense of irony at this situation.

"It will be an honor, and of some interest to talk to you, Baji-Ney. And I wouldn't mind learning of your people."

"I would like to have you promise not to attempt to escape—"

He was leading the way to his tent as he spoke, and the shrug of his shoulders revealed that he didn't expect me to promise anything.

I stopped, said: "I cannot promise that. If the chance comes, I will take it."

"My son will guard you well," he shrugged. "You will not escape!" He pulled me into his tent, which was unpartitioned, unlike those of the Diano. Just an open space of sand served as a floor. There were three bed-mats and a skin bag in which a goodly portion of desert water-plant liquor was kept. "Sit. We will talk like friends; and forget the cruel necessities of life which force us to do acts against our will. You will try to escape. Right?"

"Let's say I don't look forward to the idea of not being my own master."

"But who is his own master? We are all slaves to our honor and customs."

"I will not accept slavery to another man who owns me against my will. To serve one you respect—that is different." I was still puzzled by this strange man who was so totally ruled by law and custom, yet quick to be friendly. It hardly made sense in one way, yet on the other hand, I felt an odd rapport with this grim, hard desert man. Possibly he had the same reaction. I don't know, but I was to discover that Baji-Ney was a man of many complexes, living vigorously within the framework of a harsh unyielding code.

We sat on the sand, facing each other, the skin bag of liquor between us.

"It's a cruel world, Torlo Hannis. I accept the realities of that world. It is foolish not to believe a captured man will not attempt to escape—or at least think of it." He shrugged. "If you escape—I cannot do anything to stop what the gods have in mind for you."

"If my success will mean your son's death—do me the honor of assigning another to guard us," I suggested seriously. "I would not want to kill him if it were not necessary, or be the cause of his death by your hand. But...I will not meekly be sold as the slave of another man."

This odd conversation seemed fantastic to me—also the fact that this man had taken me alone into his tent. Did he not fear I could easily overpower him? Or was he not such a fool as it might appear? I decided upon this latter impression. Obviously he was no fool.

A grim smile played on the corners of his lips. "I know you will attempt escape—and would not expect anything else from such a mighty fighter. And of course my son will die if you succeed. I do not want that, naturally. But I would not hold you to blame—for no man worth his sword would let such considerations stand in his way to freedom. Rha-Ney has requested the honor—knowing you will attempt escape, and aware that if you succeed he will die most horribly, in shame before all the members of the tribe, and that his women and children will be sold into slavery. But he honors you and me and himself by taking on this responsibility. He is as much as saying: This man was my responsibility, I should have killed him—he could have killed me, but let me live. I will guard him and his slave-woman and if it is to be that they escape then none will suffer other than myself who was defeated in honorable battle with a great warrior. But for him, I would not be breathing the desert air at this moment. It is his right to take my life at any time he is able to do so—and it is my obligation to see that none of my father's people will die or suffer because he allowed me life beyond this night."

Baji-Ney placed a hand on my shoulder. "But, beware he will not allow you to escape, and if you try, he will kill you if it is necessary, without notice, without a chance to defend yourself. And he would do this to keep his family from slavery. That is our code, too. So, for the life of my son I warn you once in repayment. Watch him carefully, for he will never take any foolish chances with you...and if you attempt escape he will hunt you down like a mad dog, recapture or kill you without mercy!" He leaned back, sighed. "So, and the Mutis say: one event leads to another, becoming the cause for another happening, which cannot be altered. The future is locked in place by the happenings of the past. I can no more save the life of my son than you can escape and gain freedom, unless it is so mapped out by the past and present that mathematically equates the future."

It was the first mention of the Mutis by those of Baji-Ney's tribe. I had almost forgotten about these strange creatures whose edicts were blindly accepted with such fatalistic and almost religious faith. Yet the Mutis are considered neither religious leaders nor even political leaders. Still, their influence over those who lived in the city-states was so immense that I instinctively felt they must surely hold vast, impenetrable powers over the human civilization on Noomas.

164

My two meetings with a Muti flashed before my mind like visual paintings. First when I was absolved of all charges of cowardliness in battle and the Muti pronouncement that Youi Janis was being taken by the Diano—and that my shadow crossed her life-path. Then the encounter with the startled Diano Muti who told me to leave, escape. This last encounter had been far more puzzling than the first one in Bel-loniea, and certainly supported the allusion that the future was immutable.

Now, Baji-Ney had made mention of the future being preshaped by past and present events, unmovable, but in such a context and manner that it was impossible to keep from seeing his total fatalistic acceptance of life. This was unlike what those of Bel-loniea believed.

Qui Shan, commander of all the armed forces of Bel-loniea, had explained it as a mathematical equation. Two and two equals four, and there was no way in the world to make it equal five or three—and thus events became causes for new events, unable to create or equal any other result. Modern belief claimed there was free choice, but that this was part of the education, too. Baji-Ney seemed to have the old-fashioned belief—as Qui Shan had labeled it—that all is pre-written, and that there is no free choice. This attitude seemed stagnant, too rigid and certainly left no room for free choice. It also explained his inability to bend custom.

It seemed to me, in this one flashing instant as thoughts whipped across my conscious mind, that there might be more than one way to make an equation equal four. Just in addition alone there were at least four simple ways to come to the figure "4". One plus one plus two equals four. One plus three equals four. Could this possibly be the answer to make possible free choice? We decide which numbers—actions—we might take. Coming to a fork in the life-path we can pick the short way or the long way, and if both paths lead to the same destination, it will still be by a different route. If that were true, then it might be possible to accept the fatalistic attitude of the equation and also admit that a person had a choice—more than one way to reach the final goal. Yet, I admitted, by that calculation there was still no way to avoid the final goal—that number four. Like there

165

was no way to escape the fact that death would come as the final end to all life-paths. But one did attempt to avoid death and put it off as long as possible. A man could take forever to gain a final total of four in an equation by the method of not limiting himself to simple addition. Take three, add three, subtract one, add seven, divide by two and you still don't have four, but end up with six, which can be played with in this manner almost endlessly—never repeating the exact combination of mathematical patterns.

All this reasoning took but a breath of time.

Baji-Ney still sat before me, his fatalistic words still ringing in my ears.

"It might be written that I will escape and that you son will live," I suggested.

"Only if he ran with you, never to return to my people again. Such dishonor would be below him!" Baji-Ney said with great emotion. "You dishonor my son to suggest such a course of action."

"It was not what I meant to imply. I but suggest that things need not be written down for the future by our past acts. Events can be changed, I truly believe this—as can customs. I see no reason why we cannot be true friends—I going my way in freedom, for surely the price that will be paid for our slavery is not so great that the tribe of Baji-Ney wouldn't survive the loss."

"One does not tamper with custom, one does not question the ways of the universe, but accepts what the gods offer."

"Yet you have offered to bless me in your prayers, to bribe the gods on my behalf—how do you equate that with your belief one cannot change custom or change the direction of the future?"

A glint flashed in Baji-Ney's dark eyes and he leaned closer.

"Torlo Hannis, you are a brave man to speak to me so. You are a stubborn man. I like you. What you have said can be explained away thus: All acts of man do end in final death, as well as directing the pathway to his final destruction. Each event is part of the pattern, inescapable. Each word, each thought, each breath is dictated by an irreversible pattern of actions, causes and effects. All is part of the pattern. Even our sitting here in the middle of the night, natural enemies, because you are captive and I am your captor. Maybe the casual crossing of our life-paths has some dramatic meaning of importance in my life. Your words, while holding logic and an intelligent point of view, do not take into account that all acts are a part of the pattern. The act of blessing you makes it that much more possible for you to experience the answering of our prayer—it is necessary that these blessings be made so that they will be causes for effects in your future—either good or bad.

"But why give prayers if they might do harm to you—while it is my wish to create a good effect? Because everything I have ever been, done, thought, eaten, experienced with all my senses, has led up to this moment, all such acts being the minor causes which create the major cause that will be responsible for my praying for your well-being, which, of itself, is an automatic effect that immediately becomes a cause for other acts." He glared across at me. 'Surely you know this, as does every man on Noomas."

"My name, in the old language, means the Lost One, I am a man without memory of even a year of my past."

"But you claimed to be a mercenary from Kanns," he reminded me.

"But even a man who has forgotten his past will remember some minor facts," I explained with a shrug, enjoying the drift of the conversation. It was so easy to lie—so simple to follow this one big lie with others. "Perhaps the Gods grabbed memory away just so that when I crossed your path these questions could be asked. How do we know what the Gods' plan for any of us is? How do we know what kind of humor might tickle their supernatural minds? Who knows what game is being played out, right now, as we sit here? If, as you say, all things are but the effects of past causes, which were in the beginning nothing other than events that were the logical results of other events—then surely the loss of my memory must have some purpose in the minds of the Gods. And who can honestly guess what this purpose might be? Maybe my sole purpose of ever living was to make this moment possible...this questioning with you, Baji-Ney." These

167

words came easily, following his reasoning; the blind fatalistic belief that all events are written in advance through some planned pattern directed by unknown Gods. It was an emotionally safe belief.

Baji-Ney put in words the exact question which was so puzzling me.

"And why should you be so important to me that these questions must be a part of my living experience?"

"I don't know, Baji-Ney. But I would be your friend—and I see that you are of a people who are proud, strong, honorable but unbending, and the tree which does not bend with the wind will break. Surely there must be some other way to survive outside of being slavers."

Baji-Ney laughed. It was totally unexpected.

"Look at the desert! Where is the living here? We would barely survive on what it offers. The city-states give us food, materials, weapons, for slaves and the sweet liquor of the desert. We live a good, free life."

"If the desert is so hard to live in, then why not go to the more fertile lands to the south? There are many ways for men to make a living. Your warriors are proud of being great fighters—why not become mercenaries?"

"No! It is not the way of my people. We live here because of the desert, the beauty, the silence at night, the freedom from the confining restrictions of a closed-in city, walled up so that nothing of Nature can come in without permission. We want freedom with that which created the world—to feel the breath of the Gods on our backs. No! The cities are for pale men and trembling women." He violently shook his fist at the night. "To fight as mercenaries—such is for fools! We fight for principle, for honor, for freedom! But we need not fight in the silly wars which the city-states indulge themselves in. They fight because they have nothing of the Gods' worlds. They frustrate themselves behind those thick stone walls, find themselves dissatisfied and convince themselves that if they had more walls, in other places, they would be happier. No! Not for men of my breed. I'll take fools prisoners sell them to one another, grow fat and wealthy off their foolishness and come out here in the desert to grow healthy of mind and spirit and body."

168

He laughed, eyes twinkling bright. "How much greater a world it might be if all city-dwellers would lose their memories as you have, Torlo Hannis. You think—because you are mentally searching for identity. You, I honor. The rest? No!" He shook his head, then picked up a skin bag on the floor, drank thirstily.

He extended the bag to me. "Drink, friend. But don't think you can drink Baji-Ney under this tent. I fear not that you might escape. And the men and women of the desert drink for three days and three nights when the circumcision ceremonies take place once a year for the young males of our tribe. We drink until vision leaves, until movement is not possible—yet if attacked, our men fight like the fury of the wind. No! Think not that you can drink Baji-Ney to a state of helpless drunkenness."

He laughed again as I tasted the liquor, which was quite sharp, burning my throat. Yet there was a very pleasant aftertaste.

"Tell me, Torlo Hannis, why is it that you do not circumcise your women?"

"I've been told that women have equal rights with men—so there probably lies your answer!"

He threw his hands up in the air. 'You are right! Of course. I had not considered that." He fingered his beard, then said thoughtfully, "We of the desert have many women, and the men treat them well, court them for a full year after getting permission from the girls' father and clan leader. Once she has considered the men courting her, she will pick one—and on the wedding night he will not force his passions on her, but rather give her time to develop fully into womanhood."

"They are not mature at marriage?" I questioned, surprised.

"At fifteen they must pick a husband within the year. Though they are not forced into a union against their wills, but I've never known of a woman not joined with a warrior by sixteen. Our women are strong-breasted with lusts to match their men! One does not hold back a spirited animal when it must run. The passions must be fed as should the belly. But a woman must be fully ripened before entering

169

into full womanhood. Thus, an honorable man waits a short time, until she is ready for the first experience of the flesh."

He wagged a bony finger in my face. "That's what is wrong with you city-dwellers. You confine the passions too long—and then put up excuses to do so. Love! Romantic love! Love comes from long living together, knowing each other's habits. But, then, the city-dwellers are all a little insane and foolish."

"No doubt we think much the same about your customs!" I suggested carefully.

"Yes! Yes! All people are fools and crazy if they don't follow your ideas of morality and honor. True. Very true. And who's to say who is right? We are all channeled by what has happened in our lives from the moment of birth, shaped and predestined to a narrow trail to death. Maybe we are all fools and the Gods sit up there in their timeless world and laugh at us mortals much the same as we laugh at ourselves and others."

He slapped my shoulder. "You are a good companion, Torlo Hannis—and exchanging ideas and conversation with such a man is a pleasure. Though," he added with a twinkle in his eyes, "not as pleasant as it might have been to spend the quiet time of night with your slave-woman."

Silence answered him, for I could think of nothing to say. Anger burned hot on my cheeks at the thought of this man and his fellow warriors degrading Youi Janis just to satisfy their physical needs. The good companionship of the moments before now slithered away. Almost immediately I was aware of this man as an enemy I would unemotionally kill if given the chance.

My eyes shifted to examine the tent more carefully, and saw shadowy figures silhouetted against the tent's yellow material. Guards had been placed close by. Baji-Ney was not a fool. Even if I were to overcome him—kill him—there would be no escape.

I turned my attention back to him.

Once again I was tempted to reveal Youi Janis' true identity, suggesting that her father and Romos would surely pay a high reward for her safe return. One question held me back: Why hadn't she done so already?

"It gets late, Baji-Ney...and the events of the day have exhausted even this warrior."

He laughed heartily. "And you have a beautiful slave woman awaiting your return. Yes, I've been a selfish host." He clapped his hands and immediately an armed guard entered the tent. "Take this man to the quarters my son arranged for him and his woman. Then have Teesiea brought at once." His eyes winked as they flashed my way. "She is a woman of ripe young body—I have saved her for a special occasion. The time is ripe to take her as a full wife—teaching the total duties of a woman, as befits a female of the tribe of Baji-Ney!"

I stood, then said: "I wish we had met under other circumstances."

"It was not written. But that we met at all, I am thankful, for you have taught me that a man of the city can be honorable and have a mark of greatness. It saddens me that your future will be the harsh life of an Arena warrior. But if you fight well, win many battles and are blessed by the Gods, you might earn your freedom with honors. Live, Torlo Hannis."

I followed the guard outside, where we were joined by an escort of three others, each holding a small Kay-gun pointed in my direction. They were taking no chances.

They marched me to a small tent a short distance away, before which stood Rha-Ney, arms folded across his chest.

"Your woman is inside," Rha-Ney announced formally. "I have attended to her needs for food and drink. If you wish, food will be brought to you."

I shook my head, for food seemed less desirable than rest.

Youi Janis was sitting on the floor, face tense. As she looked up at my entrance, her eyes widened with relief and emotion.

"What's happened?" was her immediate question.

I told her of the fight and my conversation with Baji-Ney. When I'd finished she said: "They have shown you high honors, Torlo Hannis. The desert people are hard, cruel, with a natural dislike of anybody who lives in the cities. You are truly a mighty warrior and a honorable man."

There was pride and something else in her voice as she spoke. Her eyes were bright as they met mine. "You were wise to call me your slave-girl." Her voice whispered the words.

"I wanted to ask you about that, Youi. Surely your father and grandfather would pay highly for your return," I stated in a low enough voice not to carry behind her. "Why not tell them?"

She shook her head. "They would but sell me to the Diano because the price would be even higher. I would rather become the slave of slaves than fall into Aoji's hands again."

"Slavery is slavery—would it make that much difference?" I countered, puzzled by her statement, even while understanding her dislike of Aoji.

"There is slavery and there is dishonor. Slavery can be good or it can be very bad. Life is harsh, Torlo Hannis. But I don't wish to make my future any more terrible than it already promises to be. To fall into the hands of the Diano would shame all the people of my nation. Life there would be the worst kind of slavery, for Aoji would publicly shame me in order to publicly insult Bel-loniea. If sold to a Lord who does not know me, there is always the chance of my bondage being no worse than being forced in to hard daily labor—and possibly it would mean a decent life in the service of some Lady."

"You accept slavery so casually?" I questioned, amazed.

"Not casually, Torlo, but merely as a part of some greater pattern which will reveal itself. I don't think I will be a slave long. I believe that in time it will be possible to arrange for Romos to learn where I am, and for him make the necessary arrangements to obtain my freedom. It has not been unknown. And as you said, Baji-Ney has promised to see that I get a kindly master—an old man or a woman—where acts of dishonor will not be inflicted."

She smiled up at me, then her face frowned in tragic concern. "It is you that I am worried for. The Arena is hard

172

on a warrior—few survive long. But if you can survive, know that I will see that you are freed, immediately, once Romos has freed me."

I felt dazed from all these startling statements, the hours without sleep, the soreness of wounds inflicted upon my flesh. Nothing made sense any more. It didn't even occur to me that Youi might be merely trying to make my burden lighter; that her light words of hope possibly were ground-less, shaped simply to hide the actual reality that life-time slavery faced both of us, until death gave the only escape from captivity.

I was too exhausted to reason any of this out at that time; and only later would I understand the true meaning be-hind her words.

Youi Janis touched my forehead tenderly with deli-cate fingertips. "Sleep, Torlo. And remember that while we live there is always hope for the future."

CHAPTER TWENTY

DEATH OF A PROCTORESS

The deserts of Noomas are bleak places of uncomfortably hot days and warm nights, but have a silent beauty which is hard to describe. There are places where nothing grows at all for as long as a day's ride, hot sands stretching in every direction. Some areas are covered by flat flaky stones, or high cliffs that strain out of the desert floor like brown twisted walls. Other parts are dry ancient sea bottoms baked hard, thin chips of brown slate-like sand curled away in massive chunks which crumble when walked upon; here the storm waters will arrive during the winter seasons to quench the thirsty land with shallow seas which are greedily absorbed within a day.

The desert is most beautiful at sunset and nightfall, or when the countless stars are looking down from a black sky, the soft night breezes whispering across the flat expanse of arid wasteland. When the sun touches either horizon it will streak the nearby sky with gold and red haze, paint all clouds with brilliant oranges, soft rosy pinks. Only during the afternoon is this parched land most cruel, the blazing heat of the sun baking all things that exist there.

But the heat is not the real threat of the desert, nor are the few beasts of prey who claw out a bare existence from its few life-giving products, nor is it man, the most dangerous animal to be created by the Gods. The nomadic tribes, who survive by slave trade and wander in this dead world of their birth, life and death, seldom threaten one another. They keep their distance in respectful silence as they pass another caravan along the many invisible trails that ages of travel have established. They are only dangerous to the unlucky wanderer who comes into their possession, while raiding small villages or during the few times that clan rivalries create a state of war between two nomadic camps, one to be conquered, enslaved and sold to lords in the cities. There is only one thing the desert people fear on the face of their dry world: the desert storm. For then the land reshapes itself, claiming life with the violent smothering force of an almost solid wall of blasting sand.

It was on our third day with the tribe of Baji-Ney that this kind of storm attacked. But during these few days with Baji-Ney's tribe I was to learn a lot about their ways, and something about the mental attitude of their leader and his son.

The morning after my fight what Rha-Ney, Youi and I had been given one of the mounts, called Jilioes, upon which was a double saddle, the one in front more delicately shaped, designed for a woman. Controlling these beasts proved amazingly simple. They are trained almost from the moment of birth to learn a few important command words. Stop, walk, run, faster, slower, left, right, turn, back. They respond immediately to a verbal command with an eagerness that reveals the total rapport between them and man. I was told about this relationship between Jilioes and man by Rha-Ney, who never was out of sight for more than a few moments, other than during the night, when the coarse-woven cloth of the tent separated us from his ever-present form.

"There is no creature on Noomas so closely attached to humans. You can beat them, mistreat them in every way— forget to see they are fed, hold them back from their mate when they are wild with passion, kill their children the moment they are born—you imagine any kind of cruelty possible to inflict upon a creature and it will not be enough to make them turn on you. The only circumstances in which they will attack and kill a man is when their master is threatened—or any part of his family. Then they will kill swiftly. All instincts are focused on pleasing their masters—and protecting them. Such blind loyalty might be questioned as in part a sign of stupidity, yet they are highly intelligent and learn fast. Many young boys will take a baby and train it to

175

understand and respond to a hundred different commands—and they will learn almost anything after being shown no more than three times. And I believe they would learn the first time if it weren't the mere fact that the very mechanical difficulty of trying to make communications with another species."

The caravan awakens early, as the first edge of light becomes visible on the horizon. A breakfast of yellow mush is served—much like that which is served in the cities—and hot Ka. Immediately after eating they break camp and start on their way to the next night's campsite, moving in a swift gait, eating up distance like a starved beast swallowing down a fresh kill.

There was little chance of conversation between Youi and myself during the long morning and afternoon rides. When the caravan stops for the mid-day meal, they form a large ring, dismount and the slave-women and wives of the warriors quickly serve cold Ka and dried meat. For a long time the warriors sit in the hot sun, talk, laugh, tell jokes, totally ignoring the women and children, who stand quietly aside, away from their men and fathers. I learned that they consider this the men's time to visit, where both social conversations and business plans are in order. Nights were for the family—unless some purely male activity, such as the fight I had with Rha-Ney, was arranged. These combats to the death are considered too rough for the eyes of women and children. But afterwards the men will go to their tents and search out wives or the slave-women.

The women themselves seem a happy group. Their cheerful, slender faces, reflect a wholesome cheerfulness and open love towards their men. They seem highly confident in their role of woman and mother and show a strong open sense of love toward the children and deep affection for their men, even in public.

The first day when the caravan made its mid-day rest, I was strongly impressed by the highly emotional out-going laughter and warmth of the men of Baji-Ney. It was so different from the night before when they had drunkenly enjoyed the combat between myself and their chief's son, lustfully taking in the savage spectacle of two men fighting to

176

the death. but among themselves, in the heat of the hot noon sun, they revealed an equal passion for friendly fellowship. They vividly proved themselves to be a people who greatly loved life, dove into each experience it offered with a complete emotional, mental and sensual attention.

As Youi and I were sitting eating of the rather tasteless dried meat, Rha-Ney came over from a group of men and squatted down beside us. He has just been taking a break from his guard duties to talk with his father.

"I'm told you had quite a conversation with Baji-Ney last night. He was impressed by you. My father is a man not easily impressed even by members of his own people—let alone one who lives in the cities—especially a warrior who repeatedly sells his sword and loyalty to any man willing to pay a price. He is puzzled—and so am I—why such a man as yourself became a mercenary."

I looked at Rha-Ney, far more puzzled than he could have been by this question—and debated what kind of answer it would be possible to give. I knew so little about the world; and the role of mercenary was a blatant farce, originally suggested by Orra Jik when we formed our plans to rescue Youi Janis from the Diano, and picked up as a quick, logical explanation as to my origin to Baji-Ney—for I had been told that mercenaries were usually accepted by all nations with open arms. But most appealing was the fact that the man of Kanns had a reputation for not liking to talk about their past; a cover which served as a means to escape any necessity to explain myself to men who might easily trip me up on a lack of knowledge of Noomas.

I glanced at Youi Janis, hoping she might guess my confusion and be able to suggest a story. She merely shrugged.

"Your father knows that I have no memory of my past. I told him as much last night."

Rha-Ney nodded. "But surely that has nothing to do with the role of mercenary, does it?"

Youi Janis was quick to come to my rescue before I had a chance to fumble out a bad answer. The subtle gleam in those dark eyes as she spoke revealed a sense of humor which had not been apparent until now.

"He has been a mercenary for as long as I've known him," she announced, eyes bright as she looked at Rha-Ney. "It is through me that he knows anything at all about his past life. He originally was a warrior in Kanns, and when the Proctor declared a state of peace with all other nations around Kanns, he left with many others to join the armies of warring nations."

Rha-Ney looked confused. "How long have you known him?"

I quickly put in, "Only since I've been without memory."

Youi gave me a quick look. Obviously I had disrupted some fantasy she had been working up.

"Then how do you know he came from Kanns?" Rha-Ney inquired. "How do you know anything about him, if he knows so little about himself?"

Youi smiled sweetly. "My last master had known him..."

"Then you know his true name?" Rha-Ney inquired, interested.

Youi shook her head. "Only Torlo Hannis...for my last master never referred to him otherwise."

"Oh?" Rha-Ney sounded a little mystified—a reaction which I could not blame him for. I was as interested as he must be to hear her explanation.

"You see," Youi quickly put in, "He was known as a fine warrior—by reputation. I don't really think my former master knew his real identity...only had heard about him. At least, there was no mention of any other name."

Rha-Ney laughed sharply. "I think you should beat this slave. She talks in riddles."

Red flushed up Youi's high cheeks. "I but tell you the truth."

"But my question is not answered. Why would a man like Torlo Hannis become a mercenary. That is the puzzle which disturbed my father. He possesses a great sense of honor—something which mercenaries never bother with, other than for the price of Proctors Tokens...and that is merely because they had learned that only through such loyalty can they remain such popular professional killers. There is no honor in this. To kill, simply for the pleasure of it."

Now it was my turn to make a conversation jab. "Yet you and your people delighted in the idea of seeing me killed. You seemed to glory in the pointless slaughter of a fellow human being. Where is the difference?"

"Honor! There is the difference. We but wished to take you to market to sell as slaves.

I turned to see a strange savage sight.

You insulted our honor—you challenged all the men of Baji-Ney. That makes the difference. We glory in physical strength, courage, the ability to stand up against another man, fight to the death and win. There is honor in that! We do not kill for the mere pleasure of killing, but for the honor it gives to the victor. Man is the most dangerous of all animals—because he is small and by nature weak, ill-fit to protect himself—yet he has survived to kill creatures far more powerful, because he possesses a brain, cunning, knowledge. To stand up against another warrior, to engage in honorable, fair battle with him on equal terms is the act of pitting yourself against the most dangerous of all creatures—and if you are victor, you stand that much taller. If you are killed—it is your time."

"You have surely answered your own question, Rha-Ney," I suggested. "Why should it be different with me?"

"I have answered nothing!" he exploded, angry for the first time. "I fight when honor dictates it as the right thing to do. I have purpose. But a man who sells his sword, and kills merely for profit plus food, drink and women is not doing so for honor. Do you not hear the words I speak—do you not listen to their meaning?"

I shrugged. "Each man creates his own rationalization!"

"Then where is yours?"

"A man without a past is a man without a country, without a home—therefore without any loyalties. He is also a man free to roam the world, sample of its wonders, look upon its natural and man-made treasures. Is there need for any other reason?"

"You could become a trader."

"Or a slaver?"

"It is an honorable profession!" Rha-Ney pointed out less emotionally.

"I'll never quite agree with that. I could not understand your father's explanation any more than I can see how you can accept such a viewpoint."

"And what is wrong with being a slaver?" Oddly enough his voice as not defensive but rather held honest puzzlement.

"Take us, as an example," I suggested, warming to the subject with some pleasure. "We were on the desert, harming no one; and in fact being attacked by those birds, who would have taken our lives in a few moments if the guns of your people had not saved us. We greeted you in friendship—and regardless of that offer, you took us prisoners and now are taking us to the slave markets to be sold into a life-time slavery of misery, and a type of captivity which is the most vile. Where is your honor there?"

Rha-Ney grinned, nodded. "You answer your own questions, too, friend."

"I wasn't aware of it."

"You would be less than slaves if we had not come along to save your lives. In saving your life we used up a large supply of Kay-pellets, which come expensively to us. It is only fair that in exchange for your lives that we should expect some payment; to say nothing about the expense of the ammunition. Nor to mention the fact that we of the desert are poor and must take the riches offered by the Gods. A man's family always comes first—unless it is dishonorable to put considerations of love before the necessities of the tribe as a whole."

"I offered my sword as repayment for as long as you wished to use it."

"But as you can see, we have no use for swords. We seldom war among ourselves—and we seldom get involved in the conflicts of your city-states, unless it is highly profitable and ethically necessary. And then only because it is a matter of Honor. So, such an offer would be meaningless."

"And if we were members of a rich family—even of the High Royalty of some nation—would not the offer of a

180

fortune in Proctors Tokens and jewels and metals sway your obsession of selling us as slaves?" I inquired, for the first time seeing possibly hope in this line of approach. Out of the corner of my eye I saw Youi Janis tense just slightly; her eyes narrowed in warning.

"Surely you are a man without memory, for how otherwise could you be so ignorant of our ways?" Rha-Ney cried to the heavens, his head raised up toward the blinding sun. He looked down again, blinked. "Any reward the family of a rich man or a Royal son might give, would be doubled, tripled, multiplied a thousand-fold by their enemies—for there is no greater insult than taking the son or daughter of Royal family away into slavery."

He threw up his hands in helplessness. "Do you know nothing of what is right now going on? The nations of Bel-loniea and Diano are at bitter war after more than a generation, simply because Aoji, son of the Diano Proctor, has stolen the Proctoress of Bel-loniea. And if that was not bad enough, it has been rumored that during an escape attempt she was killed by Aoji's own hand."

I saw Youi Janis relax with quick relief at this last statement. It wasn't hard to blame her, for even I had begun to feel a plaguing doubt that they might guess who she was.

Her voice was light, a little on the amused side as she said: "I would imagine this woman was disappointed by such a turn of events. Surely slavery, under any circumstances, is better than death."

"I can see," Rha-Ney observed with an edge of contempt, "that you are of the low born. Such ignorance could come only from the mouth of a slave girl who was born as a slave girl."

She nodded her head respectfully.

"A woman of the Royal blood would rather die than fall into the hands of her nation's enemies, for being such a slave is the highest insult to her and her people. Death was probably exactly what she wanted if escape were impossible. In fact, I would not be surprised if she actually killed herself—and Aoji took the credit. It was common knowledge that she had sworn before a Muti that, in the event of her possible capture, she would kill herself before falling into the

181

hands of the Diano. But, so the story goes, agents of the Ka-sha managed to capture her right out from under the very roof of her father's palace, past the crack personal guard of Romos, her grandfather, before she had a chance to even consider the possibility of such danger. I feel sorry for her—for they say she was the most beautiful woman in Bel-loniea—a nation known the world over for its highly bred and attractive women. In fact," he said directly to me, "your slave might easily have come from that nation, for she is by far the most beautiful woman I have ever seen."

Youi smiled. "My mother was born in Bel-loniea and taken as a slave by raiders much like yourself when she was traveling to visit her husband, a mercenary like my master also born of Bel-loniea blood. He was my father. So...you have guessed right."

Rha-Ney accepted that with great pleasure, obviously pleased with himself. "If this Proctoress was more beautiful than you, then surely she must have been far too perfect for any man. A woman should not be flawless."

"Oh, I have flaws?" Youi retorted with sudden femi-nine fury in her eyes.

"None that I have seen, other than the mere fact that you are a slave-woman—which is flaw enough," Rha-Ney assured her. "But, of course, I have not seen all of you."

The expression on Youi's face was such that I believe she would have stripped bare of all clothing if it had been possible to do so honorably. Such great emotion implied to-tal confidence in the fact that if Rha-Ney could see all the evidence he would find no fault. The idea of being witness to such proof more than intrigued me.

At that point the conversation was halted by Baji-Ney's cry to break camp. Immediately every member of the tribe stopped what they were doing and went to their mounts.

CHAPTER TWENTY-ONE

"I AM STILL PROCTORESS!"

Once I slipped into the saddle behind Youi, the caravan was prepared to begin its journey. For a long time, while helping to support Youi in front of me, I was painfully conscious of the fact that she was so sure of the total beauty and perfection of her body. The fiery love which possessed my emotions and mind for this frail woman now became overwhelmed. All the raw male passions were savagely alert and aware that this was truly the most beautiful woman in the world. But there was now a natural desire to see the actual proof; a sight which seemed forever denied me, because she was a Proctoress and I nothing more than a mere warrior without status enough to be even considered a proper suitor for her affections. And only the man she would marry would gain the right to have the proof of her physical perfection.

It was then, while riding behind Youi, right arm about her waist, that I realized no matter what the true events of our status in Bel-loniea, to Baji-Ney's people I was a mercenary warrior from Kanns, and Youi Janis my personal property, a slave-woman, over whom I had the total power and authority to possess unconditionally until the day they took us to the slave markets. What hurt was the fact that no matter what I did or didn't do, Youi Janis, Proctoress of Bel-loniea, would be sold into slavery—and it would not be a man of her picking or her father's or grandfather's picking who learned the perfection of her form, but some unknown Lord who had paid the small price of a few Proctors Tokens—and no matter how great the amount it would not be enough—and became her real slave master.

In all honesty, these thoughts tempted me beyond all considerations of honor. Only a fool would not be tempted—or a warrior who was not a true man. Along with this fact was the added temptation of her own words, which subtly suggested that if she were not the Proctoress it would not be wrong to offer her my love.

What made this even more irresistible was the fact that in a couple of days it wouldn't matter. And though I could not remember my past life, nor any of the women I must have known, there was an instinctive awareness of the fact that any woman would welcome the man she loves as the first to possess her—especially if the future held as little promise as Youi Janis'.

With every rapid step the mount made across the desert sands, one question kept repeating itself with maddening rhythm. Could it be that she might actually want to share her last nights of freedom in my arms?

Darkness fell quickly on the desert, and the caravan pulled to a stop in front of a large cliff which rose high above the desert like some gigantic warped wall. Camp was speedily set up around a small sunken well where the women hurriedly gathered for their supply of water.

We ate a dinner of roasted baby Jilioes flesh. The meat of this desert mount is delicious—and forms the basic food for the nomadic desert tribes. How they can slaughter and eat these beasts which are so attached to them was explained by Rha-Ney.

"You survive. You take the food the Gods offer, and you don't question it. We have always eaten of their flesh. In the beginning they were bred merely for the flesh—training them as mounts came afterwards," he explained when I had inquired about it. "We kill every third baby born—the others are considered riches with which to trade to a father for his daughter's hand in marriage."

While we sat there before the small fire built in front of the tent assigned us, I could not keep from being obsessed with the logical rightness of making these last nights with Youi as full and happy as possible. It was then that I determined to bring up the subject to her.

Our situation was unique; and thereby required a more flexible attitude. Such thoughts would never have come close to becoming temptations if things were different—or there was even the slightest hint of hope.

I knew what must be done. And so, when Rha-Ney stepped off a short distance, as Youi started to retire in our tent, I approached him, said: "Could I ask one favor?"

Youi hesitated at the entrance to the tent.

"Go on in, I'll be right there," I told her, urging Rha-Ney further away. Several of the other guards drew Kay-guns.

He hesitated, then followed me a short distance. "What is it?"

"Soon," I announced in a dry, thick voice, "you will be reaching the slave markets, is that not true?"

"Yes. Tomorrow night," he announced with a grim nod.

I hesitated, unsure how to ask what I wanted. The idea of coming right out and suggesting that his men move further away to allow us privacy seemed crude. Then I realized that they already believed that Youi, being my slave, would naturally be spending intimate nights in my service. "If your men could be posted just out of hearing of our voices, I would be in your debt," I finally said. "A little more privacy."

"You promise not to attempt to escape?" Rha-Ney countered.

"I promise."

"It will be as you desire, Torlo Hannis, for I know you would not promise my father that same thing. I believe that you will keep your word—my own life hangs on this belief." He slowly smiled. "It is little that you ask."

"But the favor is great," I assured him, turning and starting for the tent.

Now, at least, it would be possible to talk boldly with Youi Janis; a necessity.

Youi was sitting on the floor, waiting for me. "What was wrong?"

"Nothing," I assured here, suddenly finding it hard to organize any words. All day they had been drumming through my brain—now they were static and meaningless. "I simply asked for privacy...that his men stand guard beyond hearing."

Maybe there was something in the expression in my eyes, or possibly it was a female's instinctive ability to guess a man's thoughts, to read subtle meaning by the shading of his voice, the all but invisible tensing of the facial muscles; but Youi immediately grew rigid, her eyes widened with alarm.

At once shame waved through me, sending a pang of guilt to icily close around the endless rationalizations which had brought on this moment. Abruptly it all seemed fantastically incredible to have ever considered the idea of taking advantage of our situation.

I stood there, hands clutched to my side, unable to move or speak, throat constricted so tightly that it pulled the inner stomach linings into a knotted ball of sick pain.

The silence pressed in so totally that it seemed like an actual physical force. I had the impulse to scream, just to kill this bestial quiet. Then slowly a more rational sanity seeped into being and made it impossible to ignore the rank foolishness of this stilted scene. Immediately rage followed, an intense annoyance at myself for playing the immature little boy. The automatic result to this flash-anger caused irrational conclusions. All I became aware of was the fact that no matter how the facts were organized, Youi would be sold as a slave to some man who didn't have the right to touch her; I would probably be dead in a very short time; we had only this moment; and foolish morality—rigid adherence to a cultural code which had no place in the immediate situation—was going to deny each of us one last night of happiness.

The thought of some other man forcing himself on Youi created a madness which killed reason. She was totally helpless to resist any demands I made.

I took a bold step forward. Youi gasped softly; her eyes froze to mine.

Then the words were flooding out.

"What twisted sense of morality can make it wrong? What perverse code of honor can argue against the two of us grabbing at least a moment of happiness before it is too late

186

to ever have a chance to any happiness? What possible argument can you offer that would make it impossible for me to claim you as mine?"

I was now standing over her darkened form, unable to see the expression on her face, but easily able to imagine what it might be. It could be shaped in horror or relief, in anger or happiness, in disgust or love. I could imagine, but see nothing.

Her voice came strong and yet oddly gentle to soothe the tormenting confusion commanding my thoughts.

"Torlo Hannis, I can give you only one reason—and though it might lack logic in your mind, I believe you will accept it." There was no doubt, no fear, not even the suggestion of anger in her tone. The caressing tenderness which embraced each word stopped me short.

"I am still Proctoress of Bel-loniea, and in every nerve of my body is the total knowledge of what that means—it directs every action and thought. What I might personally desire can have no bearing on my actions. What happens to me against my will can never change what I am to myself, or my people. Even as a slave-woman it will be impossible to change this conditioning. No matter what is commanded of me, it will not bend my own personal code or make me less of a Proctoress. I know what is in store for my future and realize there is nothing I can do to alter or control it—other than killing myself. My body will become the plaything of many men—if I don't find some way of ending life. But it will never be so degraded that if freedom were offered I could not return to my place as Proctoress.

"In simple, undistorted terms, Torlo Hannis, I am what my culture has made me, and so completely that nothing—no matter how physically destructive—can change the course of all acts and actions over which I have control."

Youi Janis stood, moved very close, almost touching me. Her eyes looked up, wide, trusting, tender, deep with emotion.

"If I was less than all this, Torlo Hannis, my lost one, it would not make any difference what took place between the two of us tonight. But if I was any less, I would not be a Proctoress—since it is impossible to be one without the

187

other. Being Proctoress is more than a title of birth, it is a stamp of personality so ingrained that to let that be killed would destroy the person. Though I might not be physically killed by it, the destructive effect would be so complete that I would never be the same woman—the one you spoke to with love in your eyes and heart. I would not be the woman you claim to love."

She slipped her arms around my neck and gently kissed me, then stepped away.

"Is it not enough to say that I wish with that basic part of me which is common to all women, that we could share all that you have asked for. The woman half of Youi Janis would find it impossible not to give of herself totally—regardless of how shallow or deep her emotions for you—simply because I know you'd be tender, and care. And because as a very human woman it is only natural to desire one last—and in my case first and only—chance to know the full tenderness and perfection of a true lover. The woman half cries to know such an experience—especially since it will now be denied her for life.

"But the Proctoress half cannot and will not allow the woman to take command. Not because of some foolish, childish morals, but simply because there are rules by which each person must live, regardless—otherwise there would be total insanity in the world. Rules bring order even out of madness. The rules for a Proctoress in matters of love are simplicity themselves: she must find a man worthy of her, able to stand at her side and rule a nation. With this man, and only this man, she will give of herself totally—but at the right time, after the marriage vows have been spoken before a Muti. To give of herself in any other circumstance would not only degrade her but her family and nation. What others might inflict upon her she is blameless of guilt."

For a moment I believed she was offering herself—saying that if I were to take her now, she could be mine without guilt. Then I remembered what she had said in the beginning.

"I am still Proctoress of Bel-loniea!" I knew now that no more needed to be said other than that to an honorable man of Noomas, for it stated simply enough that as Proctoress it was impossible to ever give herself totally to any man who had not stood beside her in front of a Muti and spoken those words which join them forever in marriage.

"And if I were a man with honors, and there was Muti here to bind us in marriage...?" I asked huskily.

"The woman in me would say you have earned the right to possess Youi Janis' love. The Proctoress would hesitate and point out that you have not had time to prove worthy of standing at her side as co-ruler of Bel-loniea."

"Then you would not even then be sure?"

"I am sure—the Proctoress is not," she admitted, turning away.

I stood there looking at her for some time, not knowing what to say. Joy should have filled my heart, for she had admitted I had won her woman's love.

Finally she again faced me. "We must not speak of such matters, Torlo Hannis. You are but a warrior in my grandfather's army—it is not fitting that such a conversation be exchanged between us...not until the time when you have received the honors you so deserve."

It is not strange that her words failed to cheer me.

"Which can never happen, now," I pointed out with an ironic, grim smile.

"Who knows what the future truly holds for either of us, Torlo?" she corrected with a sweet smile. "I think it is best that we tell ourselves there is always a chance—at least until we are slaves."

"Of course, you're right," I admitted, though inwardly unable to convince myself there was any hope.

We were silent after that, for it seemed each of us had become trapped by the conviction there was no hope.

As for my part, I didn't have the heart to continue a conversation which would, by necessity, have to be filled with blatant lies.

When Youi finally curled up on the blankets which Rha-Ney supplied us, I felt a sense of relief and followed her example.

Life held many wonders, hiding endless tricks up its sleeves—one being my advent on this planet, falling in love with a woman who was impossible to possess, only to see her life shattered by the cruelty of man's selfish struggle for survival which left no room for considerations of the single life when the majority might suffer as a result. But as mysteriously tricky as life might be, I could see no possible escape from our fate—and therefore wished only the unconscious blank of sleep.

During the night, winds breathed heavier across the desert, building slow force as the stars moved their laborious way across the heavens to make room for the morning sun which would be blanketed by the beginnings of a naked desert sand-storm. It was a night that interrupted sleep countless times.

How Nature has a way of equalizing all Man's problems into a shapeless and meaningless neutral clouded thought. All that is left is the primitive instinct of survival. And this exists, naked, screaming to be heard above all other anguished fears for the future. How simple a man's motives become when faced with the final destructive form of the elements grinding mindlessly away at the surface world on which all living things exist.

As I pointed out before, neither man nor beasts nor the hot sun is the real danger in the desert—only the sand-storm holds any actual threat of total disaster.

CHAPTER TWENTY-TWO

ESCAPE IN HELL

My first awareness that things were not going to follow an orderly pattern was when I awoke to discover it was no longer dark outside. We had already spent two nights and more than one full day with the nomadic clan of Baji-Ney and learned there was a strict, almost military pattern to their daily routine, never broken for any reason short of some major necessity such as attack from an outside source, the capturing of slaves or acts of the Gods. The necessities of survival in the desert left no room for deviation from a set inflexible formula. The distance between water-sources in most parts of the desert were such that a caravan on the move must keep to a tight time schedule in order to reach the next campsite. The fact that much of the desert had the water-plants scattered did nothing to make flexibility possible, since their liquid was usually reserved for emergencies or gathered for distilling the desert liquor so popular among the tribes.

From the few conversational exchanges with our guards, who were cheerfully willing to answer questions—though careful to keep their guns ready for instant use—I learned that many times they would be forced to give up the popular midday stop and continue late into the night in order to reach the next area of safety and water. I also knew that our planned destination that day—the slave market in Katoria, located just on the outer edges of this vast northern desert—was a long hard journey, necessitating a very early departure for a late arrival without any noon rest.

191

My first impression upon waking took into account this fact along with the immediate awareness that our tent was violently straining against the deep driven stakes that held it tightly secured to the desert floor. The flap which served as an entrance was whipping angrily back and forth like the explosive sound of a Kay-gun discharging. It was this latter that startled me from the exhausted sleep which had finally claimed mind and body.

The deep-throated howling of the wind swelled in force even as I lay there still dazed from the aftermath of deep sleep. The eerie loneliness of that invisible, almost animal sound created a sense of being totally alone in the world—cut off from all living things.

The tent swayed, the material buckling in; sand swept through the entrance with a blasting force, cutting out all visible shapes other than the gray-orange mist of its attack.

I heard a human scream nearby and recognized it to be Youi Janis, apparently startled awake.

Then the tent collapsed with swift suddenness, blanketing down upon us like a smothering layer of dirt tossed into a grave.

Immediately I clawed to where Youi Janis had fallen asleep the night before.

It was more her struggles against the entrapping tent walls than any sense of direction which brought me finally to Youi's side. When she became aware that I was there, her arms clutched blindly out and, like a frightened animal, clawed close in an instinctive need for protection from a terror which the naked mind, when stripped down to its primitive core, is not equipped to cope with or understand.

I held her trembling form in such a way that it was protected by my own body, yet at the same time allowed room enough so that an air-pocket could form between us.

The world outside our cloth enclosure kept up a constant screaming as sand and wind pressed the tent's material hard around our bodies. The only thing which saved us from total suffocation was the fact that the desert tribes make these tents of coarse woven cloth that allows air to seep through, while holding back sand—though fine particles of dust attempted to contaminate our meager air supply.

I felt helplessly trapped under the smothering folds of cloth; though realized this was probably better than open exposure to the raging elements.

Above the tormented roaring of the wind and sand I could hear shouting voices, screaming animals, all edged with stark fear. It was hard to imagine how anything could survive in the open, and equally as difficult to visualize our own survival while so totally embraced within the folds of the collapsed tent.

Dangerous as our situation was, I could not ignore the pleasure of Youi's soft form clutching against mine. I remember thinking that for this privilege alone it was worth dying; my only regret was she might also pay the same price.

A man can face death in many ways; but the most pleasant is in the arms of the one he loves—though hardly if it means both must die.

The storm was now only in the early stages of building violence, though I had no way of knowing this. I felt almost an insane urge to strike out blindly in desperation to escape our immediate danger. The only thing that made me resist this mad impulse was the belief that even during this premature phase of the storm it might be impossible to safely change our positions. Already I could feel the sand piling up around the tent's crumbled ridges. We were being buried alive by a storm which gave no evidence of reducing its force, but instead offered unrelenting promise of increasing violence.

Memory of the sharp terror which possessed me during the electrical storm which had drowned the southern lands after our escape from the Diano served to sharpen awareness of the far greater danger of our immediate situation. While the solid walls of a grav-disk flyer would easily serve as protection from these grinding sands, as it had against the flooding force of a tropic storm, there would still be no way to avoid total burial under a mountain of sand. Obviously under mere cloth that tightly embraced us we had less chance of being buried alive.

Vaguely I heard Youi's voice sobbing near my ear, and had to strain to catch even a part of her words, which made little sense.

"I...want...know...you...don't want...to die...you... knowing this." How things might have been different if I could have known what she was attempting to tell me!

She trembled, shivered convulsively. Her arms choked around my neck with such force that it seemed she had gone mad with terror.

I became conscious of the fact that slavery might surely be better—no matter how degrading—than immediate death. Life even without hope of freedom offered more than death. This realization proved that I had never totally accepted the concept of life after death. The fact that nobody is really able to accept their complete and final end, where all conscious awareness of being has eternally stopped, held little comfort. For a brief instant I found it possible to almost visualize death as total destruction of self awareness; the mental impression was so sharp with vivid understanding of what this must mean that it sent my mind screaming away from contact with this suicidal concept. That part of the mental process whose sole purpose for existence is the impressing of the survival instinct into every nerve, muscle and thought, now rationalized away all conscious acceptance of death as a total end of being, while at the same time it forced to the surface and encouraged the demand to clutch onto life at all costs. The argument was simply to avoid the unknown, regardless of any promise of another kind of existence after death. The experience of death will come soon enough, the argument insisted, something we all must face. Now it was not the acceptance of some eternal nothingness that kept me from giving up all hope of escaping our crushing death-trap but the awareness that no matter what death might offer, any kind of life-time torture was better than discovering what lay beyond the grave before this was necessary—no matter how pleasant that might be.

Oddly enough, even this total fear of death was not great enough to ever shake the unquestionable willingness to die in an effort to save Youi Janis from the smallest amount of harm. Such is the extreme irrationality of a man's love for a woman.

It occurred to me that while the storm pinned us helplessly down, those of Baji-Ney's tribe were equally trapped.

194

Immediate realization followed that we would never have a better chance to escape. The fact that success would mean Rha-Ney's death and slavery for his family touched me no more deeply than the idea of stepping on a harmless but annoying insect—but not pity, regardless of the fact I had learned to like him and the other members of the nomadic tribe, since they knew the rules in which they must live, and accepted them. I would unemotionally kill every man, woman and child in the tribe for as little reason as to avoid momentary discomfort to Youi Janis.

Even as these combined thoughts formed, my mind was automatically seeking some possibility of escape.

Desperation will drive the mind into irrational pursuits, blindingly focused on obtaining its object. We had nothing to lose but a questionable future. The interesting thing is that almost as fast as the concept of attempting escape was accepted, a means to that end solidified. I don't really know if the plan came before or after the idea of escaping seemed worthy of consideration

What takes a long time to explain took little actual time to mentally react to.

The awareness of Youi's physical nearness, the fleeting terror of death to be replaced with an acceptance of life under any circumstances, the recognition of the sound of screaming voices around us and the realization there was now a possible way to use the storm to our advantage, came in such rapid sequence that they must have been absorbed in one large mental swallow, as a man drinks the countless millions of atoms in a mouthful of water. I couldn't have been holding Youi much longer than it would take to gasp in half a dozen breaths before the plan had formalized in my mind and was instantly accepted for immediate action.

There was no way to communicate what I planned, other than to press close to Youi's ear and say: "Don't struggle!"

At once I began working on the harness strap which is a loop of leather wrapped around a warrior's middle and used to attach him to one of the many rings placed along the inside railing of a flyer. This I finally managed to loosen, then work free at one end. The first part of the plan was to slip this about Youi's waist and up to be attached to the other side of my harness, so she would be safely bound to me.

This seemingly simple act took a long time to accomplish. The tent's material had been pressed in tight by the weight of quickly gathering sand. Sweat covered my body by the time the strap was free to be worked under Youi's back.

What little air was still seeping through to us had already become stale. Heat pressed in with a stagnant force. I readjusted the impulse to tell Youi to raise up, and began to work the strap under her with the hope she might understand and make some helpful effort. The moment I began, Youi guessed what I wanted, though she could have had no idea of the true purpose behind this act. With her help it became less difficult. Shortly after that the clasp was clipped to my left side. The fit was snug.

Now, placing my hands on the sand about her head, I pressed downwards, straining against the heavy weight that had already piled on top of us.

If there had been time to put any deep thought into what I was attempting, it is highly possible the whole plan would have been rejected as fantastically insane. So-called logic when fully applied can shatter plans that illogically become workable when impulsively acted upon.

One concept had impressed itself upon me during that flash-moment when desperation insanely searched for escape: anything loose on the face of the desert would be torn along the course of the storm's virago. What might happen to such objects along the way was of far less importance than the fact they would be carried rapidly from their point of origin before the storm would abate. Any dangers that might follow, I conveniently ignored by believing they could be handled when crossed. How a man rationalizes under pressure. I'd accepted life under any conditions rather than death, yet at the same time preferred to risk far greater dangers in the hopes of improving our momentary situation.

As I strained to press up through the slowly rising sands, all thoughts were blindly concentrated on this single effort. Once the inrush of sand slipped from my back to flood into the area created by this upward lift, I immediately

196

pulled my legs under me, grabbed blindly at the tent material which was pressed about both of us. Now all muscles strained to pull at the cloth in order to gather it all into a bundle lump around our bodies.

This stage of the operation proved even more difficult than expected. The weight of sand was of little importance now. The basic problem was the fact that these tents are firmly pinned deep into the desert by long stakes. It was this that kept us from being immediately picked up by the storm once it gained enough force.

Youi had kept her arms about my neck up until this moment, but now though not able to guess why I was trying to ultimately do, she began adding to my efforts, unquestionably supporting an unknown plan with blind confidence in my judgment. I believe this action on her part did more to my morale than if a thousand Bel-loniea warriors had swooped in and magically rescued us.

Strength which should not have existed now surged into power. I felt the sudden false conviction that nothing was beyond me; that all the Gods in the universe combining together against us would not be powerful enough to defeat our purpose. Such total confidence comes from the mind, not the pitiful muscles of a man's mortal body; yet it makes possible deeds that would otherwise be impossible to accomplish.

Abruptly only one point of resistance held us pinned to our position.

We were already feeling the violence of the storm attacking the bundled shape of our bodies. Sand was piled up to the level of our waists, yet it was almost beyond our power to resist being slammed flat by the harsh force of the screaming wind.

With one last, determined surge of strength, I battled both the storm and the stubborn stake which continued to defeat the raging elements. Almost immediately it became obvious that nothing was going to move the stake. Then with a sudden wrenching tear, the combined strength of storm and human muscle proved too much for the tent's remarkably tough fiber, and it tore from the deeply anchored stake as if slashed by the mighty swing of a razor-sharp sword.

197

From the moment we were cut loose, the real dangers exposed themselves.

Almost immediately the wind-powered sands grabbed our bundled bodies like some gigantic hand, struggled to lift us upwards, then abruptly succeeded in pulling us free of the sand, and threw us savagely forward. It felt as if we were being kicked, hit, tossed by that invisible ungodly giant, in an insane frenzy of destructive violence. Yet these endless blows were unrelentingly shoving us along the course of the storm and away from the band of desert slavers.

We'd just had enough time to clutch one another before being taken into this new cruel captivity: the malignant mercy of a distorted mindless beast of Nature.

Now I realized the insane rashness of my plan. An image of our battered, torn bodies being crushed against the high cliffs or, at best, slowly battered to death by the desert floor, left little room for any consideration of survival long in the wake of this sandstorm. The only excuse that offered itself for having so impulsively secured a ride on this new journey to ultimate death was the fact I'd had absolutely no way of imagining how powerful the storm actually was.

I don't know who lost consciousness first. It was inevitable that neither of us could retain awareness for very long. Our bodies were slammed and tumbled along the course of the wind, sometimes hitting the hard desert bottom with stunning painful impact, only to be once again thrust upwards by another sandy arm that took perverse delight in throwing us down again, to repeat this over and over as if possessed by some insane rage for this ragged bundle which had dared to challenge the deathly malignance of this face of Nature's violence. The amazing thing is that we did not suffocate.

Each numbing collision with the solid desert sent dizzy blackness tighter around me until finally one final bow closed off all further thought.

CHAPTER TWENTY-THREE

HIDDEN MEMORIES

How long it took for conscious dreams to take shape upon the black screen of my mind, I don't know. There was no immediate knowledge of what had last taken place; only a dim recognition that I existed took focus. Following this acceptance came a broad series of quick, disconnected impressions. At first there was a lack of any organized pattern; then the pieces slipped into a vague semblance of logical order, consciously reshaped to create a solid continuous sequence.

I know now what wasn't obvious at the moment of realization: that a small segment of my past life had forced its way to the surface revealing a total piece of information that in itself made sense but left too much out to explain the full significance of its meaning.

I was sitting in a darkened lounge room of a large space liner, whose roof was a transparent dome through which reflected the glorious spectacle of galactic interstellar space, unfiltered by any planetary atmosphere. It was a sight that my eyes casually accepted through years of past exposure—yet there was an ever-present inner memory of a first impression as a young man of seventeen on the first trip off his native world. There is no greater sight in the universe than seeing the stars like specks of pale multi-colored dust against total black, marred only by distant cosmic clouds, touches of hazy star-substance which one knows to be remote galaxies.

Knowledge of being a professional soldier in the Federation Space Force was as much a part of me as acceptance of being alive. I'd trained in all forms of killing, from

199

primitive knife-fighting to laser-guns, from swords to hand-to-hand Karate, Soliam, Judo, Torsa. This fleeting knowledge was just a part of an all-over awareness of being, the automatic reflex memory that is a total part of what you are, what your life has been and means.

I was waiting to see an old man who had just been released from the Penal Planet around which the space-liner orbited while awaiting a passenger shuttle-ship.

This scene abruptly flashed out of being to be replaced by the image of an aged, wrinkled face of angular bone structure, marked by scarred cheeks, accented by contemptuous lips that sneered on every word. The washed-out gray eyes were nervously alert but held a deep imprinted weariness created by twenty years of hard labor as a Federation prisoner.

"Don't know how you learned 'bout me, spacer," the man growled in a harsh voice.

We sat in a small room, along a wall of auto-bars—a series of slots under a square plate of buttons which served out drinks as dialed. I was carefully supplying him with a continuous series of drinks to be charged to my spaceman's credit account.

"I told you, sir..."

"Don't sir me, spacer," he snapped between gulps of Galactic Cocktail. "Might like a bit of respect—but none of that sirrin'—had enough of that down there!"

"I discovered from a friend that one of the crew members of a pirate ship had been sentenced some twenty years ago for involvement in the destruction of the liner upon which Dal Sorla and his wife were traveling. They were reported dead. I merely thought maybe you could give me information on them. This friend introduced me to a prison mate of yours, Squail, you called him."

"Squail! Space rocks, we had to laugh." He slapped his knee. "Tell you 'bout—"

"Dal Sorla! Squail got the idea they hadn't been killed."

The man frowned with annoyance, studied me momentarily, then grunted: "Only ones survived that was this man and his wife. He helped the Chief. We let 'em go." He

200

laughed harshly again, as if at a private joke. "No chance of 'em returnin' to civilization. Dropped 'em in deep space, off the travelin' lines—with a bad shipper. Had one chance to live. We'd learned of this planet by accident—a healthy one for humans—unhealthy to 'tempt landin'.'"

"You can tell me...where it is?"

"Let me think some. Been years. Ain't no air outta my space suit if you wanta buy one-way ticket. Cost you some, you can bet your spacer's oxygen on that." He laughed again. His laughing face continued to mock me as it slowly faded away.

Thoughts reorganized themselves, new memories shaped to smother his dreamy phantom from the past.

The throbbing pain of my body pressed aside all dreams as slow consciousness ebbed into being. I remembered the sandstorm escape from the nomadic slavers.

For a while this was as far as my thoughts could travel. The elements of the dream returned to take focal possession of thought. Immediately I accepted it as a piece of past memory. I probed deeper, attempted to uncover some other facts to join with these, but they were locked securely behind the misty wall which held all memory of my past life beyond that on Noomas. The name Dal Sorla meant nothing other than acceptance that it must be important. Immediately the story which Andon Janis, Youi's father, had told me during our last conversation, sprang into mind.

He had been on a space-liner with his wife when it was attacked by space pirates who killed everybody except the two of them, saving him because he was a doctor.

Every other detail fit Andon Janis' own story about being left adrift not far from the world which he later learned to call Noomas. They had managed to reach the planet and crash land—as I was told had happened to me.

Sudden doubts plagued the acceptance of this dream as returning memory.

Had the dream been only a fabrication of a slowly returning consciousness conjuring up a fantasy out of pieces of disconnected factual information? Could there be a blend of facts symbolically interwoven into this dream illusion? Or was it a moment of total recall of some event which had actually taken place? Then why hadn't Andon Janis referred to himself at least once as Dal Sorla? And if I had come to this planet, seeking Dal Sorla, who now called himself Andon Janis, why was it impossible to even recognize his importance?

The information was again too incomplete to form any useful answers either about my past or to supply logical reasons to motivate a search for a man I was not now able to place nor relate specifically to a young soldier in a vast Galactic Federation Space Force.

A quick awareness of the problems which involved me and Youi Janis made it necessary to simply label the whole thing as either a dream-fantasy or incomplete evidence about a past life that now held no real importance—and never could so long as it was impossible to leave this planet as Andon Janis had implied. Logic forced me to attempt to forget the whole thing.

Still, the speculation continued as a nagging undercurrent to all surface thoughts, even as I struggled to center attention on Youi and the problems which must now be faced and solved.

The need to make a survey of the immediate conditions surrounding us proved unexpectedly difficult to achieve, for total consciousness was still reluctant to open up. It was like being at the bottom of a deep lake, whose depth is questionable, and no amount of struggling to swim upwards offered an end to the pressing water.

Dreams had come first, followed by the determination to face present problems, but all this took place in a totally mental plane that resisted all attempts to evolve to a point which included the physical world.

A sense of frantic impatience created momentary panic. Emotions were swollen to overwhelming dimensions by an anguished need for urgency.

Sound filtered into this lightless mental void. At first it was difficult to understand the sound, then like eyes straining to focus on a distant blurry object, a world became recognizable, surrounded by an eerie quiet.

"Torlo..." The word weakly repeated itself several times.

I tensed, fought desperately to control disconnected senses and muscles. It was not until the animal panic gave up its insane fight that it occurred to me to simply open my eyes.

The simplicity of this idea was startling, for it brought realization that I was fully conscious, alive to the surrounding world. Dull pains splotched large areas of muscle and flesh. I became aware of a soft, yielding form pressed against my body. Sand supported my back like a form-fitting bed. A cool breeze sent a shiver through aching muscles.

My eyes opened to see a brilliant display of stars gathered together to form a massive irregular hazy bright island in the black heavens overhead. A dark silhouette blacked out part of the sky; pale moonlight painted delicate strokes, only suggesting the lovely features of Youi Janis, Proctoress of Bel-loniea.

A fluttering, unreasonable nausea chilled my stomach. Some unconscious current of perverse fear smothered the deep love I felt for this woman, then flashed away as if pulled by invisible strings.

I shuddered, equated this as a reaction to returning consciousness.

Then the ghostly clutch of fear returned as the features of Andon Janis filled in Youi's shadowy face. The illusion passed, flickered out of being as if snapped away.

"You, are you all right?" I weakly questioned, hands searching for the harness strap which secured her body to mine.

"Yes...I don't think any serious damage was done," she answered in a cautious voice.

My fingers tangled with the folds of shredded cloth. It was some time before I could find the harness clasp and release it; these moments were far from unpleasant. If Youi were not Proctoress, I was sure that our physical closeness would have offered temptations neither of us could possibly have ignored. Our total devotion to controlling any suggestion of temptation was almost as fantastic as the rigid codes that man has always seen fit to inflict upon the members of his culture in the blind belief that this proves him better than the unreasoning beasts. But even the dumb animals have their rules of courtship.

After I unlatched the harness strap, Youi rolled away with a sigh of relief. I sat up, forcefully ignoring the pains which bruised my body with throbbing regularity.

We had taken a brutal beating, but miraculously managed to elude death. The storm had passed by, leaving the desert in just about the same condition as before its coming.

For some time we sat on the desert sand, merely aware of one another and the realization that life and freedom were at least momentarily ours.

The cool night was bathed by three radiant moons which cast triple shadows around all objects which stood above the flat sandy world. A soft breeze moaned on the crystal air like some distant ghostly voice, to remind us that life was a gift which could be easily taken away by the mindless will of Nature. Yet this windy murmur offered strange comfort, suggesting that no person was totally alone while in the wilderness of some planetary surface. The wind brought life, as well as destruction, seeding fertile lands with the tiny germs of future vegetation upon which countless living creatures would feed. Even the desert was vibrant with vigorous life; a multiple scattering of water-plants gave undeniable evidence to this fact. Without the wind to gather their tiny seeds they could not be spread so generously across the dry parched sands to spring forth into natural water-absorbing vegetation which took moisture from the air and from deep within the sands.

Perhaps the narrow escape from eternity made even this sight seem so bountiful to my gaze.

It seemed as if we were the only people on the world. As I turned to look once more at Youi, I knew such a fate would hardly be unwelcome. The two of us would then become the promise of a future race of men, planting our roots in this wasteland to form the foundation from which later generations could, in some distant future time, spread across the world.

Our total isolation made the mental fantasy seem almost real. An acceptance of her helplessness against the brute strength of a man's muscles made it easy to imagine how simple it might be to find some isolated place, away from all contact with other humans.

I was not restrained by a sense of false morality, or loyalty to the cultural moral codes for royalty on Noomas, but rather by my own respect, love and worship for this woman who called herself a Proctoress. I could look upon the confining restrictions of her cultural codes with objectivity and see they were at least honorable—though no more so than endless varieties of other standards which must have existed throughout time in many distant places across the universe. I could also accept with equal conviction the morality of a mutual sharing of two humans in live with one another, for I believed that the real ties between two people was their mutual feeling for one another; nothing more. All social, legal and so-called moral ethical conventions could never change what was felt by the heart and mind. Possibly the rigid rules which so completely sealed Youi Janis within an invisible shield—simply because she was a Proctoress of some miniature nation, located on a single continent, marking the surface of some unimportant world—were unrealistic in a purely humanitarian way. But they bound her totally within their grasps. I could never dishonor what she held to be sacred.

Youi smiled shyly in my direction. "Torlo, how is it that a mere day can bring on so many changes in a person's life? You think you know everything, are sure of yourself and then...one day can change all that."

The question was so unexpected that I foolishly stated: "It only proves what you told me last night. We should never give up hope—for there is no way of knowing what the Gods have in store for us. Rules contain the seeds of sanity-control. I don't believe I ever had any strong convictions of a God, otherwise it would have been impossible to accept our fate as hopeless. Faith in a God gives faith in life; and that creates hope when there is none."

Her mood changed with whip-like quickness. The soft tenderness in her eyes washed away. She seemed to stiffen just a tiny bit. But her voice remained much the same.

"There's a lesson in that for you—both of us—not to ever let emotional impulses strip away our sense of honor."

It was tempting to point out that honor was a relative thing—for what was considered honorable in one society and culture would be impossible to accept in another.

Instead, I said: "About last night. Though my thoughts were not selfish...I was wrong to make such an attempt. I can only beg your forgiveness. A man will do desperate things when hope dies."

She nodded, impersonally. "Fear gathers up emotions to a point where the logic and refinement which makes Man different from animal almost disappears, so the Mutis say."

She hesitated, looked down at the sand. "In that we were both guilty of being too human and lacking acceptance for what the future holds."

"I won't accept a pre-set future," I argued, defensively. "We are moved by the accidents of Nature, the whims of selfish men. It's impossible to be anything but totally human, frightened of death and susceptible to reacting to apparent defeat. If I offended you in wanting what any man might desire under such circumstances, I am sorry. But I'm not excusing myself."

"Your desire—as pointed out," she retorted savagely haughty, "was no better than one could expect from any man! Under such circumstances!"

The hot bitterness in her words was startling. I felt as if struck bodily with a whip. Something in my expression must have revealed this pain, for she almost immediately said: "I'm sorry, Torlo Hannis—but we have both been through a lot—and there's more to face. It is not honorable that I reward your acts of bravery with such anger.

"When we return home," she continued, after turning away, "the Proctor will see that our debt to you is paid in full!"

I merely nodded, hurt by her anger, for I could not understand this sudden change in attitude.

Now a wall of cold isolation surrounded her.

I felt utterly cut off, convinced there would never be any chance of regaining the ground lost.

How those last words had lowered my status to the level of all male creatures who merely think of a woman as an object upon which to force their physical passions.

In one simple announcement, she cut away the friendly bond of companionship we had shared in the last days.

In such a manner she might deal with a Commoner who had overstepped his social bonds and needed to be harshly reminded not to speak unless given Royal permission.

I was numbed by her words and tone of voice and could not understand what might have brought it on.

Such rapid change, from the woman who had the night before admitted love for me, to Regal superiority, was numbing.

This sudden reversal left no room for any other considerations but to get her back to Bel-loniea and then try to forget I had ever met her. All ambition to receive any rewards and honors was now shattered with the force of this realization she would never be mine.

"Which way to Bel-loniea?" I demanded, impersonally.

Her lips parted, then she looked away to our left. It was some time before she spoke, and when the words came they were level, flat. "Towards the Southern Star." She pointed to the bright star which I had recognized as a supergiant. "That direction,. But we must go west, to the coast, first, to avoid the jungles."

Swift irony made me face the fact that the last couple of days had not only changed our relations but stripped us of weapons. We were naked to the attacks of any predatory creatures wishing to make a quick meal of our bodies. Suddenly it seemed the tribe of Baji-Ney would almost be a welcomed sight. At least they had food and water—even slavery as an Arena-warrior would give honorable death, which I might well have embraced at that moment.

It was then, for the first time, that I could have given Baji-Ney and his son the answer to their question as to how an honorable man became mercenary by choice. Slave, warrior, mercenary, any means which might offer death. Even

207

though that subconscious voice within me would scream to hang onto life and force my body into physical acts of defense, I would in time be defeated and killed. Thus would end my adventures on Noomas. I embraced such an event for I could not live without hope of possessing Youi Janis on terms she would accept fully.

Yet how perversely tricky the mind can be, one moment totally submerged with the death-wish, unable to imagine any future worth existing for, then the next reversing the process with no more hope than before to be responsible for the change.

If there are Gods, they certainly must look down upon us poor mortals with great mirth, enjoying our comic antics.

Events were destined to strip naked all considerations of self-pity before the next day was half finished.

Chapter twenty-four

Desert madness

The sun was blazing hot by midmorning. The two of us were already feeling the effects of not having anything to drink or eat. We moved across the desert with stubborn, silent steps. Conversation had been limited to the social necessities since our last exchange the night before. The first water-plant I had come to proved one unexpected fact: Without a sword, or at least a sharp pointed object, it was impossible to open these natural bowls of water. If our situation had seemed difficult before Baji-Ney's slavers had captured us, it had been at least more hopeful than what we now faced.

Youi merely shook her head when I asked about breaking open the plant. One quick glance at her face revealed the impossibility of doing so without a sharp instrument.

After that the heat pressed in around our bodies with intense force like the blast of a furnace. We continued toward the west simply because it was better than standing still; in time either the heat, thirst and hunger or some desert creature would claim our lives. I wished there was a way to hide this fact from Youi. We both moved like people who lack expectancy of escaping the desert, but too stubborn to admit defeat without a struggle.

During most of the morning my eyes kept scanning the skies for any signs of a flock of birds like the ones which had attacked us that first day. The only defense we might have against them would be to lay flat on the sands, frozen as if in death; though even this seemed to offer little hope. Finally the knowledge, that if such desert birds found us there was no way of protecting ourselves, caused me to forget any dangers from that direction. If they came, we would die.

By midday we staggered to a stop, sitting down under the hot rays of the huge orange sun.

"I should have brought that tent material along with us," was my only comment. "we could have at least covered from the heat."

Youi shrugged. "It wouldn't have made much difference in any case."

We sat there for some time, too exhausted to continue. Thirst had made our lips and mouths bone dry.

"We should have stayed with them," I cursed half to myself.

After some delay Youi shook her head, as if my words had just made an impression on her. "No!"

I cursed under my breath, then forcefully stood. Moving to one of the water-plants a short distance away, I dumbly studied it. One of our guards had told me that deep roots searched down into the sand for moisture. My mind struggled to admit defeat but a stubborn need for water drove desperate thoughts in search of some way to get at the trapped water. The plant is covered with countless little needles, long thin thorns as tough as metal. The shell they protected was fibrous and strong.

Falling to my knees, I started digging around the plant's base in an effort to move the sand away from around its roots. My purpose was uncertain, other than making a search for some avenue which might give entrance to the water. It proved a far more difficult task than expected, since sand would keep slipping back into place. Finally it occurred to me to start making a huge ditch around the plant. How long this took, is hard to estimate. Youi sat watching, as if I were some interesting mad creature. When I had exposed the lower portion of the water plant, revealing a massive network of hair-like fibers that drove their way downwards into the sand, Youi revealed a spark of interest.

"What are you doing?" She moved to my side, looking at the purplish fiber-roots.

"We can't...just give up! There has...to be a way!"

210

She appeared on the verge of shaking her head, but instead reached out, touched the roots in a gentle exploration. "They're soft."

Quick inspiration moved me. I took the harness buckle used to attach a warrior to a grav-disk ring and, holding the metal clip, smashed it against the water-plant's side, striking at the long thorns, breaking them away.

I'm sure Youi thought I'd gone mad.

Once one side had been partly cleared of needles, I worked to clear the other. Sweat was drying out my body by the time this had been accomplished.

Placing a hand on each bared side, I strained with every muscle, pulling, rocking back and forth on the plant in an effort to uproot it. This quickly proved impossible. Standing, I kicked at the plant with the bottom of my foot. Time and again I struck at it, moving from one side to the other. It continued to stubbornly resist even these efforts. After while, I bent down and once more attempted to manually uproot it. This time there was just a sluggish suggestion of a lessening resistance. Standing I repeated the process of kicking the plant. Countless times the remaining needles cut into my flesh. Again I grabbed the plant, strained until the blood rushing to my head created such dizziness that it was necessary to stop. Exhausted, breathing heavily, I fell back against the sand.

It seemed hopeless.

Youi suddenly bent low, studying the roots. A gasp sounded from her dry, cracked lips. "Torlo! Look!"

I slid weakly to her side. She was pointing to a small portion of root which had been broken; at the end still attached to the plant, a small drop of water slowly formed. On such slender encouragement hope gathered itself into a last mad determination to make a total attack at the plant, fighting until it came loose or I died.

Perhaps insanity had taken momentary possession of my senses. I'm not sure to this day. However, all muscles followed orders from a nervous system suddenly gone wild with rage. I retain only a vague impression of what happened next. One moment I was frantically kicking, the next instant clawing hands were wrapped around the bottom of the water plant, muscles straining, body pressed into the sharp needles which slashed my flesh until blood flowed freely over them. Then again I'd be kicking, sometimes in a standing position, at least once with both feet while lying back against the sand, supported by stiffened arms. Little gasps and cries of encouragement from Youi kept the fiery fever of my efforts at a constant high peak of desperation.

Finally, when even the mad animal determination had drained away from pure exhaustion, my body continued weakly against the resisting plant, automatically fighting without any real awareness of what was happening. It was much like following the rhythm of drum beats, dancing on and on, unable to stop even though it is obvious that to persist will bring on ultimate death.

Youi's voice continued to encourage me, but it became a sound from some other world which had no place in this totally personal fight to the death against the plant's mindless, stubborn will.

When I suddenly felt an abrupt break in the resistance, and felt myself tumble over, away from the area of conflict, my mind could not at first recognize what had happened.

Then slow realization came.

Dazed, I sat up, pulled the bulb away from my chest, where the spiny needles had planted themselves. Turning the plant over, I examined its base, where it had been finally torn away from the roots. Slow moisture was beginning to seep up through the white pulpy area that had been the root-bed out of which grew the tough purple fiber-roots.

Youi stood beside me, eyes wide, breath heaving. A slow smile broke across her lips and suddenly both of us were laughing hysterically. Thirst was forgotten; everything was forgotten other than the joyous relief that coursed through us at the basically simple victory against a small desert plant.

Finally I extended the bulb to Youi and she greedily sucked on the soft area through which moisture struggled to bleed out. After she had finished obtaining the pitifully small amount of water, I ravenously sucked on the exposed root-base, which gave out a miserly, reluctant supply of moisture.

212

It merely soothed the dry ache of my lips, tongue and mouth. It was so little for such an anguished struggle. Yet it meant the difference between life and death Unfortunately it would merely give a short extension to our lives.

We rested for a long while after that, then finally started once again to cross the hot desert. I carried the priceless water-plant, from which we kept moistening our lips, absorbing every drop of liquid before it had a chance to evaporate in the burning heat. Once this supply was gone there wouldn't be any more, for I knew it was impossible to uproot another plant; by the next day, exposure, lack of food or any water supply would have claimed too much strength. We had merely prolonged our torture. The gain was highly questionable. Since neither of us had a concept of how far the western ocean might be, we were able to fool ourselves into believing there might still be hope. And if a person possesses hope, no matter how little, it is possible to continue even a useless fight for life.

At last darkness descended, to give relief from the unrelenting heat of day, but we continued as long as it was possible to move. When total exhaustion drained Youi's last gasp of strength, we finally fell to the sand, sleep immediately claiming our bodies.

That night a feverish delirium took possession of me, caused by the wound inflicted by the water-plant's needles and heightened by the exhaustion and lack of food.

I have little memory of the next day, other than a vague awareness of Youi always nearby. The few mental images of this period were highly distorted. Later, Youi admitted to having held my head in her lap most of the day, nursing my parched lips with the meager water supply. There were times when she was convinced the fever would turn out fatal.

During the next night, I suddenly awoke. I was convinced the fever had been a nightmare. Almost immediately sleep reclaimed awareness. The sun was just creeping over the horizon when consciousness returned. Youi's face, drawn and haggard from the long exposure to the desert, leaned close.

213

"Are you feeling better?" Her voice was strained with physical and emotional exhaustion.

When I nodded, then asked what she meant, Youi explained about the fever.

"I'm sorry," I told her, thinking that it would have been better if she'd left me there to die. We had lost one whole day, the water-plant was already showing alarming signs of drying up—a danger which I'd tried not to think about. The amazing thing is that it had lasted even through the first day.

Without another word, we stood and once again began our journey across the desert.

Rest periods became more and more regular, until by midday neither of us could go farther The sand had given way to the more hardened dry flakes of parched dead sea bottom. It was night by the time I awoke, even weaker than before. The idea of standing seemed at first too difficult to consider.

Then I heard Youi moan, turned, sat up to look in her direction. She was lying so close that I touched her while turning. Her eyes opened, then closed.

"Youi!" I cried, alarmed.

Slowly her eyes fluttered, then opened to look up into mine.

"I can't go...on!" Her voice was hardly a whisper.

"We have to!" I insisted. "Can't give up!"

Reaching for the water-plant, I started to lift it to her mouth, only to discover that the wound had finally sealed itself up into a bone-hard surface.

Disgusted, I tossed it away.

Youi merely watched it roll over the dry sandy chips, breaking them apart to form a thin trail.

"Come!" I reached for her and somehow managed to force Youi to a standing position. Without a word we started walking. Each step was more a staggering fall forward, topped by an extended rigid leg. The night progressed slowly without any stops for rest. If we had stopped, it would have been impossible to get up again.

As dawn was beginning to work its way above the horizon, I saw to the right, out of the corner of my eyes, a

214

gathering of low brush clumped together over a small depressed area. If our progress had been any faster, we would have passed this by in the darkness.

It was impossible not to recognize the signs but I refused to allow them to build any hope.

"Youi!" I said, starting to change the direction of my course. She followed like a living dead person, totally unaware of what was happening.

I half ran, still reluctant to trust the evidence before us. By the time the first low lacy brush was scraping around our legs, I could see the gleam of moisture on the sand ahead, yet didn't have the will to accept even this obvious fact.

When water splashed around my ankles, I cried out in sheer joy. Youi laughingly fell face down in the shallow pond. Without a pause, I followed her example, drowning myself in the sweet cool water.

It's well known that a person can survive for some time without food, but water is the very essence of life. Weakened as our bodies were from lack of food, the sudden quenching of intolerable thirst brought an amazing renewal of strength.

For a long time both of us were totally involved with the necessity of absorbing water in small amounts.

Finally we dragged ourselves out of the water and sat at its edge, happily wet.

"I'm for staying here," Youi announced with a weak smile. "I don't even want to think of leaving."

It was a statement hardly meant to be taken seriously; yet the horror we'd just passed through made it sound highly appealing.

"If we had food," I countered in a quite serious voice, "I think it would be an excellent plan." My eyes were searching for some possible food supply in the surrounding area. The leafy brush which clung around the tiny pond offered no promise. I'd been told that such plants were inedible.

For the first time since we had escaped the desert nomads I seriously considered our chances of living through even the next couple of days. The thought of leaving this water supply behind seemed insane—yet it would be sheer madness to remain, for without food to supplement the water, death by starvation would soon claim life. How much longer we would last without food was questionable. My own stomach was a continuous hollow of pain which had become almost numb by the passage of time. But now the pangs of hunger were sharpened because of the satisfaction of thirst.

Youi said: "I'd willingly submit to slavery for just a container in which to carry water."

I studied her face. It was marked by the long strain of the last few days, yet still held the stamp of beauty that had such an amazing effect on all men who gaze upon her.

"We need food!" I blurted out, angered by the fact that nothing I could do would produce it.

Then a thought occurred to me. "Surely other living creatures come here to drink."

Youi's face lighted with sudden hope. "If we could stay here...waiting...some animal's got to come!"

We talked it over and decided to stay there for at least the rest of the day, then leave, traveling by night, when the sun wouldn't drain what little strength was left of us.

The day drifted painfully by, each of us taking turns at sleep, while the other watched for a desert animal to approach for water. When the sun began setting, hope slowly died.

I was last to keep watch, Youi sleeping quietly, as night began to fall upon the quiet world. The effects of gaining a water supply had slowly faded away as hunger replaced the frantic need for drink. I sat scanning the immediate area, now convinced that it didn't make any difference if we stayed there to die or continued in a pointless search for the ocean and escape from the desert. It was as good a place to die as somewhere in the middle of dry sands, tortured by thirst, dying because strength had not been replaced by food. That we had survived this long was remarkable.

I turned to study Youi Janis, and remembered the pulsing passion which had possessed me a few days back. Then came the hurt her words had inflicted. All that seemed unimportant now. If dying here would save her, I realized without emotion, then I'd embrace death.

216

At that point the idea that my dead body would serve as food for hers became fascinating. I sat there for a long time while darkness became total, overcome by the interesting idea of so completely becoming a part of Youi Janis. Not only would my body serve as a food supply, but she could easily make a survival kit out of skin and bones—the major part of my flesh could be enough food to subsist upon her journey to the ocean and then south into the fertile lands where her people would welcome their Proctoress—not caring what foul means were used to survive. If my skin was dried properly she could make a water bag, then another one for carrying strips of dried flesh. Surely there were human bones which would easily serve as weapons. All one would need was a sharp pointed bone to serve as a means to open a water-plant. The visions were highly exciting to my almost feverish mind. It didn't occur to me that she might find it impossible to devour human flesh, even to save her own life. Nor did the grisly horror of the idea really have any meaning. Logic supplied the only answer: this would make survival possible for Youi Janis.

CHAPTER TWENTY-FIVE

CAPTURED

My mind was quite feverishly imagining ways to kill myself when sudden movement caught my attention.

Turning, I saw a darkened shadow slither along the ground toward the water. At first I didn't want to believe the reality of the sight. Then disappointment gnawed at me as I accepted the fact that food was making its way toward us. Now I wouldn't become a physical part of Youi's body. Now my skin would not form food and water bags, my bones weapons. These disappointments held a perverse grasp of my now quite irrational thoughts.

Acceptance of this disappointing fact centered the realization that I would accept the desert offering and kill the tiny creature if it was possible.

The moving shadow was no longer than my forearm and only twice as thick, with a narrow pointed tiny head.

I watched it inch along, not moving, my breath caught into a tight hard ball, hurting the center of my chest.

The shadow crept closer, tempted by the scent of water, but apparently puzzled by the strange frozen shape of man so nearby.

When it had finally come within reach of a quick leap, I moved.

Body, mind and muscle united into a massive machine of destruction. The move was so quick that I fell bodily upon the creature before it could even recognize any sense of danger.

218

Immediately I rolled, clawing at the quiet form of my catch. Fingers found and encircled the scrawny neck, squeezed into a crushing vise.

It was some time before I realized that the animal had been killed by the thrusting weight of my body falling upon it.

Youi was now sitting up, gazing wide-eyed in my direction, apparently unable to understand what was happening.

Coming out of the daze, I lifted the limp form of the animal high in the air, shouted: "Live, Live! Live!"

It didn't make much sense, but Youi understood the meaning. She squealed in delight and came forward, fairly whimpering with pleasure. Here was a young woman who had been destined since birth to rule a rich nation, lead her people with wisdom and strength, willing to sacrifice all personal or emotional desires in picking a man to stand beside her, completely overwhelmed by the idea of one small piece of food. Yet the needs of the flesh will, if allowed to become too possessive, overwhelm all cultural patterns of moral training, taking control like a conquering force.

Even while I was painfully possessed by the personal need for food, a quick realization of these facts flashed across my mind as I looked at Youi Janis' almost frenzied expression. I remember the two other faces I'd seen exposed: the woman who would not completely free herself from the restrictions of Royal birth though it went against every basic feminine desire, and the Proctoress whose superior voice of authority had shown so cruelly that I was beneath social status.

At that moment it was obvious that Youi Janis, woman, Royal Proctoress—even goddess, if that were the case—would have departed with honor or anything else necessary to share this pitiful, scrawny desert animal.

Such quick observations of the mind were utterly beyond control of conscious will. What makes the difference between a man of honor and one who lets his own personal ambitions claim all sense of decency is how he reacts to such undeniable conclusions. How we all are a double entity, the physical body, nakedly wanting to fulfill all its animal hun-

219

gers, and the mental network of emotional needs, all controlled by the logic of mind, motivated by a maze of ethical morality. The senses observe the world, the body screams like a hungry beast for the satisfaction of its needs, the emotions tangle up these complex necessities of life, then the logical mind weeds them out, deciding which acts are either morally or physically safe to exploit.

Regardless of the fact that a man starved for food, exhausted from lack of such substances, is not driven by any strong physical passion for a woman, these facts did slash through my thoughts in quick succession while Youi fairly lunged forward.

But also came the recognition that all civilized polish and conditioning had been carved away from us, to expose raw animal motivation—leaving only the very inner core of what we call personality to direct our actions. While Youi's need for food was great enough to possibly throw aside all ethical considerations—this was no weaker than the fact I was not tempted to demand such a price. Naked though our needs were, the hunger instinct was stronger in each instant. Her hunger-need was greater than some distant ethical reasoning fashioned by a culture which could offer nothing to the basic creature screaming for survival within her mind; my hunger was too great to be driven aside by thoughts of physical possession of the only woman I would ever desire. Honor actually had little to do with either one of our motions.

The two of us crouched over the small grayish animal, eyes gleaming with the brightness of near insanity. The first problem of how to prepare the meal held little immediate consideration above the fact that we possessed this meal.

If anyone had been witness to this scene, they might have believed we held an endless supply of food in our hands, a certain survival for the next days which faced us, instead of just a meager few swallows of flesh which could do no more than hold off starvation by only a wretchedly short period of time.

Youi caressed the animal as if it were her fondest friend returned from the grave.

220

After a few moments, I faced the problem of how we were to eat the flesh. Considerations that it might be poisonous never suggested themselves, and if they had, I don't believe it would have caused even a moment's hesitation.

"Fire," Youi suddenly demanded, taking command of the situation in a manner which revealed a natural womanly instinct.

I dropped the animal onto the sand, then started gathering pieces of dry wood. When there was a large enough pile, I searched in my warrior pouch for the flint and striking stone. Shortly we had a little fire greedily eating wood almost as fast as we could supply it.

Then I turned to the problem of preparing the animal. Why any civilized sanity kept us from considering the possibility of merely stripping the raw flesh off and eating it uncooked is a mystery neither of us were later about to understand.

At once the idea occurred to me that this animal might serve more than one purpose. The mad explorations of my mind previous to spotting the animal now returned to take a saner shape. The fur-covered hide might easily serve as a water-bag, the bones, small though they obviously were, could be examined with hopes of finding one to serve as an instrument for probing through the hardened outer shell of the water-plants.

The first problem was stripping the skin from the flesh without a knife. This alone served as a major difficulty which almost frustrated our attempts to preserve the hide as a water-bag. I quickly explained my purpose to Youi, then proceeded to attempt the impossible.

The easiest method was breaking back the small jaw, then with pure physical strength attempting to rip it away, in order to create the first tear in the flesh. This required the combined strength of both Youi's arms and mine.

The sheer insane necessity made possible a feat of strength which sanity might have surely withheld, since both of us were already drained of any physical muscle power.

After that, my efforts to strip the hide away were almost constantly discouraged by the difficulties of doing so without some sharp instrument and Youi's insistence that we

221

should give up, throw the animal on the fire and let the flames eat away the skin so we could eat.

Finally, half in anger, I cried out: "Look for a stone, a stick—anything I can use!" This was partly stated in order to get her away, occupied, and quiet.

She immediately began a search which took surprisingly little time.

She returned with a broken branch from one of the bushes; the branch's end was nicely pointed.

After that it was only a matter of controlling the impatience of gnawing hunger. When the hide had finally been stripped away, Youi fairly leaped at the skinless body, half flung it on the flaming coals.

I examined the animal hide momentarily to see how much damage had been done. Amazingly it had been possible to preserve about two-thirds of the hide in one piece, which could be easily tied closed at the top, serving as a small bag in which water might be carried.

The flesh was not even half cooked by the time hunger made it unnecessary to wait longer. We pulled the meat from the flames, burning our fingers in the frantic effort to obtain this much-needed meal. By pure muscle force, I ripped the body into two shredded parts, extending the largest to Youi, who grabbed at it without question.

This meal was by far the tastiest any person in the universe has ever experienced, even though the flesh was sharply bitter, tough and dry. Hunger would have made burned wood seem like a banquet of delicious fruits, vegetables, meats and wines.

Afterwards, our desire for food seemed heightened by the small meal, but strength did show signs of slight revival.

Before starting on our night time walk across the desert, we tested the bag and then filled it with precious water, tying it at the top with a strip of Youi's gown. Then I picked the longest bone which promised to serve best as an instrument for digging into water-plants.

After completely satisfying our thirst for the last time, we started walking away from this small oasis, neither making any comment. I felt like a doomed man continuing an endless trek through some kind of purgatory that must be suffered before death gives final rest. In leaving that water-hole, a sense of complete depression set in, for I was convinced this would be the last time we would see any water of such quantity, as if it had been the last outpost of life before slow death finally crept up and claimed what was left of our bodies.

Mocking laughter sounded from some deep, hidden chamber of my mind, at memory of the swelling relief that escape from the slaver's camp had created. How impressed I'd been by the fullness of life even within the confines of this wasteland; how grateful I'd been for the promising gift of that life which could reach all corners of the world, no matter how bleak, spread by the generous breath of the winds. But Nature was highly jealous in creating and sustaining life; she picked what areas one form could exist in and with her uncompromising set of laws drew lines of division over which other life forms were not allowed to pass unmarked by the pains of anguished suffering. Life was here for the desert creatures, for the man who could bring the necessary equipment to claw out an existence, but not for the nakedly unassisted human.

I pulled my thoughts away from such gloomy activity, forced all senses to examine the cool night, domed by the spectacle of the starry universe which gazed blindly down upon itself from eternity. A sense of timelessness assailed me as I thought about those distant stellar bodies, whose light was ancient beyond the ability of the mind to understand. Events, once passed from present to past, could never be recaptured except through memory. Yet any creature looking into the sky was in a very real sense looking across the hallways of time, observing objects as they existed a year, a thousand years, millions, billions upon billions of years in the past. The light of stars recorded the history of the universe backwards to its very beginnings for all to read who had the intelligence and knowledge to translate their meanings.

Two things happened to me at this moment. The sense of smallness that the universe gives to any rational being became a real thing. How unimportant even our struggle here was when placed against the vast endless time of eternity. This ready acceptance soothed a blanketing of calm over my nerves and thoughts, bringing into focus the fact that harsh as our survival had been, we had survived; we were still living—miraculously clawing moment by moment a bare spark of life from an unrelenting grasping environment. The second point to impress itself upon me was: all this automatic intimacy with scientific knowledge of the universe had not come from any informant on Noomas, but from a slow supply of tiny little facts learned in my past life, forcing their way subconsciously through the misty screen which continued to resist memory.

I remember the sudden acceptance of the dream that had come upon returning consciousness after our storm-powered journey from Baji-Ney's camp. There was now little doubt that it must be some event from my past life.

Where did Dal Sorla fit in my life, and what connection did his story have with that of Andon Janis' journey to Noomas? Were the two men one and the same?

At this point I was not questioning the authenticity of the dream; I accepted it as a piece of total recall of a past life.

As we made our way across the desert, my mind was lost in this other world, blocking out the reality through which I walked.

If I had come to find the man called himself Andon Janis, what possible motives could have been responsible for this search?

Apparently, I'd been a soldier in the Galactic Federation Space Force. Might it not be possible that my journey was connected with this profession? Dal Sorla was a doctor, traveling with his wife. Was it merely a vacation trip, as Andon Janis had suggested, or was he escaping some Federation authority? Had my job been to find the man and bring him back to face legal justice?

Somehow, though this theory held the seeds of reasonable logic, I felt a lack of conviction about its validity. This, in part, I recognized, could easily be motivated by my love for his daughter and respect for him. Yet the very fact that this reasoning had presented itself forced me to consider

224

the possibility that it was caused by some subtle piece of past knowledge.

My speculations served little purpose in forming any conclusions or gaining any further information about my past life, other than to begin the nebulous beginnings of a foundation that could, once solidified, serve as a magnet toward which the rest of my memory might be slowly pulled.

I'd grown up with some relative other than my parents.

I'd become a soldier in the Federation Space Force.

I'd searched for a man named Dal Sorla and ended on an unknown, apparently forgotten planet called Noomas by its human inhabitants—whose ancestors had probably originally been some lost Federation colony.

These few pieces formed a partial beginning, middle and end, needing only the flashing out of details to make them tell a complete story.

It was probably not long before such mental activity exhausted itself and the real world pressed itself once again upon my senses.

Youi was walking just a tiny bit in front of me, in such a position that it was possible to just make out her profile in the bright triple moonlight. The delicate face, with its upswept nose, the high cheek-bones, the wide, pouty mouth, straight, firm chin, upwards sweeping jawbone which gracefully pointed to tiny ears, were all painted with soft, golden, pale lines. Her slender shoulders, the frail, but well-filled out figure, reflected a natural health and stamina which even this ordeal in the desert had not as yet completely defeated.

How dear and wonderful she looked! Feminine, yet as fully able as a man might be restricted to the limits of strength which her woman's body was able to produce.

The little threads of emotion slowly attacked me, twining around until all those elements of love that had been so powerful within my breast now rebuilt to overwhelming proportions.

Again the resolve the never leave her side, either as slave or lover, as guard or guardian, solidified.

The night was slowly drawing to a close by the time we were too tired to continue. Without any conversational exchange, we both lay down on the sand and went gratefully to sleep.

I couldn't have been unconscious long before the sound of something totally alien to the desert came whispering softly from above.

My eyes weakly opened. The first reaction was a feeling of complete physical exhaustion. I realized that we would probably not last many more nights without food. The sun was only half way up from the horizon, already beginning to create a blazing heat.

The sound which had drawn sleep away grew, coming from the right. I turned, looked up, puzzled.

Immediate relief slashed wildly into being at the sight which met my eyes. Unable to restrain a yell of wild pleasure, I leaped to my feet.

Youi, startled by this yell, stood, saw what had caused my reaction and threw herself happily at me.

"Torlo! Oh, blessed, Torlo!" she fairly sobbed, overwhelmed with relief and joy. "Live! Live! Live!"

The two of us began dancing around like two people gone mad, yelling, laughing, unable to control the surging pleasure of relief.

The huge flyer was already beginning to lower towards us. Then it circled and finally began to prepare for a landing.

"You see," I shouted, "we made it."

"Yes, yes, my Torlo," she fairly sobbed joyously back. "We made it!"

The interesting thing is that it did not occur to us to question the appearance of a lone grav-disk flyer so close over the desert floor; nor were we about to even question the unreasonable luck which now had brought it our way. Death had been too promising; the flyer meant rescue from starvation and thirst. That it might belong to a nation unfriendly to Bel-loniea would have meant little to us at this point.

As the giant flyer landed a short distance away, sand billowing up around it, Youi suddenly stopped dancing. Her face went ashen, then with a short gasp she slowly slumped to the ground, unconscious.

226

Alarmed, I rushed to her side, looked toward the half dozen armed warriors leaping from the flyer, and almost immediately understood why Youi Janis, Proctoress of Belloniea, had passed out. Already weakened by our horrid struggle to survive this nightmare desert, starved to the last ounce of strength, driven by near unreasonable mad obsession to survive had taken their toll and now this last reality had broken even her grand spirit. No wonder she had fainted in a moment realization of the horrid irony now facing us.

The warrior harnesses were those of the Diano. What fantastic freak of fate had brought them to our rescue was surely some mocking trick of the Gods playing games with their mortal underlings. Everything we had done, suffered, was now in one instant made useless.

The moment the warriors reached us, two of them roughly dragged me away from Youi.

The chief warrior-at-arms looked at Youi Janis, then shouted over his shoulder to the flyer. "It's them!"

Chapter twenty-six

Nightmare revelations!

The officer's face was grim, fat from overeating, the tiny eyes wicked as they snapped to Youi's still unconscious form, held up by two Diana warriors, then shifted back to me. We had just been dragged aboard the huge battleship.

"You," he snarled, "must be the one who caused all this trouble."

"What do you mean?" I demanded innocently.

"I'll ask the questions." He stepped forward, his heavily jeweled harness sparkling in the hot sun. "You've given us a Korda's chase. Just finding the flyer you stole was difficult enough. We were able to follow tracks away from the flyer—then saw that mounted men must have captured you. Later, the sand storm wiped away all trails. Just last night we came across the band of slavers who had captured you." He gloated for a moment. "They said you'd disappeared in the storm—the chief's son was surprised to discover who she was." A cruel smile twisted the man's bloated lips. "They were furious to discover what a fortune they'd lost."

"Then Rha-Ney still lives?" I inquired, actually relieved at learning this fact.

"If you mean was he killed for allowing your escape," the officer sneered, "I'm sorry to disappoint you. Acts of the Gods are not considered within the powers of man to combat. We were almost as convinced as these desert slavers that you'd died in the storm—and were merely making double certain before returning to report to Aoji. I can assure you, he was furious to learn about the Bel-loniea Korda

228

slave-woman escaping. You really didn't think you would actually get away with it, did you?"

"We almost did!" I spat out.

"But you didn't. It's not hard to cover a lot of desert territory in a flyer. It was only a matter of time before you would have been discovered—one place or another. Agents were sent out to every known city, prepared to pick you up no matter where you went."

"Other than Bel-loniea."

"But you would never have gotten that far, I can assure you," the man mocked, with a thick oily grin. "Aoji is a very powerful man."

"One would think he was Proctor!"

"His father is weak, old, tired. Aoji rules Diano by methods far more powerful than the mere holding of the highest title. Power is the real key to leadership! You will learn the power of Aoji before he is finished with you!"

He turned away, said to his men, "Take the Korda warrior below. The woman goes to my quarters, under constant guard." Then as an apparent afterthought, he added: "Feed them both. Aoji wouldn't like his new slave-woman dying before he has the pleasure of her undivided services. As for this warrior—that will be an extra treat for our leader. Aoji will reward us all well!" The officer once more faced me. "You'll wish the desert had claimed your body before Aoji finishes with you!"

I stared through him, not caring what happened now.

The two warriors at my side shoved me across the deck of the huge Diano battleship, then down below into the gloomy corridor. One of them opened a door, the other threw me into the small room, then closed the door, bolting it.

Exhaustion and bitter realization that there was nothing I could do to change our situation, left me emotionless. Possibly this was for the best. I fell on the small bed lining the right wall, sleep immediately smothering all thoughts.

Mental and emotional stress, physical exhaustion and time all play a part in helping some people who have lost their memory to regain it. Almost every time a piece of information returned about my past life, my mind and body were beyond resistance of any conscious or subconscious pressures. If I probed, attempted to force memory, it drove recall further away like an illusive shadow set in total darkness.

This time while I slept, the wall of misty black fell away to reveal one of the largest and most important pieces of memory to return to me since my arrival on Noomas.

I was approaching a strange solar system, after weeks of being confined within the cramped quarters of a small one-man stellar scout ship which had been assigned me for the last few years of my service, since holding the rank of third-class Command Pilot. That dimensionless void popularly known as hyperspace—though scientifically shown to be something totally different—had been a gray sheet of nothing for what the ship's clocks claimed to be a little over a week. The turnover in speed from hyper drive to normal space brought the small one-man ship well within the confines of the six-planet system which was my destination. Ancient star chart information, from a report made by an exploration team, fit all evidence the ship's sensors reported.

Two planets were gassy giants, farthest from the large reddish sun. The inner three worlds varied from each other. First came the small, quickly orbiting planet without atmosphere, its rotation frozen, one side molten rock, the other iced by its eternal night of deep space. The second and third planets held atmospheres, one thick with a heavy cloud covering, the other, closer to the sun, a burning world, slowly rotating so that all sides were ultimately baked by the star's intense heat and radiation. Both were devoid of any suggestion of life, or the ability of sustaining what we might call living matter.

The fourth planet was without question Earth-type, containing three major continents and two smaller land areas. I fed statistics to the computer about orbit and rotation of the fourth planet, data extrapolated upon information given by the ex-convict space pirate about the course which Dal Sorla had taken. A moment later estimates were offered as to which area his ship must have landed. The old convict had claimed they'd kept a tractor beam upon the doctor's ship, out of curiosity, but partly because their leader was to a certain extent concerned by a morbid sense of twisted morality

230

as to their safe arrival; this was his way of clearing a guilty conscience about so ill-rewarding the man who had possibly saved him from death. Some mention of a polar disturbance on the planet had informed me that any landing might turn out to be difficult.

The ship's computer indicated three possible landing sites for Dal Sorla's ship. One was on the snow-capped south pole, another in the middle of an ocean. The third seemed a more logical choice—if he'd survived the landing—since it was off the coast of a large continent. From space, the area below revealed rich fertile lands, bordered on the south by tropic jungles, and on the north by a jungle strip which bordered a dry desert; to the east was a range of mountains, beyond which open fertile lands extended a great distance to be stopped by a huge inland sea.

As the ship orbited around the planet, I studied the other continents to discover evidence of a scattering of civilized areas, even spotting a large port city in a small bay. Then ocean spread out across the world until the coastline of my destination slipped up into view. Through telescopic lens, I was able to take in great detail, locating a small walled city not far from a natural bay, along which there was evidence of a settlement surrounded by farmed lands.

Again the ship slipped around the world, now beginning to lower into the atmosphere. It was then that I first felt indication of static interference. The ship's instruments swung from left to right, and some of the dials spun insanely. By the time I had reached the huge blue ocean between the two northern continents it was almost impossible to hold a true course.

Only by a quick burst of rocket-power was it possible to leap spaceward and out of the immediate influence of this mysterious force which made flight so difficult. Once I had reached a point where my continental destination could be spotted below, I lowered the line of flight, heading with computer accuracy toward the coastal settlement which matched the extrapolated landing site of Dal Sorla.

The braking rockets roared into fiery action, slamming an invisible hand against the racing dive of the ship. Then suddenly it seemed as if something had struck the scout

231

ship with tremendous force, knocking it sideways. My head snapped against the side of the controls. All senses numbed. With a frantic attempt to avoid total disaster, I struggled for consciousness. The last few moments of flight were seen through a red haze. Hands moved with automatic skill which had been drilled into them over years of handling such spacecraft. The retro-rockets were the only thing which saved total destruction of the ship. I managed at the last moment to pull its nose upwards, just as the highest trees of a forest loomed across the ship's nose. It was the last act of the man I'd been all my life. The world that man had known slammed away after one brief awareness of a twisting, convulsive collision with dark purplish trees, followed by the explosive impact with sold ground. Later, Torlo Hannis, the lost one, was born in a small room in the ancient palace of Romos, Proctor of Bel-loniea.

I now awoke screaming, sweat dampening my body. For a brief moment a sense of confusion set in, and it was difficult to recall the surroundings. The dream image was too vivid, as if just lived through for the first time. Then slow memory returned, flooding together in such a confusion that it made little sense. Thoughts swam with mental visions from two different lives, which would not solidify into a reasonable pattern. It was like watching two separate, disconnected video dramas at once, projected on top of one another.

Then slowly, while lying back on the hard shelf-bed, I relaxed to the memories, letting them flow freely through my mind like countless eddies rippling along a rock cluttered brook. Finally a general realization formed.

Past memory of the life I'd experienced before coming to Noomas, while returning in great detail, was not total. Yet there was enough to piece most of this life together into a general connected pattern, having large blanks to be left unexplained.

I'd been raised by an elderly aunt, sister to my mother. A trust fund grant left by Dal Sorla sent me through school and then into the Space Academy. I'd left as an officer and served in several campaigns of Federal police control. The Galactic Federation was the central government which kept an uncertain peace between the thousands of planetary governments throughout the known civilized universe. When any two political powers became involved in warlike disputes, it was up to the Federation Space Force to enforce peaceful solutions. If two political powers were at war, then they were stopped by the Federation Army—a job which many times involved conquest by means of bringing a superior force to actually conquer the warlike governments, using solar atomics when necessary.

The disappearance of my parents had created a natural interest in learning what actually happened to them. After having invested much of the money in hiring detective services, I learned about the convict on Tious III, one of the many Federation Penal Planets. This was the first lead, and required years of search. The man's name was Hanna Jasson. Taking an indefinite leave from the services, I went to question this man upon his release, to learn the location of the planet where Dal Sorla and his wife were supposed to have disappeared.

As all this information pieced itself into an organized form, I slowly felt the shock of sudden anguish. If Andon Janis was Dal Sorla, the man for which I'd searched, the father I'd lost as a small boy, then Youi Janis, his daughter by the Proctoress of Bel-loniea—since his first wife had died as a result of their crash-landing—would have to be my half-sister! This realization was shattering.

One slim hope suggested itself. Andon Janis might not be my father. But the evidence seemed all too conclusive. How could he be other than Dal Sorla? Though Hanna Jasson had not been able to remember the doctor's name.

I tried to hold to the belief it would turn out he wasn't Dal Sorla; but this was hard to accept.

Youi Janis must be my half-sister!

CHAPTER TWENTY-SEVEN

AoJI

Youi Janis must be my half-sister?

I played with this thought with great anguish. Then remembered that history was filled with Royal men marrying half-sisters, even full brothers and sisters had many times joined in marriage. But logic and personal morality fought against acceptance of such an idea when it involved myself. If she was my half-sister, that would end any possibility of ever possessing her. Oddly enough, this realization did nothing to lessen my passion for Youi. For the first time since finding myself on Noomas, I wished that memory had remained locked away forever, for I knew it would never be possible to accept Youi Janis on the level of a sister. Too much had happened, my emotional needs had developed beyond the point of ever considering a brotherly affection for her.

In this depth of mental torture, I kept feeling that I was missing something, that a very important piece of information had not yet been revealed.

Sometime later the door opened and a man stepped in. He placed a bowl on the floor and then retreated, his left hand holding a Kay-gun leveled my way. When he disappeared, I fairly leaped at the small bowl that contained a thin soupy substance in which floated a few vegetables and little drops of fat. They weren't wasting valuable food on me; yet even this seemed like a generous banquet. It served to satisfy thirst and hunger for at least the present.

The effects of getting food resulted in a far better frame of mind. The facts that had revealed themselves about

234

my past life were irrevocable; though some mental block made it possible to ignore the emotional implications at that moment. The subtle hope that some minor piece of important information might change my conclusions held enough hope to focus upon. Nonetheless, half-sister or not, I was devoted to Youi Janis and determined to somehow make possible our escape.

A rush at the guard while he brought food would hardly have much chance of success, for I'd seen in the hallway another guard carefully watching everything we did.

They weren't taking any unnecessary chances.

My mind centered upon the possibility of escape when we reached our destination.

In the meantime, I decided, it would be best to build up the picture of a man who accepts defeat. If they believed me to be without hope of escape, there was the possibility that at one time or another they would make a slip, then I would leap through the opening.

The next time the guard came to bring food and take away the empty bowl, I was sitting dejectedly on the bunk, head in hands.

Looking up as the door opened, I quickly whined: "What're you going to do to me?"

The man was square-faced, with cruel thin lips that sneered at me. "You're going to die, horribly, warrior."

"But why?" I cried, alarmed. "I don't want to die."

"Should have thought about that before going up against Aoji!" He placed a new bowl of soup on the floor.

"She's not worth dying for! I'm only a mercenary!" I cried like a man on the brink of insanity. "Surely you see that. A mercenary just does what he's paid to do."

"Don't defame us mercenaries, coward!"

"Tell your officer I'll sell my sword to him...anything."

"Shut up, coward. Shut up or I'll forget myself and kill you with my own hands. You're a disgrace to us mercenaries. I've heard of such cowards—but never thought I'd see one."

The man backed out, slammed the door closed.

A slow smile formed on my face. "Give me a chance!" I cried. "I don't want to die! I'll serve your master well!"

I took the bowl and started eating hungrily. Later I banged on the door from time to time, yelling for the officer in charge. Nobody answered.

Now I began a program of rebuilding my strength, exercising every muscle until they became sore from use.

We couldn't have been in flight for more than a full day and night before the ship landed. The room in which I was being held was windowless, so it was impossible to tell where we were.

A short time after landing, the door opened and a small unit of guards waited outside as two of their fellows were forced to drag me bodily out of the room. I repeatedly screamed that I didn't want to die and that I'd join their armies. One of them hit the side of my head with a Kay-gun. After that I remained silent, as if sulking in cowardly terror. The contempt of the men was ill-concealed as they escorted me roughly down the hall, up a flight of stairs and to the top deck of the flyer.

Through narrowed lids I searched the deck for some sign of Youi, and was almost relieved to discover she wasn't there. To build a convincing picture of a coward it would be necessary to go through acts that would be difficult in her presence.

There were several other warriors on deck and a couple of officers.

I screamed, "Don't kill me! I don't want to die!" It was the cry of a hopelessly tormented man, holding no rational motive other than total terror.

"Shut up!" A warrior hit me with his Kay-gun.

I whimpered, covered my head with trembling arms. They shoved me forward, down the long ramp which led to the ground.

Through the narrow space between my forearms, I noticed we were in a rocky open region. A camp of tents had been scattered over a large area. Obviously the Diano were still on their way back from Bel-loniea. Realization of this fact reminded me that the armies of Bel-loniea were supposed to follow and attack the Diano. Where were they?

The escort revealed great delight in shoving me forward. Meekly, whimpering with apparent terror, I took all they could hand out. It served my purpose well.

They finally came to a stop in front of a large tent which I recognized as being that of Aoji's. One of the warriors extended a foot so that I tripped over it. Falling face down in the rock ground, I yelled, then curled up into a tight ball.

"Get up, you Korda coward!" a voice commanded.

A foot kicked into my side. I merely cried in pain. Rough hands pulled my body up.

An authoritative voice said: "Tie the prisoner's hands behind his back."

"He's too cowardly to need such respect, sir," the escort leader announced.

I looked at the officer he was addressing. The man was tall, well-built; a pointed black beard gave his face a V-shape. The dark eyes studied me for a long moment. "Tie him, nevertheless. He looks mad. A mad coward can be dangerous."

Disgusted with myself for having played the role too heavily, I helplessly submitted as two warriors twisted leather straps about my wrists.

Then they took me inside the tent. This was where I had found Youi Janis. The escort shoved me down a corridor of cloth walls and then into a large chamber in which over a dozen officers stood. A small throne-like chair, covered with precious jewels, carved from what might have been solid silver centered the room, upon which sat a young bearded man, hair falling to his shoulders as black as the piercing deep-set eyes. Thick lips curled back to reveal uneven heavy teeth. His barrel-chested body was covered from neck to ankles by a finely woven silvery gown, drawn tight about the rounded belly by a leather belt which supported jewel-hilted sword and knife. The man's face was heavy, but had a hardness which comes only from long years of harsh cruelty. There wasn't a feature, from stub-nose to receding chin which reflected a gentle emotion. The eyebrows frowned together, thick and heavy.

"Bring him forward!" he cried in a high-pitched child's voice.

It was with difficulty that I restrained the fury of emotion which burst into being at sight of this man who could be no other than Aoji. Here was the person responsible for all the horrors and suffering inflicted upon the woman I loved. I still refused to think of her as a half-sister.

Visibly trembling—but from rage rather than any sense of fear—I allowed myself to be shoved face down before Aoji.

The man stood, stepped forward, placed a stoutly sandaled foot on my neck.

"Thus do I conquer our enemies!" The foot twisted back and forth with what I was sure must be most of his weight behind it. The pain inflicted made hardly any impression.

He stepped away. "Stand!"

I didn't move.

"Stand!" he screamed. When I didn't respond. he screamed to one of his guards. Out of the corner of my eyes I could see an officer hand him a short leather whip. This he skillfully swung in an arc which slapped down on my naked back.

With a real yell of surprised pain I quickly allowed myself the luxury of standing. The whip struck across my mid-section, wrapping around in a painful snap.

With a satisfied grin, he tossed the whip back to the officer.

"That's better!" His manner abruptly changed. A glint of pleasure, almost friendliness welled in those dark eyes.

"Well, now!" he exclaimed in an expansive voice which easily reached everybody within the room. "This is the man who has caused such problems."

His beefy hands slapped his thighs. "One finds it hard to think of him as a man, considering the manner in which he now carries himself."

238

Silence met every statement. Obviously his officers were used to this little play.

"Tell me, warrior...no, I can hardly call you a warrior...for you whimper much too generously." He squeezed his face up in a mocking thought. "Korda would insult such a grand fighter. But...then, you did accomplish much for a— well, coward. How'd you do it?"

I ignored the question.

Aoji swaggered forward, his face thrust almost against mine. If my hands hadn't been tied it would have been a simple thing then to grab and overpower him. "How'd you free that slave-woman—the one they call Proctoress of Bel-loniea—out of this very tent? Kill three of my best warriors—steal a flyer?"

When I didn't answer, his right hand slapped across my face. "Speak, coward!"

"You have the wrong man!" I cried too loudly, hoping it sounded highly unconvincing.

"There was but one warrior reported with the woman! You were found with her. The slavers spoke highly of your fighting ability They called you Torlo Hannis. My informants say that a Torlo Hannis made a mysterious appearance in Bel-loniea not long before our attack upon the city. This Torlo Hannis, they claimed, was from off-world, like Andon Janis. You can be no other than this Torlo Hannis. Don't take me for a fool!"

"I'm from Kanns, a...mercenary. I but sold my services...the Bel-loniea. I'll sell you my services." I had allowed my voice to gain some strength, as if sure he would accept my offer.

His laughter rang out like some insane beast dying in agony.

"Such cowards we don't need!" he finally sneered, once control had returned. "Even a mercenary from Kanns cannot believe I'd hire a coward."

"I fight well," I announced in a small voice.

"You will die even better, Torlo Hannis," he fairly screamed. "That you are a coward...I can believe. That you are a man from Kanns, I won't accept. That you are a mercenary from this world I will not accept! That you stole Youi

Janis right out from under my swords, I do accept! What magic trickery might have been used, I will find out before you die in slow pain this very morning. Even a coward can show bravery when the odds are on his side—and obviously they were that night, for no one man, even a brave one, could have done what you did without magical help."

He turned, spoke to the officer still holding the whip. "Bring the Muti. He'll get my answers quickly enough, so that we can immediately deal out punishment to this man!" He faced me again. "A punishment which, I'll admit I have not as yet decided upon. How does one devise the most terrible form of death imaginable, overnight? But I'll think of something to start with."

He turned and stepped to his throne, sat down, arms resting in his lap.

Almost immediately a hooded figure stepped into the room, moved in front of me.

A shiver coursed through my body at the sight of the Muti face. The leathery purple skin pulled tight around the angular bones. Where eyes should have been were two skin-covered sockets. Above the thin slit mouth two holes served as nostrils over a flat expanse of flesh. I tried to remind myself what the first Muti had told me about not judging a man or creature by the outer shell, but to look deeper to see what was inside the surface. There were many indications that the Mutis were to some extent highly gentle, loving and dedicated to a life of giving fully of themselves. Their amazing, subtle power over the humans on Noomas was the only glaring inconsistency.

"Muti," Aoji swiftly instructed in a surprisingly respectful voice, "read this man—tell me what you learn."

The Muti placed a small, gnarled, bony hand on my forehead, then drew rapidly away, as if he'd been burned. Slowly he replaced the hand, and if the features had been able to show any real defined expression, I was sure they would have reflected horror.

240

CHAPTER TWENTY-EIGHT

THE MUTI'S WARNING

Twice before I had been confronted by a Muti, the second time it was very possibly this same one now before me. The sense of automatic revulsion was less each time, but still hung over me like an eerie shadow. There is a feeling of strange forces about a Muti; a sense of being nakedly exposed to a probing mind. This awareness is based on reality, for while the Muti has no eyes as we know them, it is able to move through the physical world as easily as a normal man, and can read minds as we read books.

Slowly the Muti lowered his head, then turned to Aoji.

"What is it you wish to know?"

I knew that no information about my thoughts, past or even future actions could be secret to the Muti. My charade would now be exposed.

"His name?"

"Torlo Hannis."

"Well, we were right!" Aoji's eyes swept around the room, then back to the Muti. "Is he the man who took the Bel-loniea Proctoress from us?"

"Yes!"

"How?"

"By freeing the other prisoners first, with the help of a man named Orra Jik. This served as a diversion for his activities. He bombed the camp from a flyer, using both Kay-pellets and Kay-bombs, to create the illusion that you were being attacked by a large force."

"Brilliant!" Aoji exclaimed.

"Then he crashed the flyer into one of your tents, while disembarking by a rope tossed over the side. He climbed down while the flyer was diving, then released his hold at the last moment."

"A sign of great daring!" Aoji voiced with delight.

"Then after killing all of your guards, he cut his way into a tent corridor, moved to where the two guards were standing outside your chambers in which the Proctoress was being held, then bluffed his way long enough to shoot them down."

"Remarkable cunning!" Aoji fairly snarled, eyes snapping in my direction.

"He shot your officer who was personally responsible for guarding the prisoner. They made their escape to the guarded flyers, posing as a drunken couple having a private celebration. The storm took them into the desert where they were captured by the band of Baji-Ney slavers and—."

"Enough! Enough!" Aoji screamed, standing. "Where did he get all this bravery? A drug?"

"No!" the Muti answered in a loud, angry voice. "You will not speak in such a manner to me."

Aoji cringed as if slapped. "I did not mean the anger for you!"

"You will listen well to what I have to say, Aoji—for I will say it but once." The Muti raised his arms high above his head. "I have looked into his mind, have seen his past, present and future—"

"Which shows him dead!" Aoji laughed, delighted.

"Silence!" the Muti bellowed.

Aoji's face turned deep red, and it was obvious that he restrained sudden anger. His temper submitted to the stark terror held for the Muti. Again I was impressed by the subtle strings of power that ebbed from the very shadows of the Mutis. That a man such as Aoji would reveal such total submission supplied even more evidence to the theory they held greater power on Noomas that anyone suspected. Yet they remained neutral to all conflicts between city-states.

The Muti continued, its voice hollow, rasping.

"Hear me well, Aoji. The words I speak are grounded on facts I read!" He moved a long arm in my direction. "The capture of this man and the woman will prove far more dramatic than you can imagine. If their release was possible, it would serve you well."

Aoji flew to his feet, face contorted with burning rage which took such possession of the man that for a moment it appeared he would attack the Muti with his bare hands.

"You suggest...I release them?" he fairly hissed out between tightly drawn lips.

"I but tell you it would serve your purpose in life far better if it were to happen that way."

A silence pressed into the room, accented by the sound of the heavy air that sucked in and out of Aoji's parted thick lips. It was a long time before he spoke.

"You drive me too far, Muti!" His voice was quiet, dangerous.

"I have seen what I have seen," the Muti countered, ignoring the man's fury. There was just the suggestion of contempt to the Muti's words.

"What have you seen!" Aoji now backed away, aware that he had pressed close to dangerous grounds with the Muti.

"I have seen what I have seen. The past becomes the cause for present events. These events now taking shape are in turn causes for new events. The future is locked—there is no escaping it. What makes a man is all that he has experienced from birth. This dictates his actions, and thus maps his future. What I have seen cannot be removed from the future any more than the past can be changed."

"What is it?" Aoji now sounded like a spoiled, frightened child to a master who held over him the power of life. "What have you seen?"

"Some things are better not revealed. It is enough to say that you are not able to release the man or woman, because of the kind of man you are. I but indicate it would be best for you if this were possible. But your own past has marked a present pattern which cannot be broken. Beware, Aoji! The hands of the Kaska have clutched their last victim. I tell you this and no more. Time is jealous, rightfully hiding its future events from such men as yourself. Nor can I reveal to you what would only be destructive for you to know. I have spoken."

With that, the Muti turned to me. Those eyeless sockets seeing in some alien fashion, studied my face. The Muti said in a soft voice which could not have carried far:

"Torlo Hannis, this is the second of three times we shall meet. I faced you that first night with horror, for I saw some of what is now revealed to me. Then the lines of the future had not reached as far as they do this day. I saw your return and indications of what might lay beyond this moment. Then, I did not know of our third meeting. That meeting will be under different circumstances, yet what takes place shall not be of either of our makings. Remember that a man's acts are a sum total of all that he is—the events he moves in are created by countless patterns crossing for the first and final time. I regret it will not be possible to avoid the crossing of our paths this third time. I have spoken."

He turned, as if to leave, then faced me one last time. "Take care, for dangers lie before you; dangers which offer death. I can not extrapolate further, for my own vision and ability to read the future is blocked—a wall cuts me from any far-reaching conclusions. At our next meeting you will understand."

With that he walked out of the room of cloth walls, leaving a stunned audience behind; none more mystified than myself.

Almost immediately after the Muti's exit, Aoji turned to his officers, screamed in that child's voice: "Get this creature out of my sight! Feed him nothing. Keep him fully bound, under a large unit guard! See that nobody sees him! Allow only one ration of water per day! Take him away—then leave me—all of you!"

He sat and gazed at the place where the Muti had disappeared. Then suddenly he leaped to his feet. "Get the Commander of Spies. I would learn the progress of Romos' armies!"

I was taken out of the room, then from the tent. The escort of guards was careful not to touch me, as if a new respect had changed their attitude—or motivated by some element of terror and awe because of the Muti's words. I made

244

no effort to continue my cowardly mercenary charade, but walked erect, proud and alert.

I was taken to a small tent, where they securely bound my legs behind me to the leather thongs about my wrists. In such a position it was impossible to do more than lie on my side, head awkwardly cocked against the ground. The tent was surrounded by twenty armed guards, which formed a solid wall of human flesh across any possible escape route, as if it were possible to make an attempt.

The Muti's words continued to ring in my ears, as puzzling and mystifying as they seemed fantastic. What harm could I do to Aoji? Yet every statement a Muti had made had, so far, come true.

Even when darkness fell, all my thoughts centered on attempts to understand the Muti's words.

They had promised nothing. Their message revealed some subtle danger to Aoji because he held us prisoners. Then there was the future meeting between the Muti and myself. Yet there had been something about this third meeting which sounded ominous. He had implied that each of us would be guiltless of what was to follow. There had been the suggestion of danger about the meeting—but it seemed more centered upon the Muti.

Helpless though I was, unable to imagine any future which could offer a means of escape or hope for Youi Janis, a sense of expectancy underlined my mood. I argued that the future could not be pre-set by any past or present acts, wanting to believe there was always a choice where human strength or weakness would decide an issue. I fought against the words of Qui Shan, when he had explained the Mutis' power of reading the future. He'd claimed that even alternate choices were part of the pattern. I told myself there was more than one way to add two and two in order to get four. The conviction of this theory, oddly enough, brought back the depressive mood. If there were alternate futures, then this could work against me. Also the Muti had not claimed I would live, nor had he suggested I might escape with Youi Janis. His statements had been warnings to Aoji; the rest seemed to concern himself more than my own future. Did I form some physical threat to him? I could not escape this

245

conclusion as the explanation of his attitude and words to me.

Sleep finally gave rest to all thoughts. The next morning camp was broken early and the Diano forces were quick to take on an orderly formation. The guards tied a rope about my neck and then freed my legs. The long day went slowly by with only a short break for mid-meal—which for myself consisted of a few swallows of water. By nightfall, I was exhausted from lack of food. The combined strain of the days in the desert and this final torture without food drained all strength. By the time they once more tied and left me in a small tent I was too tired to even think about the questionable future.

The next day it must have been obvious even to my guards that I could not last long without food. They handled me a little more gently, when binding my legs, and that night didn't make any effort to tighten the leather ropes.

I had fallen asleep almost immediately on this third night of captivity with the Diano. What seemed but a moment later, and could not have been long, a hand touched my shoulder.

"Warrior. Wake up!" a gruff voice demanded.

I was too tired to even be annoyed by this interruption in sleep.

Several guards were crowded in the tent, the man leaning over me was dressed in finely woven cloth that covered him from neck to ankles, a star was embossed over his right breast, indicating the rank of doctor.

"You did well," the man announced to another to my right. "He can't last much longer. Whatever he went through before his capture has brought on almost total physical exhaustion. The human body can take only so much punishment. I'll report to Aoji, immediately."

The man left.

One of the guards said: "It won't do good to starve him to death! That's why I reported to the medical man."

An officer leaned down over me, his face masked all expression; but there was no hatred in his eyes.

"We are not all like our leaders. War does terrible things to men. National loyalty comes before all other con-

246

siderations. Though you are an enemy, I feel respect for you. The deeds you accomplished were brave; even though against our commanding officer and Proctor II of Diano. We mercenaries can respect the brave. It is a shame you are with the enemy instead of on our side." His statement was surprising, but later when I thought it over the words were not out of character for a warrior mercenary of Noomas. One thing is constant among these fighting men: respect for bravery, honor for a good fighting man.

I weakly asked the question which Rha-Ney had put to me. "What makes you mercenaries?"

"Why would you ask that, being a mercenary?"

I managed a bland grin, revealing nothing. "Act as if I were a stranger on Noomas—for I remember little of my past."

The officer stared blankly at me for a moment, then shrugged, grinning toothily. "Many things. Some of us are killers at heart, some are running from dishonor in their own lands—or their families were stripped of honor through no fault of their own. Some had tragic personal experiences and seek escape from either responsibility, memory or whatever makes them run. Some like the challenge of a good fight—some are trying to prove themselves men, because of a demanding father.

"There are as many reasons as there are mercenaries, each carrying their secret motivations within themselves. There are even those who just like the life of adventure, going from city to city. Some are commoners who would never have a chance of advancement because of the social structure of their home nation. A mercenary is nothing more than a man searching for something in life. They are in most cases not much different than other men—except for the means of discovering a solution to their problems." He broke off. "Enough of this. Come, men, we must leave. Aoji would not approve of our talking to him."

They left, and I lay there thinking about what had been said. Obviously these hard-fighting men were not above a sense of humanity. The picture of the mercenary which the officer had presented was hardly different than I had imagined that one time when shattered by the realization that Youi Janis was rejecting all advances of love from me.

Sleep returned and was broken only by the sounds of camp breaking up.

One of the guards came into my tent, untied my hands, presented me with a hard Mio-stick. "Aoji's orders are to keep you alive for such time as he has decided what form your death will take."

He watched as I ate, then tied my hands in front of me.

This and the next day I was fed three Mio-sticks, one in the morning, midday and night.

Strength returned quickly, though I was losing weight. The leather which bound my wrists had become loosened. When the guards made casual examinations of these bonds, I managed to make them appear tighter than they were by lightly flexing all arm muscles. But each night I struggled for a long time to loosen the bonds. It could only be a matter of time before I would slip out of the leather straps. This possessed me totally on my sixth night of captivity. The food substance of which the Mio-stick is made has amazing powers of restoring the body strength. Later I learned that they contain the youth drug which made possible an extension of life up to almost a thousand Federation years if taken in a man's daily diet.

It was on this sixth night that the bonds seemed on the verge of releasing their hold, and hope formed. I was working my right wrist against the leather when suddenly a unit of warriors marched up to the tent. I stopped just as two guards stepped in.

"Aoji has summoned you!" one announced harshly.

I stood and followed them out, where the warrior unit formed around me.

There was a quiet upon the men, and I guessed Aoji had decided upon my fate. We marched across camp, through the thickly grown trees of the lower mountain forest. Finally the escort drew up in front of a large tree-lined, rocky area which held Aoji's quarters. I had been gently working free of the bonds about my wrists; but this seemed a mock-

248

ery. Even free and armed, what could I accomplish, one man alone against a whole army?

CHAPTER TWENTY-NINE

A MAN WITHOUT HONOR!

The area surrounding the huge tent was crowded with more than a hundred officers. Banquet tables had been placed along the edge of the clearing. In front of the tent was the throne chair upon which Aoji sat like some savage warrior demon. On the ground at his feet sat Youi Janis, silvery irons around her wrists, a plain tavern girl's gown draped loosely about her body.

"Bring him forward!" Aoji cried upon seeing my escort. Behind the son of the Proctor of Diano stood a hooded figure. The Muti.

This was to be the third and final meeting of which the Muti had spoken. My senses became immediately alert.

Youi looked in my direction and the expression on her face was tense with emotion and strain.

I refused to believe she could be my half-sister. No ungodly mockery could create such an inhuman situation where a man would fall so desperately in love with his own half-sister. There had to be some other explanation. This conviction was so strong that I became momentarily convinced it was motivated by some subconscious knowledge.

Then my eyes turned to Aoji. He appeared to have been drinking a lot, but when he spoke there was no indication that it physically affected him. The hateful expression in his small eyes leveled at me.

"Have the guests brought forward!" Aoji cried in a voice thick with amusement.

As I was brought to a halt in front of Aoji, guards at either side, I believe his comment concerned me.

Then out of the corner of my eyes I saw two yellow-robed slavers. The second recognition came as the two figures approached closer to stand at my side. I turned to face Baji-Ney and his son, Rha-Ney,.

Aoji leered at the two slavers, his features creased with gloating pleasure.

"Well, now, aren't you glad you made the trip, my two friends of the desert?" He directed his statement towards Baji-Ney.

The desert clan leader shrugged. "You offered a fair price for the slaves we had—the bonus of a celebration and exciting entertainment, a feast of three days, all the drink a man might wish, the use of your tavern girls for my men."

He indicated me with a wave of his hand. "As to this...well, it explains much—for you are one to rob us desert folks when it is within your power...the temptations of your grand and generous offer had to be tainted with some ulterior motive. I am only surprised to see the two of them alive."

"One will not be living to see the next day!" Aoji laughed.

"For that I am sorry this is the way the Gods have written his end," Baji-Ney countered. "He is an honorable fighter. His only fault is not being of the desert clans."

Aoji's face contorted. "Yet you were furious to learn they had tricked you. Your curses were directed to the Gods. Your wishes have come true."

"I but cursed their dead bodies. I cursed the Gods because we did not know their true identities. I have no anger against these two who were smart enough to continue to survive even when the fury of the desert storm ravaged our lands."

Baji-Ney shrugged again. "But as you said, he will be dead before morning. It is so written, then. There is nothing that can be done to change what must happen. So we of the desert believe. We accept."

"Enough!" Aoji cried. "I wish entertainment."

He slapped his hands together, sat back against the throne, grabbed a goblet held by an officer at his side. Liquor slopped down his face.

I said to Baji-Ney, "I am glad your son lives."

251

Baji-Ney nodded. "I am sorry that you have fallen into the wrong hands. But...don't give up hope, yet."

Rha-Ney slipped quickly close, hissed under his breath, lips touching my ears: "Romos comes within the Unit. Survive."

Then in a loud curse he cried: "The Diano wishes to gloat! He but mocks us. He says we are fools with every word." Then facing me, he added: "But know, Torlo Hannis, I will enjoy your death, for you deceived us. I am not my father!"

Aoji frowned. "Quiet. I grow eager for death."

Baji-Ney bowed. "We are in your service." There was something about Baji-Ney's voice which struck me as threatening, but Aoji did not seem to notice.

At that point a giant man stepped up to the throne. His head was bald, shining greasily, large greenish eyes bulged from a round, muscular face. Lips pulled back to reveal sharp, pointed teeth. The man's shoulders, arms, chest and stomach were a mass of huge rippling muscles. He was dressed in a gleaming red loin-cloth, belted in the middle by a spiked leather strap. On his huge fists were heavy metal rings, in which were set jagged slivers of glass-like jewels. He was a walking instrument of death. I could not imagine a normal warrior defeating him.

Aoji stood, patted his giant's shoulder. "This is Tor, who has served me well in giving entertainment fit for Royalty. He has gone up against twenty men at a time, killing them all with his metal rings and spiked harness. I have never seen him so much as hurt in such an encounter. I have decided to use his skill in entertaining us with the killing of two slaves. To demonstrate his ability and to allow him to work off some of the pent up anxiety, I believe it would be in order to have an immediate demonstration with another slave—before the main event."

Aoji laughed while making a nervous motion with is right hand.

I was pulled to one side and all eyes turned to Tor, who stepped forward to the middle of the clearing.

"Where's the slave?" Tor bellowed in a deep-throated, roaring voice.

252

A man about my size and build, armed with a small club, was pushed into the clearing by two guards. A roar of laughter sounded as he clambered to his feet, trembling with terror. He turned and faced the giant, Tor, who stood a head taller and almost twice as wide.

Aoji cried: "Tor, kill this one fast—we don't want to wear you out!"

Laughter met his statement.

The giant grunted, his huge pop-eyes glared with violent pleasure. He waited for the doomed warrior to approach. The other man visibly trembled, yet he stepped forward. There wasn't anything left for him other than to die as honorably as possible, and he knew it. Who could be a match for such a man?

I watched Tor, hoping to see some defect in his tactics that might be used against him.

The giant crouched slightly, legs bent, arms dangling at his sides, huge hands clawed. As the warrior came close, club-arm cocked, ready to snap out in attack, Tor made a quick back-handed move with his left arm. The blow connected with the club, snapping it in two. Another swing landed on the other's head, knocking him down with such force that the impact of his body against the ground made a loud thud.

The man attempted to get to his feet, but was obviously too dazed by the blow. Tor leaped easily forward, grabbed the poor fellow's body and lifted it high in the air, then with a mighty grunt he threw the other forcefully to the ground.

The snapping of bones cracked loud.

Tor picked up the limp form by the legs, spun around and around, swinging the body in a wide circle. Then he released the unconscious body; it shot toward a large boulder a short distance away. The popping sound of his head smashing against stone sent a shiver through me.

Youi had covered her face with trembling hands.

Aoji rose, a wide grin on his fat face, lips opening over thick teeth. "Well done, my friend. Now I believe we are ready for the main event. How do you want to fight this man?" He pointed toward me.

253

Tor shot a glance in my direction. "Give him a sword. I want a challenge."

A roar of laughter burst from the warrior audience. Aoji patted the giant's shoulder.

"Bring the prisoner forward, arm him with a sword of great strength, with the sharpness of razors. And my good Tor, if you make this man suffer greatly, I will reward you with the female slave woman they call Proctoress of Belloniea."

Youi Janis turned ashen. I felt convulsive sickness eat at the pit of my stomach. Aoji couldn't have designed a greater insult or cruelty.

Aoji grinned. "If she lives after you, my good friend, what's left of her will be given to the officers and warriors, and later to the slaves of slaves."

He turned and faced Youi Janis, his eyebrows drew tightly together, eyes blazed hatred. "You turned me down twice, slave-woman, once by your words, then by your escape. Aoji is never turned down twice! Before the night is up you'll wish you'd embraced me, for life could have been pleasant as one of my slave-women; a life of luxury. My favorites are rewarded with gifts, good food, lovely clothing and quarters—even slaves. This you turned down, and now you will learn the full punishment of gaining Aoji's hatred."

I was shoved forward, handed a sword, hands still apparently bound.

Controlling the rage in my own voice, I asked: "And if I kill this man—what will be my reward?"

The question took Aoji totally by surprise. He jerked around as if slapped. For a moment it was hard to guess what he might do next. Then a slow grin opened his lips. There were several chuckles from the men around us.

"If you kill this man...what would be a fitting reward?" His voice was a mockery.

"The woman called Youi Janis and our freedom to return to her country." I was going through this charade in the hopes of merely gaining time. Rha-Ney's whispered words offered the only true hope of survival.

"A fitting reward, I must admit," Aoji announced, his face a mass of grinning wrinkles. Apparently this game pleased him.

"A fitting reward. The winner to get the woman; interesting idea." His laughter bellowed loudly, was taken up by most of his men. "Why should I offer this to you?"

"Because you know it is impossible for me to kill this man!" I pointed out. "And if you don't make such an offer under these circumstances you stand as a man without honor."

"And that is your reason for asking? Not because you believe you can win, but to prove me dishonorable?" His voice still held humor, though now a little strained.

"Which is exactly what you are," I retorted. "Without honor!"

His face went livid with quick rage. "How dare you!"

"I dare to call you a Korda who wars only against helpless woman, behind the swords of bought men, too cowardly to fight your own battles. You have defenseless men fight against this creature you call Tor. If you were not a coward you would fight your own battles. You would draw your sword now and engage me in an honest, honorable duel, the winner to have the woman."

His mood changed from rage to amusement with lightning swiftness. "You don't call me a coward, but suggest that I am a fool! What would I gain in such a duel?"

"The satisfaction that you were the one who killed me. Man against man." A glance at Youi revealed she must think me totally mad, for obviously Aoji was not about to enter into such a match. "Muscle against muscle. Skill against skill. The honor of proving yourself a great warrior, able to stand up against all others. That's what you'd prove! You'd be showing those who follow you that you've got the guts to enforce your leadership and win followers because they admire the man, not his Proctors Tokens."

"Such do the desert men speak. You are a fool. I'm a realist. The heroes are the winners. The cowards and villains are those who are conquered. There is only honor in winning. The winner writes history to suit himself."

"To win a battle is not to win a war. To defeat men who are helpless is not to even win a battle. You but show yourself as a coward, and rationalize to save face. But nobody here is really fooled. These men present all know the truth, for they are professional warriors who will fight against others in honorable combat. They know I speak the truth!"

For a moment there was a little doubt that Aoji was about to leap at me. His right hand reached for his sword, drew it half out of the sheath, then suddenly released it. The raging face relaxed, then smiled.

"You bait me to fool's plays. To kill such as you, who holds no honors, who is already defeated and captive, a mere warrior without Royal status, would not be honorable, only murder. I've had enough of this. We'll begin immediately."

Hoping to kill more time before entering into a battle from which it would be impossible to survive unless help came to stop it, I said: "You have avoided the question, Aoji."

He was in the process of sitting down, and froze in midair. "I've avoid nothing!"

"If I kill Tor, will freedom and the woman be mine?"

Laughter fluttered from the Diano warriors.

Now even Aoji grinned. "You surely believe you can kill him?"

"I know nothing. What is written in our past and this present will create the future. I but wish to make the point that you are a man without honor."

256

CHAPTER THIRTY

"KILL HIM!"

Silence became heavy, flat. Aoji's eyes flashed around the clearing. Then he laughed again with even greater humor, but there was a nervous ring to it.

"Yes, yes. By all means. If you survive to live this day out, the woman and freedom will be yours, warrior!"

"And will I survive if I kill this man?" I pushed, aware that his choice of words promised nothing.

He frowned, then grinned again, lips pulling into thin strained lines. "If you kill this man you will have what I've promised."

"My life and the woman's life and freedom?" I demanded.

"What would you have me say?" he screamed. "Begin!"

An officer stepped to my side to cut the leather thongs. I shoved him away with my now free right hand which held the sword. All that effort to escape the bonds had served only as a mockery. Yet a gasp of surprise came from those around.

I stepped toward Tor, immediately, intent on two things: If possible to kill the man right off, if not, to avoid death.

I hoped that surprise would work on my side.

I swung at Tor's head. The giant moved with a swiftness which proved that size has nothing to do with speed. My sword point cut through empty air.

A shout of approval came from scores of Diano voices.

Tor faced me, his features twisted in fury by the un-announced attack.

Instead of retreating as might have been reasonable. I moved in closer, sword point weaving in and out, just missing the fast-moving man. The attack surprised everyone present; Tor most of all. He was used to men trembling in fear of his great strength. Perhaps this was his greatest weapon against any warrior. Yet I knew it was not possible to defeat him; he surely wouldn't have allowed me a sword if he thought there was any danger of being killed.

In the next moments he proved the reason for his confidence. His movements were extremely fast and would have been graceful even for a smaller man. Because of his large size he could move greater distances with each step.

Then, just as I was about to give up this line of attack, Tor stood his ground. Instantly I lunged, the point darting for his exposed chest.

Tor waited until the sword had almost reached its mark, then jerked to the left. His right fist armed with the metal rings, rammed down on the sword's blade.

The snapping sound of metal was the only indication I had that the blade was broken, for Tor's other arm slapped out, back-handedly hitting the side of my head. I was knocked half way across the clearing.

Stunned, I tried to stand. A screaming buzzed in my ears, vision was only a blurred sensation of light.

Unable to stand, I rolled away from the direction of Tor's approach.

A sound of surprise announced that I had just barely escaped Tor.

Thoughts settled into a firm pattern, the dizziness lifted. I managed to slowly stand. Vision revealed a gigantic shape lunging forward.

Then something swung from the left. I ducked. Wind breathed through my hair.

Instinctively I attempted to strike the only target which might disable Tor. My right fist slammed up between his legs, driving with brutal force. Instead of hurting the man, my blow connected with hard metal.

Agonized, hand numbed, I crumbled to the ground, rolled away, stood, face the grinning Tor who now turned to attack.

Aoji laughed from his throne. "You speak of honor, but attempt a dishonorable blow!"

I ignored the remark in order to avoid Tor. He leaped, both hands slapping together where my head had been. I struck the edge of my hand on the side of his neck. A normal man would have been stopped by such a blow. Tor merely jerked to one side, surprised, but hardly hurt. His muscles armored the huge body like steel plates.

Repeated blows at the same spot might injure Tor, but probably would fail to defeat him. Yet I decided to center all efforts on this area.

He lunged, left hand feinted, right came up at my face.

All I could do was move against his left hand to avoid the more dangerous blow. At the same time I struck at his neck again, then slipped away, hurt by the jagged stones in his knuckle rings.

He came in, swung, the metal rings dug deep at my right shoulder. Falling back, I hit the ground, the wind knocked out of me.

The feeling of something cold and hard at my side caught immediate attention; my fingers discovered the hard metal shape of a sword blade. It was the broken point, about the length of a man's forearm. Taking it, I swung the blade upwards as Tor reached out to grab me.

The point slashed through his right hand.

With a scream of rage and pain he retreated holding his bloody hand.

I came to my feet, rushed in to attack, ignoring the sharp edges of the blade which cut the palm of my hand.

Tor met me open-armed, then I felt the crushing power of his embrace as it folded painfully around my body before it was possible to bring the blade into play. Somehow he had skillfully avoided the blade's point.

The spiked belt dug at my harness; it was the only thing which saved me from serious wounds; but the pressure closing in around my body like a metal vise would soon break bones and press the spikes through the tough leather harness.

Screaming out in agony, I attempted to use the bloodied blade to some advantage, but my arms were pinned down. I moved the blade, bringing the edge against Tor's left side. Spinning in dizzy pain, I struggled to slice the razor-sharp blade through flesh and muscle.

The squeezing pressure about my body was creating a terrible agony which ripped up through nerves and mind. The world spun in black throbbing pain. Thoughts screaming, swimming in total awareness of death so close, suddenly broke through the memory barrier.

I saw a fleeting figure of a man whom I called father; but the face had an angular bone-structure, probing sharp blue eyes, black curly hair; the body was pressed into the uniform of a high-ranking Space Force officer. The image flashed away in a childish image of a small spaceship toy exploding against a black screen of starless space. This was replaced by the shape of a red-headed woman huddled against a window, sobbing, holding a video-wire crumpled in her hands. The image of another man formed, but faded as the whole memory sequence disappeared.

Death was crushing my chest.

Remembrance of the blade in my right hand brought reality into sharp focus.

I struggled to saw the blade against Tor's side.

A yell of startled pain sounded from above, then Tor's arms released me enough to make it possible to swing away from him. I struck the ground hard, numbing my right shoulder.

I swung the blade to my left hand, throwing it forward, but Tor saw it coming and ducked.

A sudden shout of surprise came from behind the giant and everybody turned to see the Diano Muti clutch his chest where the blade now protruded. In that instant I knew what the Muti had seen in the future: his own death.

The effect on all present to the Muti's slow death-struggle was an amazing tribute to these creatures. Nobody moved. They seemed paralyzed.

This was my chance. A short distance away was the other half of the sword, its blade snapped at a slight angle. In a whirl of action I stood, grabbed it, then rushed Tor, who, like the others, was staring at the now dead Muti, mouth open in amazement.

Why I yelled in warning, I don't know. It didn't make much sense, since there was little chance of killing the giant if he could defend himself. Yet I hated striking down any man from behind.

He whipped around. My left hand smashed out, thrusting the blade deep into his stomach, clear to the hilt.

His face gasped in one surprised breath, then he slumped to the hard-packed ground, clutching at his bloody guts. A moan trembled from his throat, then he died.

Killing an unarmed man in this manner might not seem the top form of honor, but to do otherwise would have been suicidal. The match had been to his advantage, regardless of the fact I had the sword. I felt more like an executioner than killer.

Aoji screamed to his feet. "Kill him!"

Baji-Ney stepped from the ring of warriors. "You promised freedom for him and the woman if he killed Tor! Honor demands that you keep this promise!"

Aoji glared at Baji-Ney. "Don't push me, slaver."

Rha-Ney moved to his father's side, Kay-gun in his right hand. "You have promised. No man here will believe your word if you do not keep this promise."

Aoji looked at the two desert clansmen, then turned and stared at his officers The stony expressions on their faces revealed the harsh truth of Rha-Ney's words.

Baji-Ney whispered to me, "Get out of here, first chance. Forget the woman. She'll be safe for the time."

Aoji shrugged. "It shall be as you say. They are free to go as promised."

Rha-Ney holstered his Kay-gun, then said to me: "The debt of honor is repaid, Torlo Hannis."

Aoji had made a quick move to his right hand towards a group of officers who immediately drew their Kay-guns, leveling them at the three of us.

"But," Aoji announced with a taunting grin, "there is the matter of our Muti. No man kills a Muti without the punishment of slow death. For that I find it necessary to detain him."

A coldness grew hard in his eyes. "As for the two of you, I'll make you wish you'd never spoken against the son of a Royal Proctor. Your deaths will match that of this Torlo Hannis. Take them!"

Almost at the same time the Diano warriors started forward the sound of Kay-bomb explosions came from the south.

Aoji cried in surprise. All of the Diano warriors turned toward the sounds of conflict which immediately surged into being.

"Your sword!" I cried to Rha-Ney, taking the hilt and drawing the blade strapped to his side.

Immediately the two desert men went into action, Rha-Ney firing the Kay-gun, his father drawing both gun and sword.

I didn't consider our chances of surviving as being very good, but hoped for only one thing: to kill Aoji before he could recover from his surprise.

I'd covered half the distance to Aoji when two of his officers sprang between us. Rha-Ney shot the one to the right, while my sword engaged the other.

Skills learned while training as a warrior in Belloniea, plus some which I now knew had been learned in training as an officer in the Federation Space Force, served me well. In three short exchanges my blade found the other's heart, then leaped out.

Aoji was grabbing Youi Janis, starting to pull her away from the field of battle.

Diano warriors were now closing in on the three of us. The position seemed hopeless until the sound of war-cries came from close by.

Rha-Ney cried: "Our men!"

Immediately the clearing was filled by yellow-robed desert warriors.

I didn't take the time to even wonder about this. Somehow Baji-Ney and his tribe of desert nomads were fighting in our defense; that was enough.

I fought through the surrounding Diano, determined to get at Aoji who disappeared around the side of his tent with Youi Janis.

Several Diano warriors quickly fell before my blade, then all at once there was clear escape route.

In the confusion of this surprise attack, the Diano forces were totally demoralized, unaware of their leader's retreat.

I rushed around the tent to discover Aoji running toward a large, unmanned flyer parked a short distance away.

"Aoji!" I called, as he was entering the flyer, dragging Youi after him.

He turned, face white. Then he pushed Youi Janis away, whipped out his sword and leaped forward as I rushed close.

It never occurred to me that he might be an expert swordsman. But in the first moments of the duel, I realized that he was a master.

My own skill was highly questionable, having been learned first during the Space Federation training, because many societies on the countless planets were a strangely perverted mixture of modern and primitive, and then by Gora, Romos' top instructor for the Special Corps of Bel-loniea.

From the very beginning I was forced to take the defensive, unable to do more than keep beyond reach of the other blade. Aoji moved forward with repeated thrusts, cuts and lunges.

I decided to play a careful retreating game on the hope that he would tire physically. He weighed at least twice as much as myself. Almost from the beginning he was breathing heavily. His body was closed in by finely woven cloth; mine was free to the night air. He had been drinking and eating heavily, I had subsisted on barely any food for days.

I kept moving away from his weaving sword. My feet danced swiftly back, to the side, swiftly circled, always far enough away so that he was forced to chase me almost at a half run.

Abruptly Aoji became aware of my tactics. Sweat was covering his face, the breath sucked in his lungs.

He came to a stop, sword thrust forward. "Come! Stand still, coward!"

Aoji edged back toward the ship. There was no choice but to move in. For the first time since we had begun the duel, I took the offensive. My sword wove through a series of swift attacks, which he blocked with amazing ease.

Then I felt the sting of his sword's point touch into my right shoulder. It whipped out again, cut diagonally. I leaped back just in time to avoid instant death.

The next moment Aoji's blade surged out like a whip, touching my body again and again, creating a series of small bloody cuts. He was skillfully slicing me to pieces and there seemed nothing I could do to stop him. Now it was obvious he'd been playing a teasing game before.

Leaping back, away from this sword point, I tried to buy time in hopes of finding some way to kill the man.

Aoji pushed in close, a tight grin contorting his face, eyes now coldly confident. "Time has run out, warrior. The game is over." He lunged with arm extended to its fullest. "You die!"

The sword moved in, its point circled around my blade, then slipped through toward my exposed chest.

If I had done anything other than step into his attack, darting to the left, his blade would have run through my heart.

I swung my sword downwards, aimed at his neck and shoulders. Then agonized pain ripped into being as his sword drove to the hilt through my right side.

The world spun, blacked out, then the ground under my feet seemed to vanish; after that came nothingness.

CHAPTER THIRTY-ONE

DAL SORLA

The miracle of life is that it can suffer great misuse and punishment without releasing its hold upon the physical body. By all logic I should have been killed by Aoji; or at least died from the sword wound inflicted by his final lunge, which had passed through my left side, just missing by a fraction any vital organ.

There was a vague awareness of voices, of movement and the passage of time; but nothing more. The next real knowledge of living came upon my returning to consciousness in a small room. Overhead, on the ceiling, was a colorful pattern of lacy designs which were startlingly familiar. For a moment it was difficult to realize why. Then as the deep fog of unconsciousness slipped away I knew where the room was.

This was the same place I had first awakened on Noomas, a nursing quarters in the palace of Romos, Proctor of Bel-loniea.

A face came into view, beautiful, delicate. The oval, high cheek-boned face was framed by long black hair which flowed down to creamy white shoulders. The large, dark eyes welled with emotion, the wide, sensual mouth parted into a generous smile.

A man's voice which I immediately recognized, asked: "How's he look?"

"Wonderful, grandfather," Youi Janis announced happily.

The heavy footsteps of Romos, Proctor of Bel-loniea sounded, then I saw his youthful features—still those of a young-looking middle-aged man, though he was well past 500 years old. His angular, brooding features took on a look of pride and gentleness. He was dressed in a simple red gown which draped from shoulder to ankles, laced with patterns of gold. There was no sign of his office, or any weapons strapped to his belted middle.

"I won't take any more time than necessary, young man. But I wanted to be here when they revived you. Enough to say that I left our vast forces which are returning home, in order to personally thank you for what you've done. It is enough to say that there will be high honors and riches bestowed upon you.

"Youi Janis has indicated that you wish to serve her, thereby, I now state before the witness of this woman, my granddaughter and her father, my son-in-law, that you will be her personal guardian, responsible for her safety, in charge of all and any officers and men assigned to this purpose. Such details will be made public in a proper ceremony of state, once you are completely well.

"It is enough to state here that you have served your adopted Proctor and country in a manner which can never be fully rewarded by mere honors and grants and titles. My personal thanks will grant you audience with the Proctor of Belloniea at any time of day or night at your mere spoken desire, for any purpose, regardless of how unimportant for as long as either of us live. Only a few persons have this right. All else is mere Honors of State." With that he touched my right shoulder. "I call you friend of Romos."

Then in a quick change of mood, he stated: "I must be going. Keep him in good health, Andon Janis. Nurse him well, Youi."

With that he left.

I was too dazed from the long sleep to have fully taken in the implications of the Proctor's words, or the high honor he had given by merely being there upon my revival.

The next thing I realized, Youi Janis was standing at the bedside, her hand clutching mine. Then an elderly man stepped up, looked down with kindly eyes. The head was hairless, except for a white fringe around the temples. A pointed white beard and thin mustache accented the startling

266

image of age. On Noomas such signs of age are exceptional. Andon Janis had said he was past thirty when arriving on Noomas, so the youth drug had taken longer to do its work. But he would live for another two or three hundred years.

In the Federation language, he said: "You have spoken some of your past life, Torlo Hannis." His words were subtly shaded, hiding all emotion. "She knows nothing...since your words were spoken in this language."

Sudden realization struck me. I sat up, too startled to realize there was only a slight pain at my right side.

I looked at Youi Janis, quick depression gnawing at my mind.

Andon Janis continued in the Federation language. "You spoke of Dal Sorla."

"What does that mean to you?" I fired back.

"If you mean, is it of some importance to Andon Janis, the answer is no. To Dal Sorla it would certainly mean something, wouldn't it?"

I stared back, trying to puzzle out the words. My brain was still fuzzy from what had been a long recovery period.

Youi Janis broke into the conversation. "I don't think it's nice for you to continue on like that, while I stand by unable to understand your words."

We both turned. I was almost glad for the interruption. Until such time that Andon Janis revealed his identity to be Dal Sorla, I could at least make believe that Youi was not my half-sister.

"What's happened?" I asked Youi Janis. "Since I passed out?"

"Your sword killed Aoji. The battle was going on in a greatly disorganized fashion on the Diano side. Rha-Ney had followed as soon as he was able, and with his help you were put in the Diano flyer. It was a big ship, luckily unmanned. Once Baji-Ney and his warriors had defeated the immediate Diano forces, they joined us, and it was an easy matter to fly the ship, since the controls are much the same as the smaller flyers.

"We left the immediate area and were able to join Romos' forces without any difficulty. The rest is simple.

With an escort we were flown back to Bel-loniea. Father has worked over you for three ten-day periods. Since Romos has defeated the Diano, his armies are on their way home. There will be great celebrations when they return in a few days."

All the time she spoke, her hand clutched mine in a very unsisterly fashion. I let myself enjoy this to the fullest extent. Andon glanced down at our hands. A concerned expression clouded his kindly wise features. He said nothing.

"What about Baji-Ney and his son. Why'd they—"

Her light, amused laughter broke off my question. In a musical voice she answered the unfinished question: "Baji-Ney was furious to discover the vast fortunes he'd lost. When Aoji sent a messenger to him, inviting his tribe to sell their slaves at a higher price and join a celebration, he guessed what had happened, knowing Aoji was not friendly with the desert clans. There could be only one reason for such an invitation: Aoji had recaptured either one or both of us, and wanted the pleasure of gloating."

"Baji-Ney did the obvious," Andon Janis put in. "There was no reward forthcoming in selling the Bel-loniea Proctoress to the Diano—they already had her—but there was a great profit in telling Romos. He had been convinced Youi was dead from the reports sent out. When he learned the truth, and that she was probably in Aoji's hands, Romos made immediate plans to attack, gathered our armies for one mighty thrust against the Diano.

"The storm had stopped all movement of our plans for counterattack—but now every man, woman and child in Bel-loniea moved to make possible an all-out encounter with Aoji's army. Baji-Ney revealed that the Diano were in the lower mountain regions, where surprise attack might be possible during the first night of celebrations. Romos paid him a vast fortune for the services of his men in this effort, since he would be in a position to attack from within. Baji-Ney still felt a sense of duty towards you for not having killed Rha-Ney, so he could with honor, within their strict code, join Romos.

"Baji-Ney had learned to like and respect you, and now jumped at the chance to save your life. Complications came when Aoji announced his decision to have you killed on the first day of celebrations, rather than keeping it for the last night as custom should have dictated."

Youi looked from her father to me. "Romos has announced publicly what he has told you. It is as you wished, Torlo Hannis, personal guardian to the Bel-loniea Proctoress, and all Royal status which goes with that position of honor."

I stared blankly back. My glance swept Andon Janis, then returned to Youi. She was leaning eagerly forward, eyes bright, lips half-parted. Her fingers squeezed mine, meaningfully.

She finally said in a hesitant voice, when the silence had become too oppressive: "You deserve even greater rewards, Torlo Hannis. You have earned all that the Bel-loniea nation has to offer."

There was no question about her meaning. Her words offered the Bel-loniea Proctoress. But instead of joy at them, I felt a great sense of total defeat choke me.

The minute the words were spoken, she released my hand, stepped back, startled by my silence. Her face showed sudden alarm as the silence continued. What could I say? Then she suddenly turned, rushed for the door.

Andon Janis called out: "Wait, Youi!"

His voice was harsh with command. She stopped. "There are some things that have to be explained," he announced. "Come back. Act like an adult, a Proctoress, not a little spoiled child!"

His face was stern as it turned to me. Youi came to his side, but remained at a distance from the bed. Her eyes revealed no emotion. My silence had shocked and hurt her deeply. How I had wanted to speak words of love, say what she wanted to hear. Life seemed meaningless.

Andon Janis now spoke in the Federation language. "You mentioned Dal Sorla. You revealed other things. Your true name, Jan Sorla, for one. You spoke of love for my daughter." The statements snapped from his thin lips like Kay-pellets exploding against a stone wall. His expression revealed nothing.

"I came to find Dal Sorla," was my only comment.

"Oh, yes. Dal Sorla. I had almost forgotten that name. Strange how time and circumstances will blur memory of the past. I should have guessed from the beginning who you were, and what your purpose must be. After all, two men landing on the same planet in the same area within a century! Rather fantastic. But, yes. Dal Sorla. A man who was a doctor of some reputation, who was husband to a woman who died on this planet shortly after our crash landing. But he had little money or position in that Galactic Federation. Like you, Torlo Hannis, Andon Janis was reborn, but willfully forgot about that vast civilization in the stars, considering his life here as having the only true meaning or reality."

"Hardly the same," I countered bitterly. My glance went to Youi Janis. "If circumstances were different—"

"I told you that once honors had been won, that a man can have a good life here on Noomas. Life can be sweet. Your position now will be as a general in the armies of Bel-loniea, a position which only Royalty can hold. With the right woman, you will find happiness."

"I'll not be staying here," I announced, suddenly making a decision. "There should be a place for me in some country as a mercenary. The life will be rugged, but it will not be necessary to face what now must be accepted." The depressive thought of Youi Janis being my half-sister made it impossible to consider being in the same city with her. The pain would be too sharp. "Maybe in time I'll return."

Andon Janis grinned widely. "You speak like a man who has given up hope before even entering into the battle. You are defeated without even asking the obvious questions. One to me, first."

I had the nagging impression he was toying with me.

"Who is Dal Sorla?" I sighed, sick inside, determined to be done with this double-talk.

"I am. Or was. Just depends on how you wish to think of it."

"I love Youi Janis—as a man will love and desire a woman. Do you understand how I must feel about your admission? My father was Dal Sorla."

Andon Janis shook his head. "Dal Sorla was married to your mother, Torlo Hannis. You were a small boy when she met me. Your father was killed in a space battle some years before. He was the one who set up a trust fund for your

270

education—out of his insurance money. That is why you were able to join the Space Corps and become an officer so easily. I but adopted you. Certainly, Torlo, you must have known that!"

I shook my head, dazed. Then I remembered the dream in which the elderly woman who had held me so close—whom I recognized as an aunt—whispering: "For such a young one, to have twice suffered so great a loss." This coupled with that flash memory-dream while fighting Tor, of a strange male face so unlike Andon Janis' and the woman huddled by a window, sobbing in sorrow, now united to make sense. That male face had been my real father—an officer in the Space Force. The images of the woman had been my mother, after having received the video-gram from Space Command Defense Department stating her husband had been killed. How could those facts have missed me so completely?

I looked at Youi, grinned with sudden relief. "That question you wanted to hear...if I have earned enough honors in your mind—"

Bitter words cut me short. "You can forget it!"

Andon Janis quickly explained what we'd been saying. Youi's expression softened. She came forward, hands clutched mine.

"I love you, Youi Janis!" My voice was torn with emotion.

"I've loved you, Torlo, from the beginning," she half sobbed. "During the desert storm I tried to tell you, but you must not have heard. I didn't realize that then."

Now I understood the rift which had developed between us after escaping Baji-Ney's tribe. She had openly admitted her love to me, and I'd not responded. If only I had known.

"Are you sure I can stand at your side to rule your people?" I teased.

"I have known for a long time—but a woman never makes it easy for the man she loves. I wanted to be sure of your love." She laughed lightly, then added, eyes twinkling. "And then, I had to talk it over with my father...and he instructed me to inform Romos about my feelings."

"Then..."

"Romos knows—but he expects a royal ceremony!" Andon Janis announced, touching my shoulder.

Youi shook her head. "Please send for the palace Muti."

"Surely a royal wedding must be held!" Andon Janis countered sternly.

Youi Janis stubbornly shook her head. "We have done everything together, alone. I want this to be ours, completely. A secret wedding. Later Romos can demand any kind of wedding he wants. I won't wait another day."

She laughed as Andon left the room. "I want it this way, always have. One impulsive act. A woman, even a Proctoress, can desire her one moment when convention is broken. You don't mind, do you?" Her eyes were bright with eager excitement.

"I'm hardly in any physical condition to..."

"As the desert people say," she pointed out, guessing what I meant, "it is best for an honorable man to allow his wife to fully mature before taking her as a complete wife. I don't mind waiting, if you find it too difficult to..."

We both laughed, and then I said: "But won't Romos be furious?"

"Of course, he made me a promise about that!"

"What?"

She half giggled. "He said no secret marriage, and I told him in no uncertain words that I would do exactly what I wanted and he couldn't do anything to stop it." Again Youi laughed. "He merely nodded, said that I was headstrong like my mother. He gave his blessings. But I made him promise not to let father or mother know. After all, they went up against him—and I think they would enjoy the idea if we were doing the same thing. They are both terribly romantic. Do you know that mother has refused to take the youth drug, just so that she would age with father? But of course not, you haven't even met her."

In silence we waited until Andon Janis stepped into the room, followed by a hooded Muti who quickly glided to a position in front of us.

"Romos will be furious!" the Muti announced in a rasping voice.

"My father and mother," Youi Janice countered, "faced you in secret, and were married because they loved one another. I wish you to do the same for this man and myself. It is little to ask."

Andon Janis had already slipped out of the room.

How strange this all seemed, yet oddly enough it seemed fitting that we should thus face a Muti together, alone, without others to witness this very important moment. For we had learned to know and love one another while going through harrowing adventures which nobody else could have shared with us.

I looked at Youi Janis's bright, eager features. She seemed like a young girl—yet long days of fighting for bare survival had proved her to be a proud, strong, brave woman.

I had no idea what would follow, but could never have guessed its simplicity.

The Muti touched a hand to each of our foreheads.

"The two of you will answer each question. The honesty of your words will reveal themselves to me—if they be true, your marriage will be filled with years of happiness—if you lie, there will be no marriage." His voice was a soft rumble, almost a chant.

"Do you love the other?"

Each of us answered yes.

"Do you both desire a lifetime of fully sharing yourselves totally with the other?"

"Yes," both our voices announced solemnly.

"Will you both be devoted and loyal to one another for as long as you live?"

Our third yes was followed by his final statement:

"You are now joined, bound by powers greater than any of those upon the world, greater than any force within the universe. I have seen your past and your present thoughts and have looked into the future and know the great binding power of the love which possesses both of you. Go happily upon your life paths together and know that not my words bind you, but only the greatness of the love you share. Remember there is no law in the Universe which can hold two people together stronger than their own lasting desires and love for one another."

His hands lifted from our foreheads. Without another word he turned and left the room, silently closing the door.

Youi came into my arms, lips gently touching mine as we kissed for the first time as husband and wife.

Later would come the grand public ceremonies of a Royal Marriage before the people of Bel-loniea. The formal marriage of State would give me the title of Proctor II. Romos would present us with a huge palace and a great fortune in Proctors Tokens, a personal household staff and a military guard.

But all this would mean far less to me than the simple words exchanged with the Proctor's Muti in the small room in which I had first awakened on Noomas, where I had first seen Youi Janis, and where we were finally united in the only way two people can truly be united: through their total love for one another.

ABOUT THE AUTHOR

Charles Nuetzel was born in San Francisco in 1934, and writes:

"As long as I can remember I wanted to be a writer. It was a dream I never thought would materialize. But with the help of Forrest J Ackerman, who became my agent, I managed to finally make it into print.

"I was lucky enough not only in selling my work to publishers but also ending up packaging books for some of them, and finally becoming a 'publisher' much like those who had bought my first novels. From there it as a simple leap to editing not only a sci-fi anthology, but a line of sci-fi books for Powell Sci-Fi back in the 1960s. Throughout these active professional years I had the chance to design some covers and do graphic cover layouts for pocket books & magazines."

Much of his work in covers and graphics are a result of having had a father who was a professional commercial artist, and who did a number of covers for sci-fi magazines in the 1950s and later for pocket books—even for some of Mr. Nuetzel's books.

In retirement he has become involved in swing dancing, a long time lover of Big Band jazz. But more interestingly world travels have taken him (and his wife Brigitte) across the world, to Hawaii, Caribbean, Mexico, Kenya, Egypt, Peru, having a life-long interest in ancient civilizations. His website is full of thousands of pictures taken during these trips.

"Discovering these wonderful places actually exist, and getting a chance to even touch those ancient stones and structures, climbing some of the Mesoamerican pyramids to their very top, has been a life-inspiring adventure! It is fan-

275

tastic to realize that our modern world is built upon such fascinating places, like the 2000-year-old Petra, which was simply amazing to see. Almost as stunning as the pyramids of Egypt! All of which, I keep telling myself, are the remains of colonies developed by the Haldolen Empire some 30,000 years ago (related in *Swordmen of Vistar*)."

www.ingramcontent.com/pod-product-compliance
Lightning Source LLC
Chambersburg PA
CBHW022003010726
47494CB00003B/872